C.M.N. ROGERS

Witchborn

Book One of The Bellarose Legacy

First published by House of Nine Press 2025

This is a work of fiction. Names, characters, places, and incidents are the product of the author's imagination or are used fictitiously. Any resemblance to actual persons, living or dead, events, or localities is purely coincidental.

Stories drawn from shadow, written in light, and stained with truth.

First edition

ISBN (print): 978-1-7641620-1-2
ISBN (digital): 978-1-7641620-0-5

This book was professionally typeset on Reedsy.
Find out more at reedsy.com

Contents

Acknowledgments

To the readers: thank you for stepping into this world of blood, shadow, and soul. If this story found you at the right time, then maybe—just maybe—it was meant to.

To my son, who is my greatest teacher, my heart outside my body, and my most magical why—thank you for reminding me every day what courage and unconditional love look like.

To my friends: you deserve medals (or at least wine) for understanding when I vanished into writing caves, forgot how to reply to texts, and ranted about characters like they were real people. Your support has been my oxygen.

And finally, to the story itself—thanks for choosing me.

One

"The blood remembers, even when we try to forget. Especially then."
— Witchborn Proverb

Maison Bellarose carried the weight of centuries. Its stone walls, etched with time, guarded secrets sealed within repose. Grand archways opened into light-starved corridors, their passageways lined with portraits of long-dead ancestors whose painted eyes tracked every step with unsettling precision.

Shadows curled at the edges of vision—too fluid, too interested. They didn't just shift. They paid attention.

The scent of beeswax polish and aged vellum lingered in the air. There was no true silence here, only murmurs from the past stitched into each beam and tapestry.

Under chandeliers casting steady golden light, polished floors gleamed. Towering mahogany furniture, carved with runes and curling motifs, stood as guardians of a forgotten era. Every detail whispered of wealth, discipline, and a reverence for tradition so deeply ingrained it had become sacred.

Outside, the estate rose in defiance—more fortress than home, untouched by the chaos beyond its borders. Ivy clung to its exterior, veins of light barely breathing beneath its leaves—residue of wards layered over centuries. Enchantments cloaked the manor in a second skin, woven to protect, preserve, and remember.

At the edge of the Crescent Enclave—a hidden district stitched into the bones of New Orleans—the house kept silent vigil.

The Enclave didn't announce itself to the mundane world. Its entrance was guarded by towering wrought-iron gates, black as pitch and etched with sigils only the magically attuned could perceive. To outsiders, they appeared as rusted fencing around a forgotten garden. But to those with magic in their blood, the gates shimmered—alive with recognition. Passing through them wasn't merely crossing space; it was stepping between worlds.

The atmosphere inside was heavier. It hummed softly, as if the ground paused in anticipation, preserving the old sorcery flowing beneath cobblestone streets and time-worn facades.

Streetlamps burned with a faint, otherworldly glow. A hand-forged sign swung gently above a closed café, its lettering shifting when viewed from the corner of one's eye. A child chased a ball of light down a quiet alley, watched by a familiar in cat form, its eyes twin moons.

Beyond the warded line, the mundane world went on with its blind rhythms—but inside, magic held court.

At the estate's heart lay the Scriptorium—a sanctum untouched by modernity. Candles flickered in sconces shaped like thorned iron branches, casting restless shadows over shelves groaning under the heaviness of grimoires and rune-etched tomes. The foundation itself radiated a consecrated, volatile charge.

Gold and silver sigils spiralled across the stone floor in sacred geometry. Ritual tables bore the marks of long use: scorch patterns, knife scores, dried wax.

In the corner, a smoky quartz scrying basin stood sentinel, its still water black as obsidian. Nearby, brass astrolabes, crystal phials filled with reactive essence, and enchanted scrolls clustered alongside jars of herbs and bowls of crushed bone and volcanic glass.

Despite its power, the room held a quiet that bordered on holy. Leather chairs and faded couches offered sanctuary between shelves. Tapestries adorned the walls—depictions of triumphs, blood-pacts, and sacred vows.

This wasn't just a library. It was a reliquary. A crucible of remembrance and cost.

This was where their legacy had been recorded, hidden, and protected since the 1600s—an unbroken chain of witches who had served as wardens, guardians, and at times, executioners. Each generation had paid its price. Not all had survived it. But none had dared turn away.

Saffron Bellarose stood at the podium. Her auburn hair, streaked with silver, fell over the plum robe wrapped around her shoulders. Emerald eyes caught the candlelight, veiled with quiet fire.

The grimoire under her hands was old. The ink writhed slowly beneath her gaze, stitched with bloodline memory.

Her fingers moved with ceremonial care across the parchment, though a tremor betrayed the unease she was feeling.

A name surfaced.

Seraphina.

Her daughter. Her failure.

That ache wasn't a wound anymore. It was scar tissue that burned when the weather turned emotional.

Seraphina hadn't just rejected her birthright—she'd walked away from Saffron.

She could still see the moment—Seraphina, shoulders squared, chin tilted in quiet defiance. No shouting. No curse. Just the finality of distance.

Their bond, once forged in ritual and love, had fractured. In its place remained careful pauses, polite phone calls, and a grief that deepened with time.

Seraphina hadn't abandoned magic.

She had abandoned everything.

Saffron exhaled slowly. But the sorrow pressed in, heavier than any ward.

Her thoughts drifted to Wiccan Whispers—the shop she had poured her soul into. Nestled in the heart of the Enclave, it had become her sanctuary. Every shelf and corner bore her touch: labelled herbs, shimmering pendulums, potions arranged in a mosaic of stained glass. Tarot decks with worn edges. Spellbooks that called to the brave.

It wasn't only a store. It was a haven.

And still, after all this time, she dreamed of Seraphina returning— not just to the shop, but to everything she'd once been destined to inherit.

Lately, that hope felt like dust.

She pulled her focus downward—beneath the Scriptorium—to the truth she rarely dared name.

The Shadowkeep.

Hidden deep below the estate, sealed behind ancient wards, the Shadowkeep held the family's most dangerous inheritance. Spellcraft too dark to teach. Relics so cursed they tore through every binding laid upon them.

Scrolls sealed in blood and ash. Whispers rose from iron vessels— low, curling murmurs from imprisoned demons, their voices threaded with torment and temptation.

A black-glass mirror loomed on the far wall, its surface rippling with a silken gleam—a portal to realms and timelines best left undisturbed.

Saffron was the gate and its keeper.

But not for much longer.

She had prepared the transfer. Upon her death, the key would pass to Seraphina.

That truth would not be welcomed. Knowing her daughter, she would rather burn the bloody estate down than wear the crown.

She caught the sound of footsteps.

Deliberate and slow.

She turned.

Julian stood in the doorway.

Taller now. Lean. Defined with a new precision. His dark hair brushed his collar in carefully crafted disarray. A tailored coat hugged his frame, and at his throat, a shard of shadowglass reflected the light.

But it was his eyes—icy blue—that made her stomach tighten.

Glacial with a whole lot of empty.

"Aunty. Father sends his regards."

Of course he did. Of course the coward sent his son to do his dirty work.

The sting of betrayal, though expected, tasted bitter.

She'd braided his hair more times than she could count—he'd never ask, but he never pulled away. Where had that boy gone?

She'd loved him. Raised him. Gave him more than Brinnan ever had.

When Brinnan cast him aside—too busy building an empire to look after a bastard son—Saffron took Julian in.

A brittle child with hollow eyes and too many questions.

He'd clung to her in silence, desperate to prove himself. She remembered how he buried himself in books too advanced for his age, how he hung on her every word.

She'd tried to fill Brinnan's absence with kindness. With safety. With structure.

But what Julian needed most wasn't comfort.

It was *significance*.

Saffron offered patience and order. Brinnan promised legacy.

Where she set boundaries, Brinnan handed him inheritance.

And as Julian grew older, so did his resemblance to his father's darker ways.

That quiet ache for a father's approval hardened into ambition. A hunger to matter.

Brinnan told him he was meant to rule.

So, when the chance came to seize it—Julian didn't hesitate.

He was willing to pay the price—to sever the one bond that had been real.

Standing in the Scriptorium now, blade hidden, treachery in his heart—he felt no regret.

Only resolve.

He'd been the outsider his whole life. The afterthought. Now, the bloodline would bend to him—or break.

They had written him out of the lineage, sealed legacy behind rituals and names that excluded him.

He would not be excluded again.

"It's time the family's power served its purpose."

Saffron's hand moved to the amulet at her throat. Its warmth had ebbed, a quiet warning.

"How long have you been conspiring with your father?"

"A while."

"And when do you plan to betray him?" This was always how it had to go. Didn't mean it hurt less.

"Ah, you know me so well. He taught me how to open the doors. But I do intend to walk through them alone."

Her chest tightened.

Julian was no one's pawn.

From her, he learned discipline. From Brinnan, ruthlessness. But he meant to eclipse them both.

He stepped closer and drew the dagger.

Made from stone black enough to drink the light. Forged in shadow.

Its edge gleamed with a curse too complex to name.

"You can kill me. But I swear—you and Brinnan won't win."

She'd already handled that.

His mouth curled at the edges. "We'll see about that."

The blade hit, and the world spun left. Her bones screamed. Her power shattered inward like glass dropped in slow motion. Her body faltered.

The spell was more than poison—it severed her ties to magic, to blood, to the wards she'd woven—unravelling, strand by strand.

"I'd call that checkmate, Aunt Saffy."

Her vision blurred. But deep beneath the wreckage, a final ember stirred—one that refused to die quietly.

She didn't fear death. But she mourned the goodbyes—the apology she might never speak, the daughter she might never see again.

Still, the legacy would hold.

The wards would remember.

And *Seraphina*... Seraphina would rise.

With trembling lips, she spoke a single word.

The wards ignited.

The room trembled.

The amulet caught fire behind her skin. The heat kicked once—twice—before ripping through her veins like molten silver. Her body spasmed. Her magic, what little remained, rose in protest, clawing up her throat in one final, feral cry.

Her spirit anchored.

Her remaining strength flowed inward.

Her knees gave way, and she fell.

Julian stood over her, unmoved.

She had given him a place, loved him and believed in him when no one else had. But belief wasn't power. And power was what he'd always craved.

Now, nothing stood in his way.

No more waiting.

No more being passed over.

This time, the legacy would kneel.

He stepped to the altar and drew his athame. A single cut across his palm. Blood dripped onto the scroll. Symbols took shape.

For a second—just a flicker—he hesitated. Not because he doubted the spell. But because for one brief, bone-deep moment, he remembered Saffron's arms wrapped around him after his first nightmare.

That memory was a weakness.

He buried it.

The ink resisted.

It writhed. Shifted.

Words emerged.

By death's decree, the power flows,
To the matriarch, as bloodline shows.
Clutch at ghosts, plot your schemes,
The key's beyond your darkest dreams.

Julian stilled.

Seraphina.

She had walked away—fled to the suburbs, rejected her blood. And yet she was the heir?

The scroll mocked him. As if her will still breathed through the parchment, laughing at the boy who was never meant to rule.

Saffron, even in death, had outmanoeuvred him.

But not for long.

He crushed the page in his fist.

Seraphina couldn't hide forever.

He would find her.

And when he did, she would open the vault.

Or he would tear her world apart until she did.

Two

Seraphina jolted awake, her heart pounding like a frantic war drum. Sweat slicked her skin. Fear curled bitter and metallic in her mouth. She sat upright, gripping the quilt to her chest.

Something was wrong.

Not just *wrong*—Saffy wrong.

Her mother's words still rang in her ears, pointed and insistent in the way only she could manage. "Come to Wiccan Whispers. Now!" No room for argument. Even in a dream, that voice could peel paint from walls.

Seraphina groaned and rubbed her temples. She'd walked away from the chaos that shaped her childhood, but Saffy didn't believe in boundaries—especially magical ones. She worked mojo strong enough to wake the dead.

Or, apparently, terrify her daughter in the middle of the night.

"Damn it, Mum." She swung her legs off the bed. "They invented mobile phones for a reason. No need to go full poltergeist."

Figures. Saffy could still haunt her sleep like she owned the place—and hit every nerve on the way out.

Her eyes darted to the clock.

3:01 am.

Of course. The witching hour.

With a resigned sigh, she reached for her phone and scanned the contacts until she found:

Mother (Answer at own risk).

Her thumb hovered over the call button but didn't press.

A knot twisted in her gut. This wasn't just a dream. Saffy was as subtle as a brass band in a monastery. If she was sending a message in this way, something was seriously off.

"Fine. You win."

She pulled on a pair of faded jeans and an oversized hoodie—the soft grey fabric fraying at the cuffs. Every motion carried the sluggish weight of a choice she hadn't wanted to make.

The sweatshirt hung loose on her frame, a contrast to the wild cascade of auburn curls framing her face. Her emerald eyes—vivid but dulled slightly by years of suppressed magic—shifted downward as she stepped into her scuffed sneakers.

"You'd better have a bloody good reason for this shit." She threw the words at the unseen forces dragging her back.

She sent a quick text to the kids:

Gram's emergency. Explain later. Don't burn the house down. Love you.

Snatching her keys off the counter, she slung her bag over her shoulder, already picturing their reactions.

Sage—the intuitive, curious one—would pause mid-step, arms crossed, brows drawn.

"Is everything okay, Mum?" She was the calm, laser-focused one. Then she'd vanish into her room to dive into whatever her latest obsession demanded—be it a Reddit thread or a three-hundred-page book.

Sebastian, steady and sceptical, wouldn't even glance up from his phone. "Okay," he'd say with a shrug. Change rattled him more than he admitted, but he'd hide it under layers of orchestrated indifference.

Her children. Her heart. Sage's quiet sensitivity, Sebastian's too-careful composure—both reflections of her in different ways. And both, always, were her greatest vulnerability.

The humid Louisiana night clung to her skin—thick with magnolia and the hint of incoming rain. Her battered hatchback wheezed to life, coughing like a chain-smoking dragon on its last lung. She ushered a prayer and pulled away.

Streetlights slid past in a slow retreat, shedding behind her in strips of fading gold. The farther she drove, the more the world shifted.

Something unseen began to gather, pressing at the edges of perception.

Turning onto Rue Mystère, everything felt tuned to a different frequency—charged and hush-held. As she approached the Crescent Enclave's entrance, its heavy gates groaned open. Sigils etched into blackened metal flushed bright beneath the gaslight, their rhythm quickening in response to her presence—an echo of breath, of blood, of something vital under the steel.

She crossed through.

Inside, the city stood weathered by time's relentless hand. The hum of crickets waned into a strange lull, broken only by the distant toll of an unseen bell. The scent of cinnamon and ozone hung low, threading through the streets steeped in what had been. The cobblestones whispered beneath her tires. Ivy-cloaked facades leaned in, conspiratorial in their silence. Moss-draped balconies glimmered with strands of floating lights. Shadows moved differently here—not merely darkness, but custodians fixed in the margins: unmoving yet never absent.

She parked near Madame Laveau's Curiosities, the window still a cluttered riot of tarot decks, bottles labelled Essence of Nightmares and Hex Breaker, and a skeletal hand waving lazily in the dim.

A voice slid from the shadows.

"Long time no see."

Seraphina jumped, clutching her bag tighter.

Malrik lounged against a lamppost, teeth yellowed in a crooked grin, coat hanging off him like a forgotten relic.

"Geezus, Malrik. Still lurking about?"

"It's not lurking. It's ambiance. Didn't think you were the witching type anymore."

"I'm not." She brushed past him. "It's family business."

"Family, huh?" he called after her. "Better watch your back. In this place, blood's thicker than water—and twice as likely to stab you."

She didn't respond.

Wiccan Whispers waited at the end of Rue Nocturne, its shutters painted a deep, enchanted violet. The worn sign creaked overhead. The place held the scent of sage and lavender—settled, deliberate, and deeply familiar.

Seraphina paused at the door, fingertips brushing the frame.

This had been her mother's sanctuary.

Now it felt... off.

"Ready or not. Here I come."

The door creaked open before she touched it.

She froze.

A chill crawled up her spine.

Shelves groaned softly, as if exhaling. A faint clink echoed—glass tapping against glass. The pendulum above the register twitched— subtle, deliberate. Her skin prickled. The shop was more than animated. It was alert.

"'Cos that's not creepy at all." She stepped inside.

Unseen intent settled into the room, dense and slow as oil. The furniture seemed to shift, narrowing the space. Shadows pooled in the corners, unwilling to release their hold. Jars and phials throbbed with faint, unnatural light.

A jolt of adrenaline hit her like a battering ram.

"Mum?"

Something was off.

"Finally," came the reply—crisp, unmistakable, and unnervingly calm.

Seraphina flinched and turned toward the voice.

Saffron Bellarose stood in the centre of the room, wrapped in a ghostly halo of luminescence. Not fully solid. Not fading either. Caught somewhere in between.

"Ironic, isn't it?" Saffron raised a brow. "The only time you bother to answer me is the night I leave the physical plane."

Seraphina staggered, catching the shelf with her shoulder.

"You mean you're... not just projecting from the house?"

"Oh my god. Mum—are you... gone?"

She grabbed the counter. Anything to stay upright.

No, this couldn't be real.

Saffy didn't die.

Saffy couldn't die.

"Quite dead, as it happens." Saffron gave it to her straight. "Obviously not entirely gone. I bound my spirit to the physical plane—hence the glowing ghost routine."

Seraphina collapsed onto a stool, dragging in air in quick, uneven gulps.

"Dead. You're not supposed to die. You're you. You're unkillable."

Saffron's mouth twitched—something between regret and gallows humour. "Sweetie, flattery's not going to help. Believe me, I was just as horrified. Turns out a magical dagger and a traitorous nephew are an effective combo."

Seraphina blinked, her tears drying in a rush of disbelief.

"Julian killed you?"

Why was she surprised? In this family, power always trumped loyalty. And she'd believed that boundaries and a good school district would keep her kids safe.

He used to flick paper spitballs at her during study sessions. His grin? Pure demon-spawn. She'd actually thought he'd grow up decent. Hilarious.

"He did." The temperature dipped a degree. "He's graduated to murder, betrayal, and a calculated grab for power. And surprise, he's been learning from the best. Brinnan has turned family psychopathy into a full-blown bonding ritual. Warms the heart, doesn't it?"

"Of course he has!" Seraphina lost it. Full stop. "Julian and Uncle Brinnan—what a bloody dream team. This is precisely why I walked away. Magic, the Enclave, the whole freak show. It's always murder, mayhem, and multigenerational lunacy!"

Saffron kept her expression exactly where it was. "Let's not get melodramatic, darling. You make it sound like we're trying to headline a horror story. Though, with this family... fair."

"Melodramatic? You're glowing like some supernatural disco ball, murdered by your deranged nephew. I think I've earned some melodrama."

Seraphina didn't back down.

The words caught, but she kept going.

"I've got teenagers at home who think their grandmother's a peace-and-love hippie into crystals and herbal tea. They don't know they're witches. They don't know anything."

Saffron didn't soften. "You bound their powers, Seraphina. You didn't just walk away—you sealed them off. Just like you did to yourself. Did you really think that would protect them?"

"They didn't need protecting! They needed normal, Mum. A life without bloodlines and curses and... and whatever this twisted legacy is!"

"And you think ignorance makes them safe?" Saffron let that one land. "Do you honestly believe Julian and Brinnan will hesitate when they realise who they are? You didn't shield them—you left them wide open."

"I made a choice!" Years of bottled frustration burst loose. "I wanted something better—a normal life for us. Something that didn't revolve around this endless, god-awful nightmare! I never wanted this life, Mum!"

Saffron didn't let up. "And look at where that choice has left you. Unprepared. And they're unprepared too."

Seraphina stared at her, chest tight, mind racing. Every wall she'd built was beginning to come apart at the seams. Reality—and fear—closed in, heavy as a collapsing roof.

Saffron flickered with the cost of it. "I never wanted them dragged into this. I never meant for you to be caught in the crossfire either. And I sure as hell didn't plan on ending up dead. But here we are."

Her light flared. "Julian and Brinnan won't stop until they've drained every drop of magic from this family—and as you know, the darkest of it is in the Shadowkeep."

The name settled in Seraphina's mind, cold and unwelcome.

The Shadowkeep.

Her hands trembled. Her thoughts spun to Sage and Sebastian.

How was she supposed to tell her son—steadfast, rational, but so much more emotionally complex than he let on—that the world didn't work the way he believed it did?

And her daughter, with her open heart and boundless curiosity—what would it do to her to learn she was part of a legacy bound by rules, expectations, and dangers she never asked for?

She swallowed hard. "How am I supposed to explain this to them, Mum? How do I tell them they're witches? That everything I tried to protect them from is coming for them?"

Saffron's gaze softened, but she held firm.

"You tell them the truth, Seraphina. Because whether you do or not, the truth is on its way. And it's better they hear it from you than from whatever monster comes knocking."

The room shifted—air thickening with quiet urgency.

"This isn't just about vengeance anymore. Julian and Brinnan want more than the Enclave. They want the mundanii too. Full domination. This isn't a grudge match—it's a conquest."

Seraphina stared at her, disbelief cutting through the fog.

"So let me get this straight. They're aiming for world domination? Seriously? That's the plan? Could they be any more cliché?"

"Seraphina, this is not a joke. The key passed to you when I died. Do you understand what that means? You're not just in their way—you are the way."

"And if they find out about the twins…" Saffron didn't finish the sentence.

She didn't need to. Seraphina's face drained of colour. A roar filled her ears.

"Okay. I get it. But tell me this—how the hell did I become the skeleton key to the family apocalypse?"

She was starting to crack. Finally.

"I couldn't risk Brinnan gaining control. By tradition, the key passes to an object when the bearer dies—then to the next of age. But that was too uncertain. So, years ago, I wove a spell. One that ensured the transfer went to the next matriarch."

Her eyes didn't leave Seraphina's.

"And that, whether you like it or not… is you."

Seraphina barked a laugh. There was no humour in it.

"So, I'm now the walking, talking passcode to magical Armageddon? Bloody brilliant."

"I understand why you're angry," Saffron kept her voice low. "You left for a reason. You wanted peace. You wanted to protect the kids. That decision cost us all dearly."

She didn't soften the next part.

"But they're coming, Seraphina. Whether you're ready or not." Seraphina stilled. Her shoulders locked, body trembling with frustration—and the first stirrings of something worse: acceptance.

"So what do I do Mum? Just roll over and play the perfectly doomed heir?"

Saffron looked at her for a long second. "No, darling. You fight."

Seraphina's lungs seized mid-draw.

"Fight how? I'm not a bloody warrior. I'm a single mother who ran from her past. I don't even know where to start."

Saffron straightened, the light around her sparking with resolve.

"I do. We start at the Scriptorium."

Seraphina blinked. "Wait—Julian killed you at home?"

"Yes, the little shit certainly did." Saffron didn't bother hiding her disgust. "My amulet's still with my body, thankfully. He didn't take it—because he has no idea what it holds. He used a cursed dagger to sever my connection to the magic. But I managed to send what I could into it before the end. It holds enough juice to unbind you—and transfer the key."

She didn't want to think it let alone say it.

"Your body? You're seriously asking me to go back to the estate… and take the necklace off your corpse?"

"Absolutely. Think of it as the world's most traumatic heirloom retrieval."

Seraphina paced, teeth sinking into her lower lip.

"Because that won't be traumatising at all! Heaven forbid anything in this family be simple."

"If I'd had time to plan my murder, I might've arranged something more convenient. Unfortunately, Julian didn't consult my calendar."

Seraphina stopped mid-step and stared her down. "This is not funny."

"I assure you. I'm not laughing. But without that little charm, you're all sitting ducks. And we both know how that ends."

Seraphina's stomach turned over.

"Great. Can't think of anything I want more than to shackle myself and my kids to the legacy I fought tooth and nail to escape."

"This isn't about what you want." Steel in every word. "It's about what has to be done. I'm not asking you to like it. I'm asking you to survive it—to protect your children, and everything tied to this family."

Seraphina blinked fast. The action didn't quite stop the tears.

No question—everything had just changed. She hated that.

"Fine. Let the record show I'm not thrilled about picking through a crime scene. And this is definitely not the mother-daughter bonding activity I would've chosen."

A ghost of a smile passed over Saffron's face.

"You've never been thrilled about anything I've asked you to do. Why start now?"

Seraphina jabbed a finger at her mother.

"When this is over, you owe me ten years of therapy, a bottomless wine subscription, and a damn good reason why this family can't go five minutes without flirting with a freak'n apocalypse."

"Deal. And I'll throw in a seance with your therapist when I'm done haunting Julian." Saffron's eyes gleamed with something fierce and proud. "Now come on. The fate of everything we hold dear is hanging by a thread."

Seraphina squared her shoulders, a restless energy surging through her. If this was the beginning of the end—she'd meet it head-on.

Three

"Those born into power believe they deserve it. Those denied it learn how to take it."
— *The Doctrine of Shadow Ascension*

The black stone desk gleamed under ambient light—an altar of precision and control. Unlike most executive offices, it held no clutter. Only the essential remained, each piece curated with deliberate significance. At its centre, a sleek laptop rested—lines crisp as origami folds. Beside it, a crystal decanter of amber liquor glinted, casting fractured gold across the dark walls. A single black feather stood upright in a rune-etched cradle, thrumming with restrained magic—a heartbeat spun from shadow. It wasn't a reminder of power. It was a declaration.

Brinnan Bellarose sat ensconced in his high-backed leather chair, the picture of composed dominance. Custom-crafted and stitched with enchanted thread to resist time, it molded to him like a throne to a king. His charcoal suit, tailored to ruthless perfection, embraced his frame. His emerald tie offered a single point of colour. Cufflinks of polished stone inlaid with green fire glinted beneath the desk lamp—subtle, commanding, an extension of the man himself.

His face was all angles and calculation, untouched by age's softening hand. High cheekbones. A jaw like it had been carved to bite back.

Lips that rarely curved into warmth. His eyes—emerald, glacial, and unflinching—dissected the world with surgical precision. Even the silver streaks at his temples seemed earned, medals of survival and conquest.

Behind him, floor-to-ceiling windows framed New Orleans in all its nocturnal brilliance. The city shimmered in electric hues, ticking along unaware beneath his gaze. To Brinnan, it was both prey and playground—an urban sprawl he had studied, shaped, and subdued. The mundanii below scurried through their constructs, never glimpsing the predator surveilling from above.

Eclipse Investments, his fortress, loomed over the skyline, a jagged spire of steel and stone cutting through the horizon. The building wasn't just designed—it was cast. Wards lined the foundation. Enchantments reinforced every floor. It didn't merely project power; it gathered and focused it. An incantation rendered in architecture.

The walls whispered faintly, pulsing with contained energy. Each office breathed its own warding—cloaked, monitored, and woven into the structure. Here, the arcane wasn't ornamental—it was weaponised.

Brinnan leaned forward, eyes fixed on the laptop's backlit screen. Charts. Numbers. Projections. Mundane on the surface—beneath, imbued with hidden design.

Scrying spells wove through algorithms, while contracts bore glyphs of obedience and binding. Rivals who crossed him saw their fortunes rot. Some met ruin. Others, worse. Coincidence was the illusion. Curse-craft was the truth.

He closed the computer with a snap of finality and reached for the decanter. Whiskey lapped at the sides of the glass, golden and smooth as he poured with ritualistic precision. The clink of crystal rang through the stillness. He leaned back, sipping slowly.

The present slipped away.

The past found him.

His childhood hadn't lacked attention—it had been sculpted from harsher materials: engineered rejection, prescribed silence. Every clipped word, every glance edged in disdain, was a scalpel leaving bloodless cuts. He was Vander Bellarose's illegitimate son, born of ambition and disgrace—his mother a witch steeped in forbidden lore, her name erased in dust and rumour. To Vander, her death had been a solution. To Brinnan, it was the final severing of warmth.

Eva had been brilliance wrapped in glass. He remembered lavender on her robes, lullabies to soothe, the gentleness no one else ever gave. And then—nothing. The Enclave gossiped: grief, madness, a curse turned inward. But Brinnan had always suspected the truth.

That Vander had ended her without consequence.

Her absence left him unguarded in a family that loathed loose ends. When his magic surfaced—wild and formidable—his father claimed him. Not from affection. From strategy. A power of his magnitude couldn't remain unclaimed.

But the price of acknowledgment was control. No love. No pride. His education was cold, efficient. Every gathering became a stage where he played the shadow. Saffron was the heir. He was the contingency. Apprenticed, but never celebrated.

Resentment grew, rooting deeper each year.

At twelve, the dam blistered and tore open.

Banished to the estate's scriptorium for "insolence"—a single question Vander had called defiance—he was left alone, hungry, and seething. In the room's forgotten alcoves, his fingers brushed a tome wedged between imposing grimoires. At his touch, a slow tremor ran through the blackened leather.

By flickering candlelight, hands ink-stained and curious, he read its secrets—binding rituals, blood spells, curses of old. His first attempt faltered. The second succeeded. A creature—mist-shrouded and cat-sized—blinked into existence and hissed at his feet.

That moment rewrote everything.

While Saffron thrived in the light, Brinnan claimed mastery in the forbidden craft. He discovered mentors in alleyways, allies in the margins. He summoned. Cursed. Broke rules. Rebuilt them in his image. The Enclave no longer spoke of him with pity.

They whispered with fear.

At fifteen, ambition turned reckless.

He tested a paralysis hex—on a servant.

Vander found him mid-ritual.

"You dare bring this darkness into my house?"

Brinnan knelt on the Scriptorium's floor, a volatile current slithering beneath his skin. The surrounding runes stirred with latent purpose. "Power like this isn't meant to just sit there. It should be used."

Vander struck him.

"Power without control is destruction. You're a stain on this family. Saffy is the future. You should never have existed."

The slap burned. But it was the words that split the world open. Not with pain—with clarity.

He'd never be enough for Vander. Not polished enough. Not obedient enough. Not Saffron.

Fine. Then he'd stop trying to be.

Power didn't require permission.

Brinnan rose slowly, contempt on full display. "You'll regret those words."

Vander shut him down with a look. "Leave. Return when you've learned your place."

That night, Brinnan didn't sleep. Rage crystallised into purpose. Legacy wasn't passed down. It was stolen. Taken from the dead with blood and will. Only fools waited to inherit.

He wouldn't beg; he would just take it.

By dawn, his path was set. If the Bellarose name wouldn't lift him, he would bend it.

Not Saffron. Not Vander. Not the Enclave.

No one would stop him.

A soft knock broke his reverie.

Julian stepped in, demeanor careful.

Brinnan didn't rise. He didn't need to. Authority oozed from him like slow poison.

"Ah, Julian." His voice wore silk. His gaze unsheathed a knife. He swirled his whiskey.

"I trust you have good news."

"Saffron has been eliminated."

Brinnan's lips curved. The smile didn't touch his eyes.

"And the key?"

Julian shifted. "That's where things get... complicated."

The smile vanished. "Complicated?"

Silence stretched between them—tight, heavy, dangerous.

"I worked the blood spell. But it didn't go as planned. When Saffron died, the key passed to Seraphina."

The crystal glass fractured with a hiss—his temper breaking first, then reassembling behind his eyes.

"You were tasked with transferring it to the orb. Explain how it ended up with my niece."

Julian held steady. "She outmanoeuvred us. Saffron anticipated our move. She bound the inheritance to blood—specifically, matriarchal succession."

Brinnan leaned back. "How annoyingly inconvenient."

A jolt shot through Julian, but he kept his face neutral. What he didn't say: the vessel had never been meant to hold it. It had been a facade—a construct for appearances. His true spell, hidden in the weave, was designed to bind the source of power to him alone.

But Saffron had seen through them both.

Julian gave a short exhale—half a scoff, half respect. "She knew we'd try. It wasn't just a safeguard. It was a lock."

Brinnan's stare bored through him.

For half a second, he saw himself in Julian's gaze—young, brilliant, overlooked. A weapon dressed as a son. He looked away. He wouldn't repeat Vander's mistakes.

Julian had no intention of staying a pawn in his father's conquest. His ambition ran deeper. Brinnan played long games.

Julian played beneath the board.

He'd been the dutiful son long enough. Now it was his turn to write the rules—in ink, in blood, whatever it took.

Julian continued. "She's delayed us. But Seraphina's untrained. She doesn't know what she carries. We can still turn this."

Brinnan adjusted his cuff. "Yes, we will. She'll open the door—willingly or not."

Julian nodded. But in his mind, plans slid free—acute and deliberate. *Saffron had altered the rules, which only made the stakes more compelling.*

Brinnan saw Seraphina as a piece to move.

Julian saw her as leverage.

As he stepped into the corridor, light fractured through the pristine air. His father's voice looped in his skull—every word a warning, every glance a judgement waiting to strike.

He'd seen the future.

And it wasn't Brinnan who ruled. It was him.

The elevator opened with a hiss. He stepped inside. Reflections warped in the silvered glass walls, shifting with a fluid shimmer—arcane light caught in motion.

The city blurred beyond the pane, but Julian didn't look at it.

His mind fixed where no eyes could follow.

A path only he could see—etched in power, carved in betrayal.

In the mirrored panel behind him, shadows bled upward like smoke.

Brinnan wanted a legacy.
Julian wanted a throne.
Only one of them was going to die king.

Four

"Those who carry the key must walk the path alone. The Shadow does not share its secrets for free."
— *The Old Tongue, Matriarchal Codex*

Seraphina gripped the steering wheel tighter as the car chugged up the long, winding drive. The pre-dawn sky barely held back the dark, like it knew better than to mess with what this place remembered. Towering oaks lined the path, their time-worn limbs twisting together in a tangled canopy that swallowed the headlights whole. She used to love those trees—barefoot summers, scraped knees, laughter echoing in the branches.

Now, they loomed—no longer shelter, but relics that recalled too much.

Beyond them, the gardens unfurled in manicured symmetry. The hedges stood immaculate. The flower beds remained arranged in untouched precision, preserved in the exact order she'd left them.

As if the whole estate had simply… waited.

A lump rose in her chest. This house had raised her and wrecked her in equal measure. And now she was back. Not as a daughter, not for closure.

But as the next in line.

Her stomach twisted at the thought of what lay inside. Her mother—

fierce, unyielding, damn near immortal—reduced to a corpse. The world felt wrong for allowing it.

She took a breath and forced the car forward.

"Home sweet home." For half a second, she was a child again—sobbing on the back steps, blood on her palms, Saffron consoling her after a disastrous tree climbing escapade.

"Glad you think so, because it's all yours." Saffy stared at it. Damn place still meant everything—and now all she could do was hover.

Seraphina dropped her forehead onto the wheel. "I hate this, Mum. I hate all of it."

She didn't even care if the house heard her. Let it. Let the ghosts judge.

They'd built this graveyard of a life—she was just here to clean it up.

Saffron was right there with her. "Oh, because I'm thrilled. But here we are. So, let's get on with it, shall we?"

With a sigh of surrender, Seraphina shoved the door open and stepped into air so thick it could've been wearing grief. Cool and damp, it smelled of earth, jasmine, and heritage roses.

Saffron floated beside her, ethereal and composed. "Come along, dear."

The front doors swung open before she could touch them, the house recognising her as its own.

"Creepy." Seraphina had forgotten about that little quirk.

"Convenient." Saffron let the word hang, smug as hell.

Inside was just as she remembered: rich, regal, unsettling. Only now, the faint tang of iron clung to the edges of the room.

Saffron glided ahead. "Hurry up, Seraphina. The body won't bite."

"That's supposed to be comforting?"

The entrance to the Scriptorium stood open.

The doorway dared her—*'cross this line and you don't come back the same.'*

She entered.

And stopped.

She'd seen the impossible. Nightmares with claws. Spells that broke physics. Men who'd sell their soul and ask for the receipt.

But nothing prepared her for this.

For the sight of her mother's lifeless body, crumpled beside the podium, as still as stone.

A sick twist pulled at her stomach, dread lodged tight in her chest. Nausea rose, swift and unforgiving. Saffron Bellarose—formidable, infuriating, indomitable—was now a husk. The deep plum robes that had once swirled with purpose hung stiff with dried blood. And the radiant force that had always surrounded her mother, once a shield against the world, had vanished.

Only the amulet on her chest gleamed—untouched, cradled in hushfire.

Saffron's ghost crossed her arms, eyeing the scene. "Well. I've looked better."

A sound caught in Seraphina's throat—half sob, half laugh. "You're cracking jokes?"

"We all grieve differently." Saffron's shrug could've come with a cigarette and a punchline.

She raked both hands down her face in pure frustration. "Let's get this shit over with."

Steeling herself, she stepped forward. Energy rushed from the pendant, its potent force pressing against her, churning with an invisible charge.

"Take it off and put it on." The candle nearest Saffron flickered hard. "Then go to the grimoire. Find the summoning rite for the Matriarchs. We're going to need one hell of a boost to make this work."

Seraphina wanted to do this as much as she wanted a hole in her head. Taking it meant owning all of it—the mess, the magic, the blood-soaked crown. The amulet didn't care. It pulsed once, like a nod. Like, *finally*. Her fingers trembled as they brushed icy skin, unclasping the chain. The moment it left Saffron's body, the atmosphere in the room shifted—the house released a long-held sigh. Shelves rattled. Candle flames stretched and snapped.

She slipped the chain over her head. The instant it met her skin, power rushed through her, bright and electric. Sound collapsed into a deep, pounding rush.

She turned toward the grimoire.

The old book sat on its pedestal, the leather cover exactly as she remembered. The scriptorium hadn't changed. Dust lingered only in the corners. Vials glinted faintly. Relics thrummed.

She used to sit cross-legged on these floors, wide-eyed as her mother traced runes and told stories of the family line. Back then, magic had carried the illusion of boundlessness. A gift. Until it blew up in her face and took the joy with it.

She was sixteen when she'd learned the truth. One spell. One mistake. Saffron's expression, stricken not with anger, but fear.

After that, magic became a burden.

Now it was back.

The grimoire's pages turned, stopping dead on an ink-smeared passage.

Seraphina stared. It remembered her. No question. "Guess this is it."

She read the words aloud:

"Matriarchs of the Bellarose line,

Spirits bound by blood and time,

Rise from shadow,

Heed my plea,

Lend your magic now to me."

A sudden force tore through the room, so intense it nearly knocked

Seraphina off her feet. The temperature plunged. Frost crept across the floor, scaling the walls with grasping intent. Candle flames shrank into eerie blue pinpricks.

Wind rose from nowhere, whispering through the quiet. Silver mist drifted in, curling and twisting. The haze thickened, taking shape—figures forming one by one from the ether. They glided forward, shifting from shadow to substance in a slow, deliberate emergence that sent a shiver down Seraphina's spine.

They didn't float. They didn't waver.

They stood—solid, silent, sovereign.

A dozen, maybe more. Some appeared young, their beauty brittle as spun sugar. Others carried centuries in their eyes, their wisdom etched into every line of their faces. Yet all bore the lineage mark—high cheekbones, piercing gazes, an air that demanded the world bend around them. Their robes, woven in the styles of their time, were laced with long-dormant enchantments. Some moved with the grace of whispers born in forgotten courts. Others wore battle-torn layers, their abilities earned through fire and blood.

Well, shit. Seraphina cleared her throat. "Whoa. That's… a lot of dead grandmothers."

Saffron didn't wait for her to process. "And a lot of much needed mojo."

The matriarchs regarded her, their expressions ranging from curiosity to quiet approval.

In a voice neither loud nor soft but carrying a weight that resonated within her, they spoke as one.

"You stand where we all once stood. Do you accept and understand what you will now bear?"

Her instincts screamed to run. To rip the pendant from her neck and hurl it across the room. But the presence of her ancestors—silent, unrelenting, absolute—rooted her to the spot. There was no escaping this.

Seraphina swallowed hard. She forced herself to meet the luminous eyes that blazed with knowing, bright as a verdict, old as creation.

"I accept."

Not that she had a choice when family duty kicked down doors and dragged you with it.

Power flooded through the space in response—a searing acknowledgment from the women who had come before.

This wasn't a gift. It was a reckoning in silk gloves. And now it had her name on it.

Beside her, Saffron stood still, gaze keen with quiet approval. With the calm certainty of someone who had carried this weight longer than most could imagine.

Saffron eyed the group. "The key must pass. The line must endure."

They turned their attention to Seraphina. In perfect unison, they raised their hands. A force tore reality open above them as ribbons of violet, gold, and electric blue spiralled through the storm, weaving into something living. It clawed at her hair, her clothes, her very soul—dragging her into its heart.

Seraphina gasped as the first wave hit. It didn't hurt. It blazed—pure light and ancient flame—an elemental current that bypassed flesh and struck the depths of her being. It roared through her veins, fusing with her core, reshaping everything she was, everything she had been, and everything she was meant to become.

Her limbs shook as the energy of generations moved through her, each wave laden with memory, each pulse resounding with the voices of those who came before. A thousand impressions collided in her mind—urgent, layered, impossible to separate. She felt them: hands steadying her shoulders, anchoring her as she struggled to remain upright beneath the storm of inheritance. She wasn't sure where her thoughts faded and theirs began. The boundary blurred—and somewhere in the roar of legacy, she felt herself thinning.

She wasn't ready for this. But readiness was no longer the point.

As quickly as it had begun, it was over.

The whirlwind vanished.

The room was still.

Seraphina swayed, her knees threatening to buckle. Her trembling fingers curled around the pendant resting against her chest.

The amulet was no longer a vessel. It was a spark—and she was the fire it had lit.

The matriarchs began to fade. One cloaked in crimson came forward, her gaze locking onto Seraphina's.

"It is done."

In a blink they were gone.

Seraphina stared at the empty space.

Saffron appeared beside her, smiling with something that was almost soft.

"You did it."

Seraphina wiped her brow. "Let's never do that again." Power buzzed under her skin—like a bad tattoo she hadn't asked for.

"Agreed." Saffron flicked a hand at her corpse. "First things first—body to the crypt, blood off the floor, maybe use something citrus."

Seraphina's brain flatlined for a full second. "Geezus, Mum. Shouldn't we—I don't know—call the cops? Report the murder? Have a funeral?"

Saffron gave a low snort. "You've spent too long in the mundanii world. Who would you call? What would you say—stabbed by a cursed dagger during a blood rite?"

Seraphina opened her mouth, then shut it. Because, dammit, her mother had a point.

"As for the funeral, no ceremony needed," Saffron added. "There's a coffin with my name on it. Literally. Bit of magic, quick cleaning spell, and voilà."

Seraphina shook her head.

Saffron made the motion of clapping—close enough. "Come now. We clean, we bury, we move on."

Grumbling, Seraphina flexed her fingers. "Let's see if I remember how to do this shit."

"Ashes to ashes, let rest be found,
To hallowed crypt beneath the ground.
Blood be cleansed, let stains erase,
Leave no mark upon this place.
By Bellarose will, by magic bright,
Let air be pure, both day and night."

Golden flecks rose from Saffron's body, drifting in slow spirals, pulsing before vanishing down the dark path to the family crypt. The blood sizzled as it evaporated, curling in tendrils laced with scorched copper. A sudden breeze knifed through the space—crisp, unnatural, infused with citrus and finality.

Seraphina wrinkled her nose. "Okay, that's almost too fresh. Did I summon a bottle of enchanted lemon spray?"

Saffron didn't even blink. "At least it's not brimstone. Domestic magic suits you."

"Don't be shocked. I had toddlers. Mastering fast cleanup was survival." And hell yes, she was proud of it.

Saffron moved toward a towering shelf, expression turning grave. "Come on. It's time you saw what we've been guarding."

Seraphina narrowed her eyes. "Oh great. Another reveal."

Every step deeper into this legacy felt like closing a door behind her. One more part of her old life bricked over. The woman who raised toddlers and dodged magic was getting smaller in the rearview mirror—and she wasn't sure she liked what was replacing her.

Saffron's fingers hovered over two books. Their timeworn spines murmured of ancient knowledge. "Push here."

Seraphina obeyed.

A click. A groan. The shelf shifted, swinging outward.

Seraphina stepped back. "Seriously? Secret passages too?"

Saffron waved toward the doorway. "After you."

A chill seeped from the opening. Seraphina paused, peering into the darkness beyond. Rough-hewn stone walls framed a narrow, winding staircase that spiralled downward, vanishing into the earth below the estate. The scent of damp soil and dust hung heavy, stale and undisturbed, time bottled and shelved like some ancient mistake.

"How long has this been here?" She rubbed her arms against the sudden bite in the air.

"Well before the house. Our ancestors built around it, expanding the grounds over centuries. But the Shadowkeep? It came first. Buried deep. Sealed and contained."

Seraphina blew out a breath. "Comforting."

"Come on. You've fought worse than stairs."

She rolled her eyes and stepped onto the stone step. Energy jolted beneath her, the fine hairs on her arms rose in warning.

She turned. "So, what's down there?"

"Things that make the devil himself tread carefully."

"Bloody hell."

With one final glance at the familiar comfort of the scriptorium, Seraphina braced herself and walked into the dark.

Her sneakers struck stone, the sound swallowed by the cold clinging to the space—a tension stretched thin, heavy with silence. Everything around her felt saturated—with history, and the residue of long-spent magic. Something primordial stirred in the shadows ahead—not hostile, but undeniably aware.

Power lingered here and not the gentle kind.

As she descended, the walls lining the spiral staircase throbbed with hidden life. Lines of warm gold and flickering white light rippled outward from her presence, responding to her as if the magic had been slumbering, and now finally stirred. Each rune flared before fading, acknowledging her as its rightful heir.

The scent of damp earth thickened, mingled with traces of scorched herbs and long buried rites. The deeper she moved, the more the quiet pressed in—close and stifling, the exhale of something old trying not to wake.

The wards lining the staircase pushed gently at her senses, probing, testing. Once satisfied, they softened. She belonged. The key had returned.

Symbols carved deep into the stone itched with latent energy, reshaping with each step she took. Their meanings unfurled in flickers—half-remembered fragments from a lineage buried under time. She didn't fully understand them, but the blood in her veins did.

At the bottom, the corridor widened into a chamber—and there, the entrance to the Shadowkeep rose from the stone, as if the ground itself had grown it to keep something in.

Forged from polished ironwood so dark it drank the light dry, the doors loomed—silent sentinels built to remember.

They weren't inert. They breathed beneath her skin, a deep thrum stitched to the very heart of the Keep. The floor registered her presence. The threshold recorded her passage.

Intricate sigils smouldered across the surface—flickering from molten orange to bloodred—possessed by enchantments too old for the modern world. These weren't decorative. They were warnings.

Seraphina approached and pressed her hand to the cool wood.

It reacted instantly—magic surged beneath her palm, curling up her arm in a rush of liquid fire. The glyphs flared brighter, shifting in a slow spiral, reforming into symbols that flickered through languages long buried by time. The threshold read her. Recognised her. And yielded.

One lock clicked. Then another. Then a third.

Each sound rolled through the corridor—heavy, deliberate, the steady rhythm of something old stirring from centuries of slumber.

Seraphina retreated as the final mechanism disengaged. A low chime rang out—a tone that resonated through the walls, through her, through the house itself. The moment had arrived.

The doors parted with a groan that rumbled through the stone—a seismic protest born of age and might.

They didn't swing—they opened as if pulled from the centre of the earth, each inch ringing with the burden of what had been sealed behind them.

Frigid air rushed out—not just cold, but the icy stillness unbroken for too long. The smell closed in: dust, ash, ruin—and a darker presence lurking below. One that clung to the past and refused to lift. The kind you didn't question unless you were prepared for the answer.

She moved forward.

What lay ahead coiled in on itself—stricture-bound, steeped in the still-before.

The floor trembled underfoot. Something long-buried stirred—not dead, only veiled.

It had never been still.

It had only held itself.

And now, it knew she had come.

Seraphina stared into the dark, heart thudding. She could turn back. Pretend none of this had happened. Pretend she wasn't one step away from starring in the worst kind of horror movie.

But she didn't.

"Here goes nothing." She crossed over like sarcasm counted as armour.

Five

"Every lock has a key. Every monster wants out. And every family has at least one secret that doesn't stay buried."
— Shadowkeep Codex, Warning Etched in Blood

The moment Seraphina stepped inside, a shiver needled its way up her spine. The darkness wasn't mere absence—it stirred, pulsing at the chamber's edge with the patience of a predator poised to strike. Whispers slithered through the stillness, curling around her ears— desperate, insidious.

Release us… Free us… We will serve…

She swallowed hard. A towering wall of shelves drew her gaze, lined with vessels of every shape and size—blackened urns, delicate glass phials, rusted iron cages no larger than a fist. Each one vibrated with restrained intensity, holding something bound—something dangerous.

Opposite them, a massive obsidian mirror stretched from floor to ceiling, its surface swirling with liquid umbra. It reflected nothing. It revealed—towering cities she'd never seen, barren wastelands, shifting figures that looked almost human. The magic radiating from it was long-sleeping and wild—a force that never asked permission. It took.

To the right, the most dangerous object in the room loomed. A glass-encased podium, its protective wards cycling in steady intervals.

Inside rested a single grimoire—stitched in what could only be demon skin, its spine ridged with bone. This book defied dust.

It brooded—feral and scented like scorched velvet, the kind of heat that curled in the throat. It *marked her*, soft as ashfall, certain as scripture.

Knowledge… Power… Just one touch.

As she drew near, the runes etched into the glass ignited. The bindings strained, recognising her.

The blackness wasn't screaming. It was seductive—sliding along her nerves, murmuring through her psyche, tempting her to open, unlock, unleash.

It would be so easy.

A twist of the wrist. A single word.

Control. Dominion. More.

Saffron appeared by the door, arms folded.

Seraphina swallowed hard. This place didn't just hold history—it *remembered* it. Not passively, but like a mouth full of broken teeth still chewing on the past. Her bravado was nothing more than tissue paper. One wrong move, and she'd tear.

"Geezus, Mum. If Julian and Brinnan get in here, the world's screwed."

"Completely and irrevocably," Saffron agreed.

Something sneezed.

Seraphina froze. That… was not on her apocalypse bingo card.

Silence stretched.

A muffled voice broke through:

"Uh, hello? Is someone finally—oh, wait, never mind. You're not here to let me out, are you?"

The last few hours had been a whirlwind of insanity—her ghost-mother dropping life-altering bombshells, wards deciding she was a VIP key to a vault of nightmares, and a whole coven of spectral matriarchs silently judging her. At this point, she might as well lean into the chaos.

The voice was smooth but edged with nervous energy—like someone trying to sell insurance while realising their life depended on the sale.

Seraphina scanned the cavernous room—past the vessels, the swirling mirror, the soul-sucking spellbook in its warded box.

Her gaze caught on something.

Crouched in a binding ring traced with gold-orange incantations, was a demon. Gangly, sharp-featured. Two stubby horns poked through a mop of messy black curls. His skin was deep, ashen red. A long tail flicked behind him. His robes—if they qualified—hung from his lean frame like a jester who'd missed several centuries of wardrobe updates.

He perked up the second he saw her, red eyes gleaming.

"Oh! A Bellarose! I'd recognise that particular blend of exhaustion and existential resentment anywhere."

"What in the actual hell?" The words slipped out before Seraphina's brain caught up.

"Ah." The demon dragged out the sound. No humility, just performance. "That would be where I'm supposed to be. Instead, I'm here. Trapped. Against my will. For—" He started counting on clawed fingers. He sighed before he hit five. "Who even keeps track after centuries? Time's an illusion anyway."

Saffron floated beside Seraphina. Her gaze carved him from top to bottom. "Samthrax."

How the hell had she forgotten this ratbag was locked up down here?

The demon winced. "Ah. Lady Saffron. Always a pleasure. And yes, still here. Still trapped. No one's more aware of my prolonged stay than I."

"You're here for a reason. My great-great-grandmother didn't trap you on a whim."

Seraphina stared at the creature, then at her mum. "Okay. Time out. Why do we have a literal hell-being stashed away in our personal chamber of nightmares?"

Samthrax tried to spin it. Cos why not?

"Technically, I may have… attempted to consume an ancestor's soul."

Saffron practically radiated disdain. "You challenged her to a duel. You lost. Then you tried to eat her."

"Yes, well. Details." He waved a clawed hand. "Bellarose women really don't take losing well."

"We don't take cheating well," Saffron corrected.

"Tomato, tomahto."

"I have got to stop being surprised by this stuff." Seraphina's new life motto.

Saffron's stare could've peeled paint. "Spare us the theatrics. I'm sure you've been plotting your escape since day one. Skip to the part where you resort to bribery."

"Ah! Now we're speaking my language. I happen to have something you want. Useful, potentially world-saving information. And I—my dear ladies—am feeling charitable."

Saffron gave him the kind of look that should've come with a hex. "Charitable? You expect me to believe you'll hand over intel out of the kindness of your demon heart?"

"Wow." He clutched his nonexistent pearls. "That's demonist. And slightly hurtful."

Seraphina stepped between them. Yeesh, this was verbal ping-pong at its most passive-aggressive.

"Enough. You—talk. And if I don't like what I hear, I'll finish what dear Grammy should've done decades ago. Capiche?"

The demon straightened. *Daughter like mother. Noted.*

"Alright, alright. Julian and Brinnan? Cooking up something big.

And let's just say… living here gives me front-row seats to every dark rumour slithering through the void."

Seraphina had the feeling there was more. *Cattle prod sprung to mind.* "Fascinating. Get to the part where it's useful."

No doubt about it—Seraphina would follow through. Time to spill.

"Brinnan's after that." He jabbed a talon at the grimoire. "And that." A tail flick toward the mirror. He leaned in, claws poised like a gambler about to lay his cards. "He won't stop. Not until he rules." His grin snapped back into place. "You know. For some light apocalyptic fun."

Saffron's whole vibe shifted. "The book alone is bad enough. But the portal—if he gets both, we're beyond screwed."

Samthrax clapped, delighted. "Oh-ho, then it's party o'clock. Picture this: realms full of unemployed demons, time tantrums instead of clocks, and physics as a polite suggestion. He could build an army. Rewrite history. Erase your whole bloodline like a badly drawn doodle."

Seraphina's stomach decided to learn interpretive dance. "I guess you were his first move, Mum."

Samthrax gave Saffy's ghost-glow the side-eye. "I would assume so. And if he gets his mitts on that book and portal—" He dragged a claw across his throat. "Let's just say your family tree's looking real flammable."

Seraphina swore. Loudly.

Saffron turned to him. "You knew this and said nothing?"

Samthrax raised both hands. *Tough crowd.*

"Oh sure, because I had so many options. What was I supposed to do—send a carrier pigeon? Maybe tap out a little SOS in the dust?"

"Okay, fair point."

"What do you want in return?"

Like Seraphina didn't already know where this was going.

Samthrax grinned. "One teensy-weensy thing."

Saffron's glare turned razor-edged. "No."

"You don't even know what it is!"

"You want freedom. Not happening."

Seraphina knew it was a bad idea before she opened her mouth.

"What if we negotiate?"

Because clearly, she'd lost her damn mind.

"Negotiate?!"

Saffron looked at her as if she'd just suggested cuddling a cobra.

"With that? He's a soul-snacking, deal-twisting chaos-gremlin from hell!"

Samthrax slapped a claw to his chest. "Yeesh. The stereotyping. For the record, I only snack on souls when absolutely necessary."

Seraphina shot him a look. "Not. Helping."

She cut back to Saffron. "Do we really have time for this? My magic's barely back online, Julian and Brinnan are gunning for us, and we're running out of options. We need every bloody advantage."

Saffron released a slow, measured breath, one meant to cage the words burning on her tongue.

"You should listen to her. The desperate ones always make the best choices." Samthrax's smile was like gravity, just waiting for someone to jump.

Saffron aimed a glare that could salt the earth. "Fine. Your decision. But if you're cutting a deal, you hold the leash."

Samthrax's tail swished. "Kinky."

"One step out of line, and I'll bury you so deep hell will need a ladder." Seraphina didn't have to say it—her face already had the shovels out.

"...Noted."

"Let's get this over with." Saffron would rather exhume her own grave.

Seraphina rolled her shoulders. "Nothing like binding a demon to kickstart a war."

She didn't trust him—but sometimes survival meant shaking hands with the thing you feared most and daring it to blink first.

She lifted her hands:

"By words alone, this pact is spun.

No blood, no bone—just will undone.

Serve me well, you shall walk free.

But cross me once? You belong to me."

Wind circled them, twitching and restless. The magic snapped into place, a binding force wrapping around Samthrax like an affectionate yet mildly homicidal pet snake.

"That has… serious 'possessive ex' energy." Samthrax looked impressed—and slightly aroused.

"So don't piss me off."

As the containment circle shattered with a shimmer and a low hiss, the pressure in the room changed. Something unseen stirred in the deeper shadows—not close. But not far.

It lingered just beyond knowing—present, and hungry.

Samthrax let out a whoop so loud it ricocheted off the walls. With limbs too long and too loose, he launched into a gleefully chaotic victory dance—tail snapping, arms flailing, legs attempting some unholy fusion of interpretive demon jazz and drunken spider.

"Oh, sweet infernal depths, that feels good! I can move! I can stretch! I can—"

He spun too fast, caught his tail, and crashed face-first onto the floor.

"Smooth." Seraphina didn't even try to hide the sarcasm.

"For the record, I've been stuck in one spot for two hundred years. I'm still recalibrating."

"If this is our secret weapon, we're screwed." Saffron sounded like she was halfway through writing their eulogy.

Samthrax bounced to his feet. "I was extremely menacing in my prime, thank you very much."

"You just pirouetted into the floor." Seraphina was thinking her mother had a point. *Shit.*

"Details." Samthrax was too happy to be offended at their mutual misgivings. "Also, my friends call me Sammy. Feel free."

"We are not friends."

"Yet."

"This is on you." Saffron's tone came with a receipt and a restocking fee.

Samthrax clapped his hands. "Let's get out of this doom dungeon before I redecorate. I'm thinking lava sconces and blood-red drapes."

That alone was enough motivation.

Seraphina led the way up the spiral staircase, gold-threaded wards whispering shut behind them, sealing the Shadowkeep with quiet finality. Samthrax stretched with every step, bones cracking in a symphony of pent-up demonic delight.

"Ahhh, freedom." Samthrax let the word roll out, indulgent as a toast at someone else's funeral. "Never kneeling to a human again—unless it comes with a throne, a foot massage, and a cheese platter."

Both women ignored him.

At the top, Saffron turned to her daughter, gaze sharp enough to file metal. "We're taking my car."

"I have a car."

"You have an affront to vehicular integrity. That thing is two bald tyres and a death wish. Even dead, I don't feel safe near it."

Samthrax leaned in, all teeth and disaster-hound curiosity. "That bad, huh?"

"Worse. I've seen actual corpses in better condition." She gestured to herself. "Exhibit A."

"It gets me where I need to go."

Not that anyone here respected functional transportation.

"Barely. And I'd rather not die again in a flaming hunk of rust."

Samthrax shrugged. "I vote we take the safest ride. Dying dramatically should be a last resort."

Seraphina rolled her eyes. "Fine. We'll take the sorceress-mobile."

Seraphina slid behind the wheel of Saffron's pristine black Mercedes, reevaluating every questionable decision she'd ever made. The leather was cool and smooth beneath her hands. The vanity plate—WICCAN—gleamed, a badge of unapologetic magical hubris. The engine purred to life with a sound her own clunker couldn't dream of replicating.

Saffron glided into the passenger side like mist that knew where to go. Samthrax flopped into the back, tail curling into the upholstery, claws already poking at every button within reach.

"This is amazing. You humans love adding complications to basic transportation. It's like a chariot and a puzzle box had a baby."

Seraphina slapped his hand away from the seat warmers. "No touching. Your infernal arse doesn't need help staying warm."

Saffron tilted her head, all judgement and frost. "If anything, you need thawing. All those years pretending to be normal did a number on you."

Seraphina gripped the steering wheel harder than necessary. "Are you two planning to tag-team my last nerve the entire ride?"

"Yes." Samthrax didn't even pretend to feel bad.

With a deep sigh of resignation, Seraphina steered the car down the long gravel drive. The estate slipped from view, swallowed by trees and secrets.

As they neared the edge of the enclave, the iron gates groaned open—enchantments humming as they acknowledged the bloodline in control.

But just before they cleared the exit, a black Escalade rolled in from the opposite direction.

Sleek. Controlled. A predator's entrance.

Saffron straightened, energy shifting. "Well, well. Killian Graves himself."

Seraphina's fingers clenched the wheel like she meant to strangle it. "Of course it is."

Samthrax leaned forward, practically vibrating with glee. "Ooooh, the infamous leader. Ruthless. Dangerous. Swoon-worthy, if you're into tall, dark, and destroy-y types."

Saffron's eyes flashed with mischief. "He's aged well."

"Don't." Seraphina pictured duct tape. Then superglue. Tempting. The Escalade passed slowly. Behind the tinted window, a face she knew too well stared straight at her.

Killian's eyes met hers head-on—ice-bright, storm-hardened, unflinching. The hit was immediate. Her stomach lurched. A violent thud, not a heartbeat. Her hands curled tighter on the wheel. Nails digging half-moons into the leather. Every buried memory detonated at once, tearing through her veins.

And then—he was gone. Swallowed by the bend.

Saffron let out a low whistle. "Still smouldering, that one."

Samthrax cackled. "That tension could power the grid."

"Shut up. Both of you." Seraphina was two seconds from driving into a tree on purpose.

Saffron leaned in. "That wasn't 'we used to date' energy. That was 'I see you in my dreams, and I hate it' energy."

"Drop it, Mum." Mortification was now a full-body experience.

Samthrax rubbed his hands together gleefully. "Oh, I am so here for this subplot."

Saffron locked on like a shark with a scent for blood and zero boundaries. She wasn't letting go. Not when her daughter's energy had changed, and not when it smelled like secrets.

"Nope. Spill."

Samthrax wiggled his brows. "Do tell! I haven't been this invested in drama since the time a summoner accidentally bound himself to a goat."

Seraphina gathered herself, her brain screaming to lie, deflect, stall— but Saffron's expectant stare bore down on her, unrelenting.

The words clawed up her throat. Admitting them out loud felt like slitting her own history open and letting it bleed. Her heart kicked hard and punishing, as if trying to warn her. But the truth had festered too long.

"...He's the twins' father."

A heartbeat later.

"What?!" Saffron hit a frequency that fried the radio.

"Holy hellfire." Samthrax reeled. "You've been sitting on this?!"

Seraphina winced. "Yes. And can we not get struck by lightning from the force of your collective outrage?"

Saffron gawked, like her daughter had sprouted horns. "Killian Graves? As in the magically gifted, politically terrifying, emotionally catastrophic Killian?"

Seraphina smacked the wheel. "Yes! And before either of you launch into a witchy intervention, I had my reasons!"

Samthrax was in his element. "This is gold. Absolute chaos gold."

"You. Quiet. Forever." Seraphina's finger was basically a loaded wand.

She was this close to hexing his soul. Assuming he had one.

"You lied. You said the twins were from a fling with some nobody!"

"Because I wanted out." Seraphina's grip tightened.

Out of the bloodlines. Out of the war. Out of watching him walk away all over again.

"I didn't want him dragged into it. And if I'd told you the truth, you'd have meddled. You always meddle."

Saffron looked torn between pride and complete exasperation. "I can't decide whether to applaud or strangle you."

Seraphina laughed. Just short of unhinged. "Perfect! That's exactly the reaction I was going for."

Saffron arched a brow. "And how exactly do you plan to break that news? Over coffee? 'Hey Killian—surprise! You're a dad. Hope you're up for some father-daughter-son bonding'?"

"I have no idea. But right now, we're about to yank the kids out of their perfectly normal, magic-free lives and drop them into a world where demons are real and family reunions come with attempted murder. I'd rather survive that nightmare first."

In truth, Seraphina was afraid of what he'd see. Of the way he'd look at the twins and know—instantly—that they were his. And take them. Because that's what Graves men did: they didn't ask. They took.

"Well, at least they inherited good genes." Saffron was all mischief and no remorse.

"Oh, I bet they're adorable chaos gremlins." Samthrax practically *beamed* corrupt pride.

"Too pretty and way too dramatic." And somehow, that was still an understatement.

"Like their parents?" Saffron's eyes sparkled with the kind of glee that usually came with fireballs.

"Don't push me." Seraphina had stopped joking.

As Saffron's sleek beast of a car cut through the dawn, a truth settled in Seraphina's soul:

This wasn't survival. It was war—stitched in silence, scarred in blood. And the deadliest weapons?

They were the ones you birthed… and buried yourself.

Six

*"Should the key awaken in unworthy hands, the bloodline will fracture.
And from that wound—war."*
— Matriarch Lore Scroll, Codex 12:41

Julian strode through the Enclave's winding streets with the quiet confidence of a predator who already owned the hunt.

Confident. Casual. Like he hadn't just poisoned something on the way in. This was a place built on secrets—and Julian traded in them.

He didn't need to chase whispers. They came to him, starved for a buyer.

Somewhere, buried under layers of curated apathy and cut-glass charm, the boy who once begged for his father's attention still stirred. Julian crushed the thought. That version of him was a liability. And liabilities don't survive in this game.

At the far end of Rue Nocturne, where damp curled into ritual-scored cobblestone and curses stitched themselves into every wall, a figure slouched against a crumbling brick façade.

Malrik—gaunt, hawk-eyed, wrapped in a coat that probably had its own rap sheet—grinned as Julian approached. The reek of cheap liquor clung to him, soaked deep into his pores.

His eyes were all twitch and teeth. The kind of man who smiled like he knew where your body would be dumped.

"Well, well. If it isn't the dark prince himself." Malrik's mouth pulled up at the corners—mockery, not amusement. "What brings you slithering back, Julian?"

Julian moved closer, with no smile, no civility. Just heat and history and the silent promise that this wasn't a reunion.

"I need eyes. Ears. And a pair of willing hands."

Malrik's grin surfaced like something dead breaking through ice.

"Oh, my dear boy—you know I've got all three in spades."

He didn't even pretend to play coy. Filth such as him didn't flirt with opportunity. They latched on and sucked the marrow out.

Julian looked straight through him; anything warm had been cut out years ago.

"I want Seraphina watched."

Malrik's gut clenched.

His grin faltered—pleasure curdling into something colder.

Even now, her name made his jaw tighten.

His hatred wasn't petty. It wasn't the type of grudge that faded with time. It burned—low and constant—lodged beneath his ribs, a shard that never stopped cutting. Each breath reminded him of what she'd taken. Any alley in this forsaken city stank of what he'd lost.

He hadn't always been a bottom-feeder.

Once, Malrik had been climbing—clever, poised, dangerous. A rising name in the Crescent's underworld. Every move calculated. Every connection forged behind closed doors.

Until she'd come crashing through.

Seraphina hadn't stopped him.

She'd dismantled him.

One brutal, righteous act—just one—and everything he'd built collapsed. She left him clawing through the ruins of his own ambition.

And he'd never crawled high enough to matter again.

Now, facing Julian, his fingers twitched at his sides, barely holding back the urge to lash out.

The years had dulled nothing.

If Julian wanted her brought down?

He'd help.

Not for power. Not for favour.

For revenge.

"I'm listening."

Julian's fingers brushed the silver signet, the way someone might trace the edge of a weapon they weren't ready to use.

"An unfortunate incident has forced Seraphina to reclaim her birthright. I want to know where she goes. What she does. Who she speaks to. Every detail."

Malrik didn't try to hide his interest. "So, you want me to shadow her?"

"Precisely, keep close. Keep quiet. Feed me everything. And when the time comes—help me make sure she's no longer a problem."

Malrik weighed the offer.

He knew the cost of being useful in this world.

"And in return?"

Julian's grin turned surgical.

"When this is done, the Enclave will remember your name for all the right reasons. No more 'Almost-Malrik.'"

He extended his hand.

"You've got yourself a deal."

Their handshake was brief. But binding.

As Julian vanished into the dark, Malrik leaned against the wall, eyes half-lidded. Memory rose—jagged as broken glass.

****

Silhouettes writhed across the apothecary's walls; the firelight restless—eager.

The place stank of desperation and magic that hadn't been cleaned in decades. Everything had a metallic bite—like spilled blood and burnt promises.

Tucked between two collapsing buildings in the Enclave's underbelly, the shop had been a haven for those who preferred their craft unshackled by Council oversight.

Here, power changed hands in murmurs. Pacts were sealed with more than ink. Every desire came with a cost.

That night had belonged to Malrik.

And he'd damn near tasted freedom.

An orb alchemists knew as the Void Seed had surfaced—an artifact thrumming with forbidden energy, said to contain the distilled knowledge of a long-dead warlock. A relic that could turn a nobody into a contender. It had practically sung to him. Spoken his name. Promised him a crown carved from bone and shadow.

With it, Malrik would pull his way out of obscurity. No more scraps. No more waiting. This was his moment.

And then—Seraphina walked in.

She hadn't been looking for him—she was after Julian.

But the second her eyes hit the orb, she knew.

Knew what it was. Knew what he was.

The damn thing dimmed in her presence. Flickered like it recognised her. Like it didn't want to be touched.

Seraphina Bellarose never could leave well enough alone. And Malrik? He'd been stupid enough to think she'd walk away.

He tried charm. Spun a half-truth into something sweet. Told her it was just an old relic. No real threat.

But she saw through the lie, right to the hunger clenching his fists around the prize.

"You're not ready for what that orb carries."

Malrik lunged for the Void Seed, desperate to vanish before she could intervene.

He could feel the energy pulsing through it. Feel it about to break open.

She was faster.

Her magic hit with the force of a storm. Raw. Unrelenting. Elemental. No warning. No theatrics. Just power—stripped bare and thrown like a bloody verdict.

The blast hurled him across the room, tearing the air from his lungs.

The orb, delicate despite the darkness it contained, shattered on impact.

A violent shockwave erupted, ripping through the shop—blackening shelves, splintering stone.

Malrik hit the floor in a broken heap.

Humiliated in front of the very people he'd spent years trying to impress.

The deal collapsed. The Council was alerted. And Malrik?

Malrik became a cautionary tale. A failure. A fool. A nearly was that never would be.

The whispers followed him for years, dogging every step, poisoning every attempt to rebuild.

Now, after all this time, Seraphina had returned.

And Julian wanted eyes on her.

To witness her ruin?

He'd do that for free.

***

Julian's black Maserati sliced through the rain-slicked streets, neon from bars and diners strobing across the windshield in feverish, stuttering bursts.

Betrayal still sang in his veins, lighting his nerves with cold satisfaction.

Seraphina had no idea what was coming.

And that suited him just fine.

He drummed his fingers on the wheel, rolling his neck to loosen the tension clinging to him. There was no finer reward for a perfectly played hand than indulging his darker appetites.

And tonight?

Tonight, he intended to celebrate.

Julian didn't chase chaos for the thrill. He crafted it.

Every move carved with intention.

He wasn't some snarling animal snapping at opportunity—he was the knife behind the curtain.

He didn't just want Seraphina defeated.

He wanted her legacy folded, pressed, and burned into something that bore *his* name instead.

Up ahead, beneath the flicker of a broken diner sign, a group lingered in the orange-hued haze of a streetlight. He slowed.

A woman stepped forward—red stilettos clicking against wet pavement, leather skirt skimming her thighs, kohl-rimmed eyes, smoky with allure. Her walk was confident. Calculated.

She leaned through the open window, her gaze taking in the crisp lines of his coat and the lazy command in the way he sat.

"Looking for company, handsome?" She purred, lips the same red as her heels.

"That depends. Do you bite?"

She laughed—low and amused. "For the right price."

He pulled five crisp hundred - dollar bills from his coat, sliding them between her fingers.

"Get in."

The door clicked open. She slipped inside, one leg crossing over the other with feline grace. "What's your name, darling?"

Julian smiled the way devils do—slow, knowing, and without a trace of mercy.

"For tonight—let's not ruin the mystery."

He didn't want her name. Didn't care who she was. She was a garnish on the evening—something pretty to mark the start of a win he already considered inevitable.

He hit the gas, the roar of the engine drowning out the city as they disappeared into the night.

***

A few miles away, Brinnan sat beneath the muted light of his study—the one place where his true nature was laid bare.

Here, surrounded by relics of his craft, where spent incantations lingered and bloodstains had long since soaked into the wood, he was unmasked. Unrestrained.

This was his sanctum. His altar.

Where the darkness he'd nurtured for decades still fed.

His thoughts were scalpels—precise and cold, slicing through distraction with surgical clarity.

Julian could not be left to wander. Ambition had always driven his son. Unchecked, it festered into disobedience.

And Brinnan did not tolerate betrayal.

He had offered Julian the illusion of freedom. Dangled power just out of reach to shape the hunger.

A leash disguised as liberty.

Julian had his father's ruthlessness, sure.

But none of his patience.

He was raw metal not yet tempered.

Still useful. Still salvageable.

But if he strayed too far?

Brinnan would break him. As he had broken others.

With measured grace, he reached for the ceremonial dagger resting on his desk—its blade forged in forgotten rites, honed by rituals older than the Enclave itself. It gleamed as he drew it across his palm. Flesh parted cleanly. Blood welled, thick and dark, before falling into the scrying bowl.

The first drop struck.

Ripples bloomed. Red unfurling through black. A stain that bled outward with slow, deliberate intent.

He murmured the invocation—voice low, purposeful—a litany carved from silk and steel. Magic rose instantly. The water twisted, darkened, roiled.

The murk receded, revealing Julian's face. Lit by flickering streetlights. Smirking. Self-satisfied.

Scheming.

Brinnan's jaw tensed.

The image shifted, displaying Malrik—a creature of wasted potential. Loyal to no one. Chained only by greed.

Brinnan studied the scene, his expression carved from granite. Julian thought himself clever. The arrogance might have been amusing—if it weren't so dangerous.

His grip on the dagger tightened, the tip digging into the desk's scarred surface.

He had built an empire from nothing.

Clawed his name into existence with cunning, cruelty, and relentless resolve.

He would not be undone by the son who owed him everything.

Let Julian ready his weapon—Brinnan would strike first, and with more precision.

He would gut his own blood if it meant the flame caught higher. Legacy meant nothing if it wasn't his name etched into history. The Enclave? Just a stepping stone toward that end.

Brinnan's true purpose moved beneath it all—vast and unseen.

Long-dormant forces were stirring.

Pacts sealed in forgotten tongues.

Old gods remembered by the desperate and the damned.

He had spent years feeding the right ears.

Unearthing secrets time had buried.

Dominion over the Crescent Enclave was only the beginning.

But first—Seraphina.

With a flick of his blood-slicked fingers, he drew a pattern above the bowl. The surface churned, spiralled—until it seized.

For a breath—nothing.

The vessel shuddered. The vision crumbled into darkness.

And the reflection left behind was his own—distorted, sneering back at him.

Not failure.

Rejection.

He had been shut out.

Brinnan's hand curled around the dagger.

The ancestors.

Even in death, those Bellarose witches shielded her. Their magic, woven through centuries—through blood, bone, and vow—stood against him.

Not a wall.

A fortress carved from time itself.

He bit down on his rage. Ground it into cold resolve.

Julian could be reached.

Bent.

Broken if necessary.

But Seraphina?

She was something else.

Cocooned in age-old protections.

Guarded by ghosts.

Backed by a legacy that refused to rot.

Fine.

Let the dead rise to shield her.

He would rip through them—one by one.

Strip their names from the spine of history.

Tear down the line they bled to defend.

Until there was nothing left.

No sanctuary.

Seraphina would standalone.

And then she would understand:

This had never been about her.

It was about breaking magic itself.

About shattering the veil between worlds.

About obliterating the lines that kept the gifted separate from the mundanii.

Once the Veilborn were unbound…

Once the Shadowkeep bent to his will…

The old laws would fall.

Power would no longer ask—it would take.

And those who stood in his way?

Wouldn't burn.

They would cease to exist.

Seven

Seraphina pulled into her street, the familiar veneer of suburban mundanii life pressing against the car windows—a suffocating weight that settled deep in her chest. The rows of houses stood in perfect, pretentious formation. Hedges trimmed within an inch of their lives. Porches draped in seasonal banners. Nothing out of place. Nothing unexpected.

This was a neighbourhood where the strangest thing to happen was a misdelivered Amazon package.

Her house waited at the end of the cul-de-sac, nestled beneath the canopy of a towering maple shedding gold leaves in slow, deliberate spirals. Painted a soft blue with white trim, it matched her intentions when she bought it—sufficient charm to deflect attention, not enough to invite it.

Once, it had been her sanctuary. Now, it felt too small and far too breakable.

She parked the car, hands tight on the wheel as though anchoring herself to reality. Each heartbeat struck like an accusation, doubt thickening in its wake until even her thoughts flinched from it.

"All right. How the hell am I supposed to tell my sixteen-year-old kids that not only are they witches, but I've been lying to them their entire lives about who they are and where they come from?"

Saffron, lounging in the passenger seat as though death was a minor inconvenience, tapped her chin thoughtfully. "Easy. 'So, funny story—your whole life's been a well-meaning lie. You've got magic, we're moving, and your estranged father is kind of a big deal. Any questions before we start loading the car?'"

Oh yeah. That would go great. Straight to therapy, do not pass go.

"I'm holding off on the Killian part. They've got enough to process."

Saffron gave her a look that didn't need words. "I'll tell them, Mum. Just… not yet."

Samthrax sprawled in the back seat, as if he owned it. "Honestly, you're overthinking this. Big reveal moments require flair. Tell them they're witches. Pause for dramatic effect. Then set something on fire. Homework makes excellent kindling."

Seraphina shot him a withering look. "Yes, because nothing says stable parenting like committing arson in your own living room."

Saffron tilted her head, amusement spreading with the slow satisfaction of someone watching a mess she didn't have to clean. "Darling, stability left the station the moment you unbound your magic. Besides, they're teenagers. They already suspect you're hiding something. At least this is more interesting than a secret gambling addiction or taxidermy hobby."

Samthrax leaned forward, interest sparking without a shred of subtlety. "Wait—do you taxidermy?"

Seraphina turned to him, face unreadable, voice built to end conversations. "Not the point."

He waved a hand. "Fine, fine. Teenagers love rebellion, right? Make it sound like they were born into a super-secret magical society. Throw in some forbidden knowledge, a touch of dramatic legacy—boom, instant cool points."

"You're assuming they won't scream, call me insane, and barricade themselves in their rooms."

Saffron gave a long exhale, every inch of it practiced. "Then you show them me. A ghost grandmother is rather hard to deny. My bet? Sage will accept it—she's always been curious. Sebastian will push back. He likes things he can see and touch."

Seraphina drummed her fingers on the wheel, thinking. "Okay, that's a decent angle. And yeah, Sebastian's going to be the challenge."

Samthrax grinned, tapping his claws together. "And if that doesn't work, you still have me."

Seraphina didn't look at him so much as reconsider his existence. "Oh sure. Because right after 'Here's Grams—dead but not gone,' introducing our resident demon is definitely the move."

He beamed, like approval was inevitable. "Exactly! I mean, look at me! I'm charismatic, approachable—"

"—horrifying," Seraphina cut in.

"—debatable," he chirped, way too pleased with himself. "But come on—a witch, a ghost, and a demon telling them this story? That's compelling. What are they gonna do, argue with reality?"

Seraphina didn't laugh—just let the sound escape before it could turn into something else. "Oh, without a doubt."

"Ah, the joys of parenting. Now, off you go to rewrite their entire sense of self." Samthrax was relishing the irony.

Seraphina exited the vehicle. "Okay, you two stay out of sight until I've explained what's going on." She adjusted her bag over her shoulder. "I'll let you know when it's safe to approach."

She walked up to the front door and pushed it open, immediately greeted by the familiar scent of vanilla and coffee.

"Mum? That you?" Sage's voice floated down from upstairs.

Footsteps thudded overhead, and moments later, both twins appeared at the top of the landing. Sebastian descended first, gave her a quick hug, and flopped onto the couch.

"So… what's the go with Grams?"

Sage followed, settling beside him. Her usual brightness had dimmed—edges smudged by worry she made no effort to hide.

Seraphina stood in front of them, fists clenched at her sides. Every cell in her body screamed to delay this conversation just one more minute.

But the looks on their faces? Waiting. Ready.

A gentle introduction didn't make the menu.

"There's no easy way to say this." The control in her voice cost more than she'd ever let them see.

Sage's wide blue eyes—so much like her father's—blinked once. "Okay…?"

Sebastian raked a hand through his dark curls, his green eyes—so damn identical to hers—pinning her in place. "Mum, you're really freaking me out."

Seraphina forced the sentence past the knot in her throat.

"…Grams is gone. She was murdered."

The world recoiled—conversation, light, time.

Sage flinched like the she had been physically slapped. Sebastian reeled back into the cushions, visibly shocked. His face emptied out. Everything in him just shut down. "I'm sorry—what?"

What the hell was his mother even saying? The thought didn't compute.

Sage shook her head, rejection kicking in before her brain caught up.

"That's not funny."

"I wouldn't joke about this." Seraphina wasn't crying, but her voice was soaked in it.

Sebastian's mouth opened, then closed. He forced the words out.

"But, we just talked to her."

"She was murdered?" Sage's thoughts scattered. Nothing lined up. This didn't happen to people like them.

Seraphina nodded once. Eyes burning.

Emotion clogged her throat, locking around sounds that refused to form. Tears blurred her vision as she watched the devastation shatter across her children's faces. Sage's breathing came in jagged, uneven bursts, her fingers digging into the couch until the fabric puckered under her grip. Sebastian stood up, his whole body straining under something he couldn't articulate, face drawn with a heaviness far beyond sixteen.

She couldn't undo this pain. She couldn't take back the words that had stolen the ground from under them.

Her arms opened instinctively. No language—only a silent plea.

Sage moved first. She launched off the couch, burying herself in her mother's embrace, her sobs raw and unrestrained, her body shaking with grief. A second later, Sebastian followed, wrapping his arms around them both. His grip tightened—strong, desperate—clinging to them like it was the only thing keeping him anchored to reality.

Seraphina clutched them tightly, her own tears slipping down her cheeks as their grief bled into her. She was their mother. She was supposed to be strong. But right now? She felt like a fault line pretending to be solid ground. She had fought so hard to protect them, to shield them from the chaos she had been born into. Now everything was crashing down around them, dragging them into a nightmare they had never asked for.

Even though Seraphina and Saffron had spent years at odds, the twins had forged their own bond with their grandmother. Seraphina had tried to limit contact when they were younger, but once they got their own phones, nothing had stopped them. Midnight FaceTimes, in-jokes only they understood—little fragments of Saffy they'd claimed as their own.

Sage trembled against her so violently she seemed on the verge of falling apart. "She's… really gone?" The words were muffled, fragile, barely more than a whisper against her shoulder.

Seraphina squeezed her fiercely. "Yeah baby, but she will always be with us." Quite literally, she thought.

Sebastian made a choked sound and pulled away first, scrubbing at his face with the sleeve of his hoodie. His usual wit had abandoned him, leaving only grief and something raw beneath it—anger, confusion, a desperate need to understand what was happening.

"Who? Why?"

Sage returned to the couch, tucking her legs under her, clutching the throw rug tightly, her fingers twisting into the fabric as if grounding herself. Both fixed their eyes on Seraphina, their attention pinning her in place.

"Julian Bellarose." Seraphina spat the name without heat. He didn't deserve the fire. "He's my cousin. Mum took him in when we were kids. He's dangerous. And he's working with his father—my Uncle Brinnan. Who is also a complete psychopath."

Sebastian made a sound that couldn't decide if it was humour or defence. "Wait. You have a cousin? And an uncle?"

"Yes."

"And this Julian—he murdered Grams?"

"In her own home." Seraphina hoped he burned in hell for this shit.

"But why?" Sage's gut twisted. None of it added up. Family didn't do this.

"Because of who we are."

Sebastian pulled at the strings on his hoodie. "What does that mean?"

Seraphina straightened her shoulders, grounding herself. She met their eyes with feigned confidence.

If there was a god paying attention, now would be a great time to pitch in.

"We're witches."

The words hung between them, heavy with implication. Not fiction. Not exaggeration. Just truth, laid bare. The world tilted, but their blood knew before their minds could catch up.

Sage stiffened, her gaze darting to the bookshelf, as though searching for proof in something tangible. Sebastian froze mid-pace, raking a hand through his hair for the third time in five minutes.

"I am. You are. Grams was."

The silence was deafening.

"Mum… I need you to start making sense."

Sage looked at her mother like she'd gone off the rails. Seraphina didn't blame her. She was starting to question her own damn sanity.

Because if this was true—if Grams was dead, if they were witches, if their entire life was a lie—then nothing was real. Every bedtime story, every birthday, every grounding for sneaking out—fake.

"Yeah, because right now this feels like some low-budget TV show." Sebastian's arms stayed crossed. His glare did the rest.

"Come on, Mum? Seriously?" It wasn't panic. Not yet. But the edges of Sage's calm were starting to go.

"I know how it sounds." Seraphina knew exactly how it sounded. "But it's the truth."

"Geezus, Mum. Any more bombshells you want to drop? What's next—psychics? A talking cat?" Sebastian didn't shout. He didn't have to. The sarcasm came loaded.

"I'm serious here." Seraphina wasn't softening this. No time to cushion or buffer. They'd understand later. Hopefully.

Sebastian scoffed, but it cracked around the edges. "Serious? You hid this from us our entire lives, and now you just drop it like a weather update?"

"Why?" Sage pushed out the question, like it hurt to ask.

"Because I thought it would keep you safe."

What she didn't say—was that if they knew the truth, they'd be hunted. Brinnan wouldn't have hesitated. Julian would've sniffed them out like blood in water. Because knowledge meant danger. And her children? They were walking fuse wires—just waiting to be lit.

"Safe from what?" Sebastian seriously wanted to punch something.

"From Julian. From Brinnan. From a power people kill for."

"You should've trusted us with this." It wasn't anger that sat behind Sage's words. It was everything after.

The fight drained out of Seraphina. "I did what I had to do." Not an excuse. Not even close. But it was the only thing she had left. She wanted to rewind time to when their biggest problem was forgotten lunch money. But there was no undoing this. No protecting them from what had already arrived. She had cracked open their history—and now they were bleeding right alongside her.

"You have no idea what I gave up." She didn't care how it sounded. Truth was truth.

"I had to make a choice—keep you in this world and make you targets, or take you away and give you a chance at something normal." It had cost her everything, and there were no receipts to prove it.

"So, you decided for us?" Sebastian aimed the words low, like he wanted them to bruise—then felt bad for it.

"Yes." Seraphina had already made peace with being the villain. "Because that's what mothers do—we protect our children, even if they end up hating us for it."

"So… we're supposed to accept this, believe it?" Sage's hands were steady. Her world wasn't.

"Right now? We don't have the luxury of easing into it."

"Why didn't Grams tell us?" Sage wasn't looking for comfort. She just needed answers.

A new voice rose, calm and deliberate.

"Because even though I didn't agree with your mother, I respected her choice."

They turned in unison.

Their grandmother stood in the corner, her presence pale and luminous.

Sage screamed.

Sebastian did the only rational thing—he grabbed the nearest object and hurled it.

The pillow sailed straight through Saffron's ghostly silhouette and flopped onto the floor.

Sebastian turned on his heel. "Bugger this, I'm out."

"Sebastian." Seraphina didn't blame him for wanting to run.

Too bad she didn't have the same option.

"What?" He spun back, throwing up his hands. "We were already dealing with Grams being murdered and witches. Now we've got ghost Grams? What's next? Zombie elves? The freaking Tooth Fairy?"

Sage, however, hadn't moved. Her mouth opened and closed before a sound finally escaped. "G—Grams?"

Saffron smiled gently. "Hello, my darlings."

Sage let out something between a sob and a laugh. "You're—I mean, obviously you're dead. But you're also here. Lit up like a divine battery pack. And—"

Sage's brain tried to file it under shock, under grief hallucination, under anything but real. But ghosts didn't care about logic, apparently.

"Defying every single law of nature?" Sebastian finished.

Saffron chuckled, eerily casual despite the whole being-dead thing. "Oh, sweetheart, you're being a tad dramatic."

Sebastian whipped around. "I threw a pillow at you, and it went through you! I think I'm handling this pretty damn well."

Sage stepped forward. "How… how is this possible?" She didn't realise she was crying.

An effervescence danced at the edges of Saffron, dimming before flaring to life once more. "Magic, my love."

Sage swallowed past the lump in her throat. "I thought we lost you forever." Everything she'd tried to hold in broke loose on the edge of that sentence.

Saffron raised a translucent hand, as if to tuck a strand of hair behind Sage's ear—though it stopped just short. "Oh, my sweet girl, I never left you."

Sage quivered, struggling to keep the sob from breaking free.

"So… what now?" The words felt foreign in his mouth. Sebastian was still catching up to the wreckage.

Seraphina rubbed her temples, wishing—absurdly—that magic was just a bedtime story, and her kids could stay blissfully unaware.

But wishes were useless.

"We're moving to the estate." Sebastian looked like he was trying to make sense of a nightmare that didn't belong to him. "But this is our home."

Seraphina didn't budge. "And if we stay, it'll be your grave."

That quieted everything.

"Maison Bellarose is where our family belongs. It's where you'll learn to use your powers. The Enclave is a community—people like us—and the estate has protections we desperately need."

"Magic we didn't even know we had five minutes ago." Sage wasn't even sure what she'd just said made sense out loud.

"Oh yeah, let's pack up our lives and move into a literal murder house. That sounds like a healthy coping mechanism." Sebastian's outburst hit fast and loud—cover fire for the panic he wouldn't admit to.

"The estate is not a murder house." Saffron cut in. The warmth was gone, and that never happened.

"Oh, isn't it? Because last I checked, you were killed in it, Grams." Sebastian hadn't meant it to come out like that, but the hurt always found the fastest exit.

Sage turned to her mother, practical instinct scrambling to make sense of fantasy. "Okay, hold on. Back up. You're seriously telling us we're uprooting our lives to go live in some secret magical commune?"

"The Crescent Enclave isn't just somewhere." Seraphina held their eyes. They could argue later. Right now, they were going. "It's the only place we'll be safe."

"So instead of living like normal human beings, we're gonna shack up in the witch witness protection program?" Control had left the building, taken the car keys, and floored it into oncoming traffic—and all Sebastian could do was stand there and watch the wreck.

"Sebastian." Seraphina baked the warning into the way she said his name.

"No, seriously Mum. Is there a cloak ceremony I should be prepping for? Secret handshake, too?"

Saffron cleared her throat, shooting Seraphina a look. "Told you he'd be difficult."

Sebastian flung up his hands again. Better than putting a hole in the wall. And he was one second away from doing it. "Sorry. Am I not reacting appropriately to being told we're witches, our grandmother's a ghost, and now we're being shipped off to a magical bunker?"

Sage had sunk back onto the couch, fingers fidgeting with the hem of her jeans. "Okay. Say we move to Gram's. Then what?"

Seraphina caught it—just the faintest shift. If Sage was in, Sebastian wouldn't be far behind.

"You train." Saffron wanted to say more—so much more—but Seraphina was hanging on by a thread. "You learn. Because Brinnan and Julian won't stop."

The words settled over them, heavy as a shroud.

Sebastian rubbed at his face. He wanted to erase the entire conversation. "Yeah, see, that's where you lose me. This sounds like the start of a bad Chosen One arc, and I'm not interested."

He kept it together on the outside, but inside? It was full-blown table-flipping mode and nobody had ducked yet.

Seraphina's control cracked, and it bled straight into her voice. "You don't have a choice."

More silence. The kind that asked what the hell came next.

"I understand this is a lot. But you have power. More than you realise. And it's high time you learned to use it." Saffron wasn't pleading. This was a door they were walking through, whether they liked it or not.

Sebastian muttered something low and useless—whatever fight he had left wasn't aimed at words anymore.

Sage didn't lift her head. She just stared at the floor. "Okay."

Sebastian turned toward her, his face said it all. "What?"

Sage met her mother's eyes, shoulders squaring for the first time since the truth had come out. "We go."

Seraphina logged the win. "Thank you."

They were still adjusting to one impossibility when another knocked over the lamp.

A low grunt followed.

"Ow—dammit—"

Something metallic and sulphurous unfurled in the room, low and smouldering.

Sebastian jumped. "What the hell?"

A groan rose from the floor. "Partially right."

Sage squinted. There, tangled in a heap of limbs and tattered fabric lay… something.

A creature with stubby horns, wild curls, and skin the colour of scorched clay. His robes hung in theatrical tatters—as if he were a broke wizard who'd lost a bet. A long, twitchy tail flicked at his back.

He pushed himself up on shaky arms, blinking glowing red eyes that sparked and faded like a malfunctioning lightbulb.

He grinned—wide and wicked, all teeth and chaos loosed from some long-sealed curse.

For a second, something ancient flared beneath his eyes. A shadow too big for the room. Too sharp for safety.

"Still working on my entrances." He straightened his robes with a flourish. "Samthrax, at your service, young Bellaroses. Temporarily, of course." He wrinkled his nose. "As per the terms of my binding—" He rolled his shoulders as if the word physically pained him.

Sebastian's brain short-circuited. "Holy shit."

Sage, who had apparently switched into trauma-processing mode, simply stared.

Samthrax rocked on his heels, tail swishing absently. "Ah, the speechless phase. Happens a lot. Don't worry. The meltdown usually kicks in right about—" He checked an invisible watch. "Now."

"Mum, why is there a literal demon in our house?" Sebastian choked on the question—half horror, half what-the-hell.

"Because I bound him to me."

"You did what?" His face did that thing it did when someone said something profoundly stupid.

Samthrax smirked. Too many teeth, all of them too pleased. "Bound. A necessary evil, my dear boy." He lifted a claw, revealing sigils spiralling like molten circuitry around his wrist—a tether etched in light. "We made a deal. And now I'm here—leashed, collared, and stuck with you until the current predicament is resolved."

"Define predicament." Sebastian crossed his arms. It was that or lose it completely.

"Oh, you know—your murderous relatives, the looming magical war, and the very real chance you'll die horribly if you don't master your powers soon." He clapped his claws together with the enthusiasm of a man pitching vacation packages. "But no pressure!"

Sebastian turned to his mother. "Mother. Dearest. You shackled a demon? Couldn't go for a puppy?"

Seraphina exhaled through her nose. Tired didn't begin to cover it. "It was the only way."

He flung a hand toward Samthrax like presenting exhibit A. "Yeah, but this one?"

Samthrax gasped—offended in the theatrical, operatic sense. "Rude! I have an exemplary track record in demonic affairs!"

Sage's mouth finally caught up with the storm in her head. "Wait—did you summon him?"

Samthrax chuckled. "Oh no, no, no. Your mother doesn't have that kind of death wish. I was already here. Locked in a charming oubliette called the Shadowkeep. You know—for crimes."

Sebastian's hands twitched toward his face—half a second from a meltdown. "Oh, for Pete's sake. You didn't just bind a demon—you bound a convicted one."

Seraphina didn't argue. There was no good spin for that.

A chill slid straight down Sage's spine. "Why was he locked up?"

Samthrax dusted off his sleeves like the question bored him. "You know how it goes—wrong place, wrong time, accidentally waged war on one of your ancestors, that led to a slight misunderstanding, followed by my imprisonment." He grinned, all charm and no apology. "All in the past, really."

Saffron eyeballed him. Hard. "Slight, my arse."

Sebastian made a noise somewhere between a laugh and a mental break. "Accidentally waged war? That's like saying you accidentally set your house on fire while holding a flamethrower."

Samthrax's tail flicked once—amused, not sorry. "Funny you mention that—"

"Enough." Seraphina was getting whiplash. "I bound Samthrax because we need him."

"For… Julian and Brinnan?" Sage wasn't sure what freaked her out more—the witch thing or how fast she was adjusting to this craziness.

Seraphina gave a short nod.

Sebastian tapped his foot, ticking off points on his fingers. "So let me get this straight. One—we're witches. Two—we have murderous relatives who have already killed Grams coming after us. Three—we are being forcibly relocated to a creepy-arse mansion that we haven't laid eyes on since childhood."

"Correct so far." Samthrax's brow lifted, almost impressed. The kid wasn't slow.

"And four," Sebastian continued, aiming for calm and missing by miles, "Mum's master plan to protect us involves adopting a demon with a rap sheet."

"You make it sound so dramatic." Samthrax could've yawned.

"It is dramatic," the words snapped out of Sebastian before he could smooth them over. He didn't want restraint. He wanted someone to admit this was insane.

"What happens when this is over?" Sage's words weren't loud, but they hit with precision.

Seraphina had no idea how to answer that.

"Now that is a very good question." Samthrax pulled something close to a smile. Close, but not human.

"See? That right there." Sebastian pointed, like naming the monster made it smaller. "That's a loophole grin. I don't trust loophole grins."

Seraphina didn't argue. She issued facts. "It doesn't matter right now. We have bigger problems to deal with—preferably before they deal with us. Go pack what you want to take. We leave as soon as we're ready."

And for the first time since their world had shattered, Sebastian and Sage realised—Normal was gone. Truth had claws. And from here on out, survival wasn't promised.

They were in it—bleeding, burning, bound.
And the real war? It hadn't even begun.

Eight

*"Exes and enemies have one thing in common: they always show up when
the house is on fire."*
— Samthrax, probably

As they pulled up to the estate's entrance, the twins took in the looming house with wide-eyed awe.

"I remember it being bigger." Sage squinted up at it. Funny how childhood made everything look larger.

Sebastian didn't respond right away—he just glared at the stone facade, demanding answers it would never give. "It's still a literal mansion."

Sage let her gaze drift past him, toward the maze of hedges and sculpted symmetry beyond. "I remember the gardens more than the house. I used to run through them because I was terrified to be inside."

Looking at it now, Sebastian wouldn't have brought kids here either. "Yeah… We didn't come here much. Grams always came to us."

Seraphina inhaled deeply, her fingers tightening on the wheel. *Because I kept you away. Because I wanted normal for all of us. Because I knew once we stepped into this world, we wouldn't be able to leave.*

She had tried so hard to keep them from this place—and now they were walking straight into the centre of it. This wasn't just an address.

It was a trigger. Every stone, every arch, every goddamn polished banister carried the echo of who she used to be. And that girl? She didn't exist anymore.

"All right." The word barely made it past everything she wasn't saying. "Let's get inside. I need coffee. Maybe something stronger."

***

No one noticed the large black bird perched high in the skeletal branches above, its eyes unblinking as it observed the scene below with eerie intelligence.

It belonged to the shadows—skimming the divide between what was seen and what wasn't. It had tracked her from the moment she crossed into the Enclave. But this… this, it hadn't anticipated.

Children.

The bird cocked its head, talons tightening on the bark.

Two teenagers. A boy and a girl. Close to Seraphina in posture and proximity.

They were hers.

The surrounding air quivered with recognition. A charge passed through the unseen threads of magic tethering this plane to others.

The bird's form fractured—edges distorting, feathers dissolving into liquid shadow—with a soundless flutter, it vanished, riding a current of sorcery back to the one who had sent it.

***

Malrik exhaled as the vision faded, mist peeling from the scrying bowl in thin, curling tendrils. His heart pounded. Revelation surged through him—savage and delicious.

Seraphina Bellarose had kids.

Children complicated things. But they also broke things wide open. And Malrik? He was very, very good at exploiting weaknesses.

He ran a hand through his oily, thinning hair, fingers twitching with the urge to act—to strike—before anyone else could.

He turned on his heel, boots scuffing against the warped floorboards of his hideout. The candlelight flickered violently—like the darkness itself had been stirred awake.

This wasn't just news.

It was leverage.

Julian needed to hear this.

Malrik snatched his coat from its hook—the leather sun-baked and blood-dark. The gloom in the room twisted with him, drawn to the scent of fresh malice.

He slammed the door behind him, his steps thudding down the stairs.

Seraphina hadn't merely returned.

She'd brought her bloodline.

And Julian? Julian would be thrilled.

***

The moment they stepped inside, Sage and Sebastian stopped cold—equal parts transfixed and unsettled.

Their memories of this place were fogged with age and childhood perspective, but now? Now the house breathed history and wealth in a way that wasn't subtle—it declared itself with every polished surface and soaring arch.

The foyer stretched wide, twin staircases curling upward—serpentine and grand—banisters gleaming beneath the natural light spilling from the skylight.

Sebastian let out a low whistle, hands shoved into his hoodie.

"Holy shit." Sage didn't move at first, like she hadn't figured out where she fit inside all this. "This place is..." she trailed off, eyes sweeping across the cavernous space.

"Off tap?" Sebastian offered. Every part looked expensive enough to hate on principle.

"I was going to say excessive, but sure—let's go with yours."

Seraphina dropped her bag onto an antique table. "It's a house, not a museum. You'll get used to it."

Sebastian studied the gallery of ancestral portraits—faces frozen in oil, their expressions heavy with judgement and secrets. Their silence pressed in around him making his skin crawl.

"Yeah, because oversized ghost mansions aren't freaky at all."

Sage brushed her fingertips over a carved wooden chair. She paused and inhaled deeply.

"It smells the same. Citrus and old books... way stronger than I remember. Maybe Grams cleaned before—" She stopped talking.

Seraphina said nothing. The scent clung to every inch—evidence of the overzealous cleaning charm she'd cast. Orange and lemon balm couldn't quite mask the prior evenings tragedy.

"Your rooms are upstairs, down the right hallway. Names are already on the doors. Unpack if you want."

Sebastian frowned. "How did our names get on the doors?"

Seraphina didn't bother answering. Her eyes said it all. Do the math.

"Right. Witchy stuff. Weird. But... I think I'm warming to it."

Sage watched her mother. Trying to read between the cracks. "You okay?"

Seraphina smiled. It went nowhere. "Just peachy."

Neither twin looked convinced, but they let it go. They took the out and made for the upper floor, their footsteps fading up the staircase.

As soon as they disappeared, Seraphina drew a deep breath.

A slow and measured knock shattered the silence.

Her blood ran cold.

She knew who it was.

Her fingers curled into her palms as she moved to the door, hesitating only a moment before pulling it open.

Killian Graves stood on the stoop.

Tall. Dark. Magnetic in the way storms are. Dangerous in the way knives are. Every inch of him wrought from menace and purpose.

His chiselled jaw was shadowed with scruff, black coat dusted in mist. But it was his eyes—piercing, unreadable, glacier-blue—that made her pulse falter.

For a long, stretching moment, they stared at each other.

The steady patter of rain was the only sound. Time seemed to hesitate, caught on the cusp of a something it couldn't undo.

His gaze shifted slightly, scanning behind her—already sensing the fractures in her life.

Seraphina lifted her chin like she had a blade balanced on it. "If you're here to say I told you so, I will throw you off my porch."

Killian gave her that maddening almost-expression he always wore when he knew he'd won a round she hadn't realised was a game.

"I wouldn't waste my breath."

That tone. That infuriating, quiet arrogance.

It made her want to slam the door in his face.

Memories shoved their way forward.

Eighteen and heartbroken.

Killian stood in the rain outside this very house, his bag slung over one shoulder.

Seraphina's heart pounded as she tried to make sense of the words spilling from his mouth.

"I'm going to Europe. The Enclave has a branch there, teachers I need to learn from. There's... a type of magic in my bloodline, Seraphina. Old, dangerous magic—which I need to master."

She didn't answer right away. Her body had gone tight with disbelief. "You're leaving?"

His hands shifted, caught between instinct and guilt—but he didn't touch her. "I have to."

"Then take me with you."

He wavered—just long enough to give her hope. Then it was gone.

"No."

It landed hard—the pull-your-heart-out-and-grind-it-under-boot kind of hard.

"Why not?"

"Because you don't belong in that world."

"Oh, but you do?"

He looked her dead in the eye, as if he'd already decided she couldn't follow him through the door he was about to walk through. "Yes. I do."

What he hadn't realised—what she couldn't say—was that she wasn't just fighting for herself.

There had been a spark—almost imperceptible—kindling beneath her ribs. Too early for certainty, but her body had known.

She was pregnant.

She'd kept pleading. Not just to go with him—but for him to stay.

He still said no.

So, she did the only thing left.

She buried the heartbreak and pulled up steel. "Fine. If you're leaving, so am I."

Something flickered in his face—panic maybe, or a truth he hadn't expected to hear out loud.

"Seraphina—"

"No, I'm done with this life. I'm going somewhere normal. Somewhere magic can't ruin everything. I only stayed this long because of us."

"You won't make it. You think you can walk away from who you are? From this?"

His hand hovered between them like something invisible was still tethering him to her.

"You'll come back. You can't run from destiny."

But she had left.

And for years, she'd proved him wrong.

She'd survived. Built a life. Kept her children safe.

And now, with him standing once more on her porch—eyes as piercing as they'd ever been—she hated the truth pressing between them.

He'd been right.

And worst of all?

He bloody well knew it.

Seraphina shifted just enough to let him pass—grace with a blade edge. "You'd best come in."

She strode into the kitchen without looking back. She didn't have to, she knew he'd follow.

He moved, a predator behind her—slow, deliberate, like sin wrapped in flesh.

She yanked open the cabinet. Screw the coffee—she grabbed the whiskey.

The bottle hit the counter with a solid thunk. She poured herself a generous glass, fingers tightening around the tumbler as a slow exhale escaped her—one she hadn't realised she'd been holding.

Killian leaned against the island with his usual, effortless dominance—like he hadn't been gone for sixteen and a half years. Like he had every right to stand there, steady and unapologetic, those infuriatingly sexy eyes catching every inch of hesitation.

Without a word, she poured a second glass and shoved it toward him.

Their fingers brushed.

It was nothing. Barely a whisper of a touch.

But it might as well have been lightning.

Heat licked up her arm—intense and immediate.

Her gaze snapped to his—he didn't flinch. Didn't waver. Like he'd been waiting for her to face him, and now that she had—he wasn't about to let her go first. The corner of his mouth curled.

The moment tightened, ready to snap.

A faultline, quick and unseen, cracked through Seraphina—pulling her out of time.

And suddenly, she wasn't in the kitchen.

She was in the scriptorium—back pressed to the bookshelf, Killian's mouth on hers, his hands unrelenting, driven by a hunger that left no room for doubt.

Seraphina flinched and reeled herself in, clutching her glass tighter—trying to crush the memory between her fingers.

Get a grip, woman.

She threw back half the whiskey. The burn didn't even register.

Killian watched her.

As if he could still read her.

And that pissed her off royally.

She'd gouge her eyes out before showing him the shake in her bones.

"Talk." It wasn't a request.

She took a sip before answering. "Mum's dead."

For the first time, something moved behind Killian's eyes.

Not shock—Killian Graves didn't do shock.

But something deeper. Like grief that never got closure.

His body leaned toward her, just barely—an instinct he buried fast.

"I'm sorry. How?"

Seraphina set her glass down with a soft clink, bracing herself against the benchtop like the counter was the only solid thing left in the room.

"Murdered." She was still wrapping her head around that word. "And I'm pretty sure we're next on the hit list."

Killian didn't move. All the violence was internal.

"Who?"

"Julian. And his father."

He should've guessed. "I'm not surprised. You said 'we', you married?"

Seraphina's stomach turned. She should've prepared for this.

But there was no graceful way to say, Surprise! You have sixteen-year-old twins who don't have a damn clue about magic and have enough attitude to level a city block.

And Sebastian?

Yeah, now that she thought about it, he had his father's cutting tongue and infuriating ability to get under her skin.

Before she could figure out how to break the news, she heard footsteps approaching.

Her heart flip-flopped.

Well. Shit.

So much for breaking it gently.

The kids strode in mid-conversation, completely unaware they were about to walk into yet another emotional landmine in a 24-hour span.

Sage stopped first. Her gaze locked on Killian—uncertain but already reaching for a truth she hadn't been handed yet.

Sebastian came in right behind. His mouth opened, sarcasm ready—then stalled. "Uh. Who's he?"

Seraphina wasn't ready for this. But here it came.

Total crapfest coming up.

Killian turned.

And the moment his eyes met theirs— instant recognition.

The truth slammed into him like lightning with nowhere to go.

He stood utterly motionless. The realisation cut through him with the cold finality of a name carved into a headstone.

Sage looked between them, brow furrowed. "Mum?"

Sebastian's stare narrowed, trained on Killian.

"Why is this guy looking at us like—" He stopped. His fists clenched so hard his fingers shook. "You have got to be shitting me."

It wasn't just anger. It was betrayal looking for something to break.

Killian's entire presence turned electric.

Sebastian's rage came hard—red-hot and nowhere to put it. "Tell me this is not happening."

Sage quiet and watchful, studied Killian. The noise around her faded under the rush in her ears. The face meant nothing, but those eyes?

"Is he… our father?"

Seraphina closed her eyes. Here we go. "Yes."

The silence could've shattered glass.

"What the actual F, Mum?" Sebastian exploded. Grief and fury collided in his voice, tangled so tight there was no pulling them apart.

Killian finally spoke. He was the still-before-the-storm kind of calm. The kind that promised destruction.

"You didn't tell them."

"Of course I didn't tell them." Seraphina wanted the truth shoved right back into the shadows.

Killian turned to them—truly turned.

And written across his face—regret. Not just for what he hadn't known, but for everything he'd missed.

Sage didn't know how to feel. Why had their mum kept this from them? "Did you know about us?"

Killian was holding onto his composure by a thread. "No. I assure you—if I had, your lives would've been very different."

He wanted to take the years back. Wanted to stand in every empty frame where his presence should've lived—first steps, first words, scraped knees and birthday candles. But all he could do now was stand still and hope his silence didn't count as abandonment.

He looked back at Seraphina.

And in his eyes, the message rang clear as a bell:

You kept this from me. You will answer for it.

"Yeah, sure you didn't." Sebastian let the venom show—straight up and deliberate.

Seraphina moved toward him, hand halfway up. "Sebastian—"

"No, I'm done with this conversation. I'm done with this whole bloody nightmare."

He spun on his heel and stormed out.

Sage lingered. Her gaze didn't waver from Killian—not accusing, not forgiving. Just measuring.

Then she turned and followed her brother without a word.

***

Seraphina pressed a hand to her temple.

Killian hadn't moved.

Still staring at the spot where his children had stood, as if their presence had left a mark too deep to fade.

She should've felt victorious—he was hurting. But all it did was reopen the wound she'd buried so deep she'd convinced herself it had healed.

When he finally spoke, his voice barely rose above a whisper—but it held the kind of heat that scorched. "You should have told me."

Seraphina met his eyes without flinching.

"To what end, Killian? You were hellbent on leaving. You made it very clear I wasn't part of your future."

Years of blame, anger, and everything they never said pressed in like a closing door.

History sparked—hot and unfinished.

She turned from him, ready to shove him out of her kitchen—out of her life—that's when the temperature dropped.

Literally.

The warmth drained from the room, as though someone had opened a door to the dead.

In the corner, a soft light bled through the join of the walls.

A beat later—a figure emerged.

Saffron, pearlescent and luminous.

"Well. Isn't this cosy."

Killian didn't bat an eyelash.

"You tethered yourself."

Saffron winked. "The afterlife is boring. This is better. It's been a long time, Killian."

He didn't answer immediately. He studied her, the way a warlock dissects a volatile charm—searching for hidden danger, for the twist beneath the surface. Cataloguing every unnatural flicker in her form, every ripple of energy that marked her as more than a residue of death. The fact that she looked him in the eye and smiled like she still had blood in her veins was a little eerie.

Finally, he nodded. "Long time indeed, Saffron."

Seraphina crossed her arms. "Great. Ghosts and reunions. Just what today was missing."

Before Killian could fire back, the front door slammed open.

Her heart kicked. Then the rhythm steadied.

Only one creature stomped like that.

Samthrax.

He barrelled into the kitchen, dishevelled—like he'd been spat out by a cyclone. His coat hung crooked, hair wild, and his face was a portrait of grim annoyance.

His eyes landed on Killian. He skidded to a halt, backing away with a muttered curse, as if he'd just walked into a live grenade.

"Oh, bloody hell. What's he doing here?"

Killian didn't move. His gaze stayed fixed, the kind of look that made predators remember they weren't at the top of the food chain.

Samthrax straightened like his instincts had clocked the crosshairs.

Seraphina tilted her head, lips curving—but there was nothing kind in it.

"Samthrax, meet Killian Graves. Head of the Enclave Council and the one person who can execute you with a look."

His throat bobbed. "Right. Lovely."

Killian didn't look at him—he assessed, like he was deciding whether Samthrax was deserving of erasure. "You're not worth the paperwork."

Samthrax's spine loosened—fractionally—until Killian took one slow step forward, his presence spilling into the room, all smoke and angles honed for damage.

"But if you become a liability. I will make an exception."

The demon—who usually mouthed off like it was his job—suddenly found the floor very interesting.

Seraphina nearly laughed. Gods help her, that level of menace should not still look that good in daylight.

Killian turned to her. "They need training. Proper training—especially Sebastian. That boy is a powder keg."

Her arms stayed crossed, her expression neutral. The silence was her middle finger.

"I can handle it."

"Not like I can."

That struck a nerve.

Because he wasn't wrong. Not even a little.

Killian Graves wasn't just powerful—he was weaponised. A warlock forged from shadow, fire and battle scars. He didn't survive magic. He mastered it. He became it.

And now, he was standing in her house… studying her like a spell written in a language he'd forgotten.

Seraphina hated the way her body reacted—how instinct overrode reason the moment he drew near.

Killian stepped closer. His voice didn't drop—it tightened, like it was locking a weapon into place.

"You know I'm right."

Her hands moved before her mind caught up. She shoved him. Hard.

Contact wasn't enough. She wanted to crack him open. Rip the restraint right off him. That calm? That steady, infuriating control? It had shattered her once. It would not do it again.

"You don't get to walk in here after all these years and act like you have a say in my children's lives. You left."

"Our children. And you never told me."

The words landed with the sickening weight truth carries when it's been buried too long.

She hated that he looked at her like that. Like she was the one who'd ended things. Like she was a puzzle he almost solved before walking away. She hadn't been a mystery—she'd been a freakin lighthouse. And he still left her in the storm.

Beneath the simmering fury, beneath the armour and searing words, there was something deeper.

Sixteen and a half years of silence.

She had never told him.

Killian had thought he knew Seraphina. Had convinced himself he'd buried the ache of her memory in the cold halls of the Enclave. He had poured his life into discipline—into control. He had left to become something greater. To master the war raging in his blood.

But now—standing here, in front of her, with ghosts and whiskey and memories playing like static footage behind his eyes—he realised he had left something far more vital behind.

Her and them.

His fists curled at his sides, the truth roiling beneath the surface of his carefully built restraint.

Saffron looked on with a glint of unholy amusement in her eyes.

"Oh, this is deliciously dramatic."

Seraphina spun on her. "Do not encourage this."

Saffron's expression stretched—savage and delighted.

"I think it's a marvellous idea. The twins need training. Killian is the best. And you two…" she waved vaguely between them, "need to work out all this unresolved sexual tension before the house ignites."

Killian didn't breathe. He recalibrated—like slamming a vault shut before the contents could spill.The rage, the frustration, the guilt—gods, the guilt—burrowed deep and clung, as if it had a right to stay.But he locked it down the way he did everything.

He gave a half-smile that didn't reach anywhere real. "Smart woman."

Seraphina groaned—not from frustration, but from the crushing realisation that this circus was only getting started. "I don't like this."

Killian rolled his shoulders, letting the arrogance slip back into place—a shield worn smooth with use.

"You'll live."

She didn't just glare—she dared him to test her. That calm? Cosmetic. The woman underneath had already made peace with violence—now she was just waiting for an excuse.

"You won't if you stay here."

He took another deliberate step toward her, the kind that wasn't about distance—it was about dominance. And underneath it, a heat he wasn't bothering to hide anymore.

She had to tilt her chin to meet his eyes. Something old and volatile stirred between them, barely held in check.

"You could always stop me." Killian's words came out as a provocation wrapped in invitation, his control so precise it cut.

Seraphina froze.

And he saw it.

The brief hesitation in her eyes.

She had never stopped him before.

And that thought? That cut deeper than he'd let himself admit.

She had begged him to stay.

And he had walked away.

Not to hurt her—but because he believed she deserved better than a man wired like a bomb and just as likely to go off.

And in choosing that path—he'd lost her completely.

He thought she'd wait.

But Seraphina had never been the waiting kind.

She had severed herself from magic.

From him.

Now, looking at her—her hair pinned in quiet rebellion, her jaw clenched against memory—he hated how familiar it all still felt. Like some part of his soul had never left this house. Like it had waited for her. And he? He'd been too much of a coward to come back for it.

She still smelled the same—that intoxicating blend of wildfire and defiance.

Killian leaned in—close enough that the space between them became a lie.

"Say the word, Seraphina. Tell me to go, and I will."

She inhaled, sharp and shallow—like oxygen was suddenly a choice.

But she didn't say it. Because she knew he was the best. Because she knew her twins—their twins—needed him. And because deep down, she had never stopped wanting him.

A loud whistle fractured the moment. Saffron stood like she'd just called lights down on an illicit affair.

"It's settled! Killian stays."

"I really dislike this." The words weren't protest—they were self-preservation gripping the last threads of Seraphina's pride.

Killian's smile was slow, unapologetic. Want dressed in arrogance. "Not as much as you want it."

Before Seraphina could unleash a verbal fireball, a voice cut through the tension with all the grace of a chainsaw at a piano recital.

"Right, well, this has been deeply uncomfortable."

Samthrax leaned on the doorframe, calm as a housecat who'd just knocked something expensive off a shelf—and was waiting to be thanked for it.

He waved a hand at the palpable charge that was barely contained.

"The sexual tension in here is so thick I could butter my toast with it."

Seraphina whirled on him. "Sam—"

"Nope!" He backed away, hands raised. "I'm leaving before the eye-fucking reaches its inevitable, traumatising conclusion."

Killian didn't deny it. He just held her gaze, that dark twist of a smile curving as if he'd already won something unspoken.

"Smart demon."

Samthrax pointed a claw at Seraphina. "And for the love of all things unholy—kiss him or kill him. I genuinely can't tell which way this is going, and it's stressing me out."

He turned on his heel and vanished down the hall, muttering, "This is why I smite."

Seraphina stared at the empty doorway.

Then back to Killian.

His grin had become positively insufferable.

She was going to kill Samthrax. Her mother next. Again. And Killian?

He was a dead man walking.

Right after he trained the twins.

Then she'd strangle him with his own ego.

Nine

"Some bloodlines are locked for a reason. Unlock them, and the world pays the price."
— *Killian Graves, Enclave Archives*

Sebastian stalked to the border of the garden, fists buried in his hoodie pockets. Humidity hung heavy, rich with the tang of loam and iron. Trees loomed around them, their gnarled branches clawing into twilight—a forest of bones scraping the sky. Crickets murmured in the distance, and somewhere deeper in the undergrowth, something rustled—too solid to be a bird.

His breath came jagged and shallow, each inhale rasping through his throat, each exhale tinged with soil and something biting beneath it—frustration, fury, fear.

"This is bullshit." He kicked a rock down the path; it skittered away as if it had looked at him wrong. "Our whole lives—a lie."

He didn't just feel betrayed. He felt disposable. As though the bedtime stories, the I-love-yous, the ordinary days spent thinking they were safe—had all been part of some long con. And now he was supposed to just... assimilate? As if the version of his life he'd trusted hadn't been fiction from the start.

Sage folded her arms, knuckles pressing white against the thin skin at her elbows. Her bangles clinked—a sharp, metallic punctuation to

92

the silence. "Yeah, it's a lot."

Sebastian barked a bitter laugh. "It's more than a lot." He jabbed a finger toward the brooding silhouette of the house. "Mum spent years lying to us, and now she expects us to—what? Nod and smile? Accept that we're witches? That our father," the word dragged through his throat, barbed and burning, "is some all-powerful warlock who decides to show up out of nowhere?"

Sage shifted, and her jacket snagged on a thorn. She didn't fix it—just stood there, caught. Her hair, once neatly tied, had started to rebel—loose strands blazing copper in the last scraps of light.

"Well, it's happening—like it or not."

Sebastian turned on her, as if he'd been yanked on a wire. "That doesn't make it okay."

She rubbed at a dirt smear on her jeans, scrubbing a little harder than necessary. "Look, I get it. I'm pissed too. But don't you want to understand this? To know why she hid it from us?"

She was more than curious. She needed it to make sense—to believe there was more behind the silence than shame. That the shadows in her mother's eyes had meaning, not just secrets.

"Not really."

She angled her head, studying him as if she was reading a language he didn't know he spoke. "Liar."

He rolled his eyes but didn't bother denying it.

She nudged him gently with her shoulder. "At least we finally met our father."

Sebastian gave a humourless laugh. "Yeah. Great. He didn't even know we existed until now."

"That's not on him."

"I get that. Doesn't change the fact he can't just waltz in and expect us to play happy families. The dude's dangerous. You saw him."

Sage braced her palms against the stone railing. Her fingers curled inward, gathering moss and grit. "You really believe that?"

"Yes."

"Then why does it seem like you're trying to convince yourself?"

He tipped his head back with a low groan—half surrender, half frustration—and dragged a hand down his face like it might smear away the truth.

"Oh, don't start."

"I'm just saying… maybe we should hear him out before we decide he's the villain in all this."

"Seriously, he's a loaded gun with the trigger halfway pulled. One twitch, and boom."

"Maybe. But did you see the way he looked at us? The moment he knew—"

"No." Sebastian didn't back down. "Don't even go there."

"Go where?"

"The whole maybe-he-would-have-stayed-if-he-knew thing." Not where he wanted his voice to go. But there it was.

"He might've."

"He left, Sage. He left Mum. She did all of this alone."

"She also didn't tell him."

A breeze stirred the leaves—rustling through the lull.

Sebastian rubbed the back of his neck. "I don't even know what to do with that. I'm mad at her. I'm mad at him. And I think…" He would only ever admit this to his sister.

"…I think I'm scared."

"Scared?"

"Of what comes next. Of who we're supposed to be now."

"Yeah." The knot in her throat almost won. "That part does suck."

What came out wasn't a laugh. Just air shaped like one, because he didn't know what else to do with the ache.

"Pretty much."

"At least we're in this together."

He made his eyes meet hers, it cost him. "Yeah. Until you sell me out to become Supreme Witch Overlord."

Her face pulled tight. "Excuse me?"

"You're way too into this whole secret-bloodline thing."

She rolled her eyes hard enough to crack bone. "So, I'm intrigued. But you're my brother and I love you. So, no betrayal. Okay?"

He sighed, bumping her shoulder with his. "Okay. Love you back. Just promise that when this all goes to hell, I get a cool title. Something noble. Like King of Barely Holding It Together. Or The Twin Who Didn't Ask for This Shit."

Before she could answer, a dissonant clap rattled the stillness, like the garden had hiccupped. Samthrax sauntered into view, horns catching the last hint of twilight. His coat billowed behind him, trailing mischief and smoke.

"I've got one for you. How about The High Lord of Snark, Stubbornness, and Deeply Repressed Feelings?"

"Finally, a title that captures my true essence." Sebastian tracked Samthrax like he was watching a car crash he couldn't stop—sarcasm doing what it always did: covering the parts of him he didn't want anyone to see. "I'll have business cards made."

"Do you ever announce yourself like a normal person?" He kept it dry—barely. The rest? A mess he didn't dare unpack.

"One, not a person. Two, normal is boring."

"You really do have a gift for showing up during emotional moments." Sage kept her delivery flat. Because if she didn't, everything under the surface might start leaking out. And once it started, it wouldn't stop.

Samthrax brightened. Whatever passed for feelings in his world, he was already elbow-deep. "I aim to entertain. So—still sulking? Or have we embraced our magical destiny yet?"

Sebastian's face didn't change. It didn't have to. The line between holding it together and breaking had already worn thin. "What do you think?"

Samthrax flopped onto a moss-covered stone, all horns and lounging-cat attitude.

"Ah, denial. My favourite brand of awakening."

He bypassed the sigh and went straight into smug satisfaction.

"So—what's the plan? Dramatic rebellion? Join a rogue coven? Tap into forbidden chaos magic?"

Sebastian didn't look at him. The feeling behind it didn't need volume—it was already deafening. "I hate you."

"Impossible. I'm delightful."

Before anyone could respond, the atmosphere shifted. Not colder in temperature—but in presence. A settling pressed into the garden, as if even the trees understood something was about to change.

Killian didn't emerge. He materialised.

The night bent toward him, as if the darkness had carved a space for him and waited for his return. His coat swept behind him, heavy with battle and responsibility.

Sebastian's shoulders drew tight. "Fantastic. The fun police has arrived."

Killian didn't speak. His gaze cut across them—not searching, not questioning. Just stripping away anything that might've passed for safety.

"I will be unbinding your powers. Right here. Right now."

Something inside Sebastian locked down hard. That thing with his name on it—the one that never trusted anyone to have his back—was already bracing.

Sage's eyes flew wide. "Wait—what?"

Samthrax was suddenly upright, all limbs and outrage. "Absolutely not! Nope and—what's that?—still nope!" He stabbed the air with a finger, too dramatic to be dismissed, too loud to ignore. "You don't do that without prep, you emotionally stunted warlock of doom!"

Killian took no notice. Whatever Samthrax was doing didn't register as a threat—or remotely relevant.

"You're free to leave."

"Leave? While you perform magical surgery on two mystically constipated minors? That's criminal negligence!"

Sebastian bristled, the comeback too fast to be anything but reflex. "Hey—"

Samthrax turned on him like he'd been waiting for that opening. "Do you even know what's about to happen? No? Then shut up and panic accordingly."

Sebastian snapped back, volume chasing the control he was losing. "I am panicking!" His attention whipped to Sage—accusation and desperation tangled in the look he gave her. "Why aren't you panicking?"

"Because, what if it's not that bad?"

"You want this?"

"Maybe a little." Sage was hella curious.

And yes, she was apprehensive—but she wanted to be all she could be. If that meant being a witch with powers? Like, hell yes. Bring it on.

Sebastian's mouth hung open. The disbelief came first, disgust riding shotgun. "Un-freak'n-believable."

Samthrax's hands rocketed skyward—pure theatre, pure dread. "This is how people end up cursed! Starts with 'Ooh, what can my powers do?' and ends with an exorcism via YouTube and a spatula!"

Killian exhaled—if breathing could sound like disdain, this was it. "Are you done?"

"Are you?" Samthrax shot back. "We can still run. I know a place. Great snacks. Hex-repelling doorbell."

The fight in Sebastian turned inward, he just couldn't push anymore. "He's right. We don't have to do this."

"You already are." Killian wasn't warning them. He was marking the point where choice stopped existing.

And the world split.

Killian lifted his hands.

Darkness unfurled—not summoned but revealed. It peeled away from his skin like a birthright, not a weapon. The grass beneath their feet crisped with frost. The chill didn't fall—it seized. Shadows flinched and fled.

Magic spilled from him—not as an explosion, but an unravelling. Ancient. Measured. Utterly inescapable.

Sebastian choked on his breath.

Light collapsed inward. Or perhaps reality narrowed.

Power touched him—not a stranger, but a returning inheritance. A birthright he'd never been told he carried. It possessed him. It had lived in him long before he'd had a name. It moved through him in slow spirals, seeping into every crevice—leaving no part of him untouched.

It didn't hurt. Not exactly. But it changed everything.

Sebastian's legs shook. His hands balled into fists. His heart was no longer beating—it was ringing. Every nerve reverberated with some forgotten note struck too hard.

Across from him, Sage stood in the same flow.

But where he drowned, she rose.

Magic didn't strike her—it moved through her with purpose—steady, unhurried, and sure of its place. Warm currents wrapped around her, winding through her being, whispering welcome. Symbols traced themselves behind her eyes, runes born of breath and bone.

No chaos. No fear. Just… home.

She looked at her brother.

And everything inside her shuddered.

Sebastian had gone pale. His chest rose and fell in staccato rhythm. Shadows didn't just cling—they clutched, drawn by something buried deeper than anger.

He was fighting it.

And something within him… was fighting back.

The guilt stung.

But beneath it, something more rusted and restless stirred.

A bond. Not just of blood—but of purpose.

She didn't just want to protect him.

Whatever had awakened in her needed to.

She stepped forward—and stopped. Not yet. She didn't know how to reach him. Not in this place.

But she would.

Killian regarded them both, his expression unreadable. For the briefest flicker, his eyes found Sebastian—and faltered.

He saw something. Something he hadn't expected.

The unbinding snapped shut.

Magic pulled back—not gone, not severed. Simply… settled.

The seal was broken.

Sebastian gasped. His knees buckled. He dropped to the grass, palms braced against earth that now hummed beneath his skin.

Sage stepped closer, hand hovering near his shoulder.

He didn't speak.

He didn't need to.

She saw it in his eyes.

Shaken, yes. But something deeper had shifted.

And she'd follow him through any wreckage that meant—because she had no intention of watching her twin break alone.

"Your training begins tomorrow. Scriptorium. Eight a.m. sharp."

Killian turned before they could see it—the flicker of dread behind his eyes. What he'd just unbound in Sebastian wasn't clean. He disappeared into the dark, taking the storm with him.

Sebastian didn't move.

Sage stayed beside him.

Because whatever was coming, they'd need to face it together.

****

Outside the Crescent, Malrik stepped through the grand entrance of Julian's tower—night, woven into motion, slipping through every fracture in the light.

Polished marble sprawled beneath his boots, far too pristine for the filth he carried in his wake. Towering glass walls clawed at the sky—cold, gleaming, untouchable. A fortress of power. A monument to a world that had long since exiled men like him.

But tonight, he stood tall, shoulders squared. A man finally off his knees.

He crossed the lobby in measured strides, his reflection bending in the chrome and mirrored surfaces until it fractured as the elevator opened with a sigh. He entered, pressed the penthouse button, and let the silent ascent drag him higher—away from the gutter where he'd been left to rot.

When the doors slid apart, Julian's private domain unfolded before him: opulence carved from precision and menace.

Floor-to-ceiling windows framed the skyline in perfect symmetry. A fire crackled low in a hearth made of black-veined stone. Leather chairs sat untouched, their stillness regal—thrones set for a gathering of gods or monsters.

Julian stood at the bar, swirling a deep crimson liquid in a crystal glass. His eyes flicked up lazily, keen with recognition but clouded by nothing.

He was dressed to command. Charcoal suit razor-fitted. Not a strand of hair out of place. Control radiated from him—not worn, but ingrained.

Effortless. Dangerous.

Brinnan's heir in every calculated inch.

Malrik didn't bow. He wasn't one of Julian's dogs.

Julian raised his glass in mock greeting. The smile didn't reach his eyes, but the warning did.

"Malrik. You have something worth interrupting me for?"

He waited, letting the moment sour enough to sting. "I do."

Something in Julian turned—a subtle shift to signal he was done playing. "Then by all means—entertain me."

Malrik closed the space between them, not to provoke—but to prove he could. "Seraphina has children."

The amusement on Julian's face didn't vanish—it crystallised. Something dark shifted in his gaze. Something fleeting. Malrik didn't miss it.

"Twins," he added, letting the word be the bait. "Teenagers. Hidden in plain sight. No magic. No training. She kept them blind."

Everything stilled. The kind of stillness that came before a decision.

Twins. Balance. Amplification. Unpredictable. Dangerous.

"Go on." Julian didn't inflect—authority speaks quiet when it's sure of itself.

"The boy's volatile," Malrik continued. "The magic in him is already showing fracture lines. And the girl is focused. Curious. She'll dive headfirst into knowledge if it's dangled the right way."

Julian set his drink down, every movement deliberate. "You're certain?"

"I saw them myself. Raw energy moving beneath their skin. Untapped. Undisciplined. They have no idea how to carry it, let alone use it."

Julian's jaw worked once—all polite restraint.

Seraphina had always been a problem. Brilliant. Defiant. Uncompromising. Now she'd become something else.

A liability with leverage.

He lifted the glass again, the motion too casual to be innocent. "I imagine she's… protective."

Malrik gave a sound that didn't qualify as a laugh—closer to a judgement. "She's barely holding it together. You can see it in her eyes—panic masked as poise. She knows it's too late to keep them out."

He angled his head, like the thought amused him more than it should. "And we both know what happens when people of her type are pushed too far."

Julian's lips moved—barely enough to register. No warmth. Only the certainty of a man who'd already decided how this ends.

"They break."

Malrik let the breath go slow, letting the moment hang—power was shifting.

At last, after all the years lost, he stood in the room with a sliver of control in reach.

"Twins are rare." Julian didn't frame it as revelation—only confirmation. "One heir is dangerous enough. But two?"

He leaned in, not for emphasis—as though permission had quietly expired. "There are prophecies that mention them. None end gently. That makes them either a tremendous advantage… or a catastrophic failure waiting to happen."

Malrik's mouth pulled back—compliance worn as a weapon.

"Exactly."

Silence gathered between them, saturated with purpose.

Julian tapped a single finger against the rim of his glass. A soft, rhythmic sound.

"You're sure they're untrained?"

"As newborns, but it's waking in them. And Seraphina brought them home, which tells me she's desperate—or stupid. Possibly both."

Julian's face didn't shift much—only enough to lose the last trace of patience. "She always was sentimental."

"And now," Malrik offered, dragging the moment out to savor it, "she's cornered."

Julian leaned back—not to move away, but to decide how far this would go.

"If she hid them… they're worth having."

He stood—not like a decision had been made, but like it had never been in question. What followed wasn't a threat. It was the shape of what would happen next. "Or destroying."

Malrik didn't need to speak. The silence between them was already working the terms.

Julian looked at him again, this time with the weight of transaction. "Bring me something useful."

Malrik's jaw clenched—but the smile stayed, razor-flat and earned. It wasn't confidence. It was refusal. He would not be small here. This was only the opening move. The beginning of a drawn-out game. He refused to remain the pawn.

"You'll get what you need. As long as you honour our agreement."

Julian didn't react. Just watched—measured, clinical, not dismissing, not amused. Waiting for Malrik to misstep. "Is that a threat, Malrik?"

"Gods, no." He tipped his head—not a concession, but a provocation dressed up in manners. "I'd never be so uncivilised. I simply value… clarity. In partnerships."

He closed the distance—not to intimidate, but to make himself unignorable. "Mutual respect."

Julian stared—not long, but longer than necessary. Just enough to show where the leash would be clipped. "Our deal depends on one thing. Your usefulness."

Malrik inhaled slowly, tension winding deeper. He wanted to

believe he could manipulate this, that he could steer Julian where he wished—but this man didn't follow music.

He wrote it.

Julian picked up his glass again, letting his finger circle the rim.

The motion was idle—the kind of idle that made people bleed later.

A note resonated—soft, near silent, dissonant.

"Tell me, Malrik—how much do you value your reputation?" The question landed like it already knew the answer.

Malrik didn't speak. But something inside him drew tight. The leash wasn't metaphor. It was a reminder. It was hierarchy.

He was still being measured. Still the mutt at the gates.

Julian's mouth curved—not with humour, but with the ease of someone bored of pretending.

"I admire ambition. Until it becomes inconvenient."

Malrik's hand didn't move, but something in it readied. He wasn't allowed anger—not yet. "You'll have your leverage. The twins won't stay ignorant forever. And when they break open…"

"They'll be vulnerable," Julian finished. "Confused. And confusion… " He didn't smile. He showed control in the shape of one. "…is very easy to manipulate."

Malrik ran his tongue along his teeth—fury lived behind the taste. But so did survival.

This man would end him the moment he lost his usefulness.

But not if he stayed ahead.

Julian turned back toward the skyline. Not to admire it. To terminate the conversation without giving Malrik anything more to look at. "Find me what I need to bring Seraphina to her knees."

He waited just long enough to make the delay feel deliberate. The next words didn't waver. They arrived like terms already signed. "Then, and only then, will we discuss what I owe you."

Malrik breathed in slow—because reacting fast would be the real mistake. He let the insult sink, deep and hot, where it could sharpen later. "Understood."

Julian's mouth shifted—not for show, but for satisfaction. "Good."

And in that moment, Malrik knew—as soon as Julian stopped needing him, he wouldn't be discarded.

He'd be deleted.

Like he was never here.

Ten

"Every lie told to protect them was a choice. And every choice has its reckoning."
— *Unknown Enclave Record, Sealed Archive*

Seraphina stormed down the corridor, her heels hammering the floor like war drums. Heat prickled beneath her skin, magic spitting sparks just under the surface—wild and volatile. Somewhere in her mind, she registered how right it felt—how natural—to have her power loose again, no longer sealed away.

Now, all that energy had one purpose.

Killian.

She'd turn his insufferable arse to stone and leave him as unfortunate garden décor.

No. Too easy.

She'd blast him across the realms—so far even time would lose track of him.

Too kind.

Better: she'd hurl him into the void and let it decide what to do with him.

Samthrax scurried behind her, flinching as a nearby candle exploded.

"For the record. I only told you because I value my continued existence."

She had built this lie with careful hands. Sealed it with silence. Refined every corner of their ordinary life until not even a trace remained. And now Killian had torn it open with the same brutal ease he always wielded—with duty disguised as necessity.

"Shut up, Samthrax."

The study door gaped slightly. Killian was inside. She could feel him.

She flung it wide. It slammed against the wall. Sparks climbed her arms, barely leashed. The current cracked at the edges of her control— feral, unstable, drawn to her like iron to lightning. Killian didn't even look. He leaned against the mantle, hands buried in the pockets of his tailored slacks, as if her whole world hadn't just collapsed in on itself.

"You unbound their magic."

Not a question.

Killian turned. A move without apology, the answer had already been lived.

"I did."

Her nostrils flared. She held the fury under pressure, but it kept looking for somewhere to land.

"You had no right."

He moved like there was nothing in her anger worth yielding to.

"I had every right."

Samthrax dropped into a chair with a wheeze. "Wow. Clearly not one for self-preservation—"

"You went behind my back." The accusation didn't rise—it was placed, exactly where it would do damage.

"You have no right to show up after sixteen years and decide what's best for them."

"They're my children too." Killian stated it as it was. "Or have you conveniently forgotten?"

"I raised them."

"Then you should have prepared them. I did what was necessary. Bound magic doesn't stay dormant. It festers. It corrupts. If I hadn't unbound them, something else would have—and we wouldn't be arguing. We'd be burying them."

His fury hit back—cut clean. The kind of truth you only throw when you're done asking to be heard.

"And you damn well know it."

The fire behind him roared.

They stared each other down, energy writhing in the walls, tension drawn so tight it vibrated—one flick, one word, and everything would blow sky high.

"Oh, for the love of all things dramatic, are you two at it again?"

Saffron drifted in, swathed in silvery layers, and flopped into the armchair across from Samthrax with a theatrical sigh.

"Honestly, it's exhausting watching you both. So much hostility— makes one wonder if we're headed for a murder or a scandalous affair."

Samthrax leaned back like the commentary spoke for itself.

"I keep saying they should get it over with and channel all that rage into something aerobic."

Seraphina turned on him—with the quiet violence of someone preparing for a live autopsy.

"What?" He lifted his hands—not in surrender, but in the universal language of 'don't shoot the messenger.' "I'm just saying what everyone's thinking."

Saffron tilted her head—part therapist, part executioner. "Ah, young love. Or, more accurately—deep-seated emotional dysfunction masquerading as sexual tension."

Seraphina faced her. "You knew?"

Saffron nodded, totally unapologetic. "Yes. And you know where I stand."

"You should be on my side."

"I am. Mostly. But on this?" She flicked her eyes toward Killian. "He's right."

Seraphina's fingertips sparked. Sweat beaded on her brow.

"Don't look at me like that." Saffron held her ground.

"You knew this was coming. They were going to awaken—whether you wanted them to or not."

"It wasn't his decision to make, Mum."

"It wasn't a decision." He delivered it like truth had never once needed her permission. "It was survival."

She wanted to scream. Shatter something. Make him feel the way she had—helpless, cornered, burning.

But the worst part?

He was right.

And Gods, she hated him for it.

Because admitting it meant everything she'd sacrificed—years of running, hiding, shielding—had led them straight back to the very thing she swore she'd protect them from.

And then, it rose—a feeling deeper than rage. Beyond fear.

Something far more crippling.

Powerlessness.

So, she did the only thing left.

She walked out, the door slamming behind her hard enough to rattle the stone.

Saffron's mouth curled—part pride, part long-suffering survival reflex.

"I think that went well."

Killian breathed out like he'd just stepped off a battlefield barely intact. "She's absolutely going to murder me in my sleep, isn't she?"

Saffron's grin sharpened—maternal, but not merciful. "Knowing my daughter? You'd be wise to sleep with one eye open."

***

The Scriptorium still smelled of orange, lemon, and lingering magic. The vaulted ceiling soared above them, enchanted skylights spilling pale morning light across timeworn stone. Candle flames flickered along the walls. Bookshelves rose impossibly high, their spines whispering secrets—a thousand voices waiting to be read.

Two circles had been drawn onto the floor—one in silver chalk, the other in deep indigo. Two training spaces. Two instructors.

Seraphina stood in the left circle with Sage, her posture relaxed but her eyes missed nothing.

Killian faced Sebastian in the right, arms folded, expression shuttered.

Sebastian wanted to punch something. Preferably his father.

Sage, practically vibrating with excitement, rocked on her heels. Sparks danced at her fingertips.

"This place is incredible," Sage allowed awe to have its way with her, drinking in every dancing candle, every book, every potion-lined table.

Her fingers itched to touch. To open. To unravel.

The books called to her, humming with secrets, as if they knew she'd come. Wisdom clung to the stone and shelves—old, untouched, enduring, as though it refused to be forgotten. And standing here, in the heart of it, surrounded by so much untamed potential, a single thought rose within her: I was meant for this.

Sebastian was not sharing her sentiment.

"We got dragged here to learn with him." Sebastian jerked his chin toward Killian, expression twisted into a look that could pickle stone. "That's torture."

Killian's mouth twitched—amused, maybe. Or just entertained by how far his son still had to go.

"You'll be grateful when your own shadow isn't trying to eat you."

"Maybe I'll let it. And drag you in with me." Sebastian invited the damage. Daring it to be mutual.

"Sebastian." Seraphina's warning came with full 'don't make me go tae kwon do on your teenage arse' energy.

He kicked the chalk line with his trainer—casual, like erasing the rules made him bigger than them. "Not my fault I got stuck with him."

"You didn't get stuck with me. You need discipline—and I'm more than happy to provide it."

He didn't say anything about being a potential weapon of mass destruction. "And Sage doesn't?" "She listens. You don't." "Yeah? Try listening when something's ripping through your insides like it wants out."

Damn.

The thing Killian had been half-ignoring, half-bracing for—just stepped into the light.

Sebastian wasn't merely losing control—he was fighting a presence.

He'd seen it the moment the boy was unbound. And now, the way the power slithered through his frame, volatile and wrong, confirmed it.

This wasn't just raw talent.

It was something old. Something dangerous.

"If you don't control it something else will."

Sebastian didn't argue. The crack was already there—hairline but spreading.

Because deep down, he knew his father was right.

"The unbinding didn't just wake your inheritance. It woke everything buried in your bloodline."

Killian kept his eyes on his son.

"You are Bellarose and Graves. Two legacies that shaped history—sorcery that spans from ruin to purity. And now it runs through you."

No sermon. Only fact. And totally inescapable.

"Neither of us knows what that makes you. Or what it could become. But you don't get to ignore it. It won't let you."

Sebastian didn't know what the hell was going on inside him. Couldn't name it. Couldn't stop it. And yeah—it scared the living shit out of him.

"You don't know what it feels like."

Killian went internal. Of course he knew. That's why he'd walked—before the thing inside him took the wheel.

"Eyes on me son."

Sebastian didn't look away.

"Magic isn't something to fear. Or to run from. You don't let it control you. You master it."

"And if it won't be mastered?" Sebastian didn't need to imagine that worst-case. It had already started to feel like a mirror.

Killian's mouth curved. "Then you make it kneel."

The words sent a shiver down Sebastian's spine.

Killian moved—sudden and sure.

He flicked his fingers.

The shadows obeyed.

They slithered up from fissures in the stone, twisting into jagged shapes that circled Sebastian's feet.

Sebastian reacted on instinct.

His power surged—a force of pure, wild energy. It didn't move with Killian's precision. It struck outward, untamed and furious.

Killian countered without effort. A snap of his wrist and the shadows wound tighter.

"Breathe. Relax. Focus on the outcome."

Sebastian gritted his teeth.

Across the room, Sage was thriving.

She moved with effortless grace, her fingers weaving golden light into delicate spirals that twirled and danced.

"This is incredible."

Energy surged in her veins—warm, responsive, eager to obey.

Seraphina joined the current, her alchemy merging into Sage's without a word.

"See? You listen. You guide. Magic is an extension of your will. Feel it—and it will follow."

Sage nodded, radiant with understanding.

Sebastian—was the opposite.

His wasn't light.

It didn't dance. It didn't yield.

It fought.

It writhed in his centre, a beast gnawing at its prison, molten and mad. A tide of power, forsaken and unclean, crawling beneath his skin.

"Again." Not a suggestion.

Sebastian braced, praying to anyone listening this wasn't about to go nuclear.

The moment he tried to summon it, the force lashed.

Not careful. Not steady.

It wanted out.

The pressure built too fast—spine to chest to arms—liquid fire flooding his veins.

He wanted to stop. To breathe. But the magic wouldn't let him. It surged like a fever under his flesh, deaf to reason, seething with something older than rage.

Surely this wasn't his.

"Control it." Issued like failing was not an option.

Sebastian growled and shoved the power forward—everything went wrong.

A guttural sound tore from his throat.

Frost spidered over the ground, driven by a force splitting open inside him.

The sigils flared violet, confused—caught between protection and panic.

The Scriptorium howled.

Whips of shadow hurled themselves across the room, feral and writhing—straight for Killian.

Killian didn't move.

The shadows weren't his anymore. They had new orders—and they weren't listening to him.

The wards screamed. Candles died.

Something laughed in the back of his mind.

Killian moved.

A snap of his fingers. A clean cut.

The connection snapped—violent, and final—leaving only the shock of being torn too fast.

The tendrils disintegrated, curling into smoke, vanishing into the floor.

The wards flashed once more, then died.

Silence descended.

Sebastian gasped and fell.

The world was spinning sideways. His heartbeat hammered—rapid, erratic, deafening.

There was something else nested within—biding time, ready to wear him like a skin.

He didn't know if it was his magic, or if he was its host now. Either way, whatever was inside him had tasted freedom—and it wanted more.

"What. The. Fuck." Samthrax called from behind the couch like reality had just rewritten itself—and left him out of the memo.

Seraphina and Sage crouched beside him, eyes wide, systems flooded with adrenaline.

Sebastian stared at his hands—shaking, scorched with the residue.

Killian gave no reaction. Not with his face. He was already rewriting the next move. He'd seen enough.

He knew.

Sebastian wasn't just fighting for control.

He was fighting for ownership of himself.

Control cost Killian. He gave the order anyway.

"Practical's done for today."

Seraphina didn't speak.

Her blood roared in her ears, louder than the echo of the wards that had just screamed through the walls. She kept her eyes on Sebastian— pale, rattled, silent. Not from fatigue, not from defiance. From fear.

She'd hidden them from this world, telling herself secrecy was safety. But this? This proved just how wrong she'd been.

Killian flicked his wrist.

A heavy tome appeared on the nearest table with a resonant thud. Sebastian flinched at the sound, his nerves clearly frazzled. Its leather cover lay scorched, gold runes slithering across the surface in fluid, animate motion.

Samthrax peeked from behind the couch, eyes wide. "So… are we sure he's not going to explode again? Or should I stay in my designated safety zone?"

Killian ignored him, placing a firm hand on the book.

"For the rest of the day, you're going to read this. Both of you. It covers theory, history, containment—"

His eyes slid to Sebastian.

"—and the dangers of ignoring any of it."

Sebastian hadn't moved. His arms stayed locked across his chest, holding himself together through sheer will alone.

"Great. Homework."

Sage was already reaching for it, fingertips grazing the cover with reverent curiosity. "Come on, Seb. This is our history—it's what we should've known all along."

Sebastian grumbled something unintelligible and dropped into a chair, flipping it open with the wariness of someone expecting it to bite.

Samthrax—having determined he was probably not going to be incinerated—flopped into a nearby seat and kicked his feet up on the table.

"And I shall remain here as your trusted advisor and emotional support cryptid."

Killian didn't bother hiding the warning in his stare. "You're here to keep them out of trouble."

Samthrax clocked the threat and vaulted right on over it. "Same thing."

The firelight still danced on the stone floor, but the warmth had long since fled. Outside the sealed doors, the manor groaned softly—old magic shifting like a sleeping beast, uneasy beneath its skin.

Sebastian didn't bother hiding his disgust. "So, we're stuck here?"

Killian got it—his son was pissed. But if he didn't get control, things were going sideways. Fast.

"Would you prefer another round?"

Sebastian cursed under his breath and sank lower in the chair. That was a hard no.

Sage was deep in the first chapter, fingers laced with threads of lingering spellwork.

Killian didn't look at Seraphina right away. When he did, the fight was already buried. "I don't know about you, but I could use a drink."

Seraphina didn't answer immediately. He looked tired beneath the arrogance. She hated that she noticed. Her gaze shifted to the twins—Sage, fully absorbed. Sebastian, still pale, still strung tight. Her mouth was dry. The worst part wasn't that Killian had unbound them—it was that she might've waited too long.

Finally, she nodded. "We need a plan. And I have questions, Killian. Ones I expect answers to."

Saffron, who had watched from the sidelines, crossed her arms, looking at the twins.

"I have a few of my own."

Killian rubbed a hand down his face. He was already bracing for what was coming next.

They weren't fools.

They'd seen what had happened.

Felt the shift in the room.

Sebastian wasn't just struggling with his birthright.

And Killian wasn't sure how much he could tell them yet.

Because if he was right…

None of them were ready for what came next.

***

The conservatory was silent, save for the low murmur of the city below. Floor-to-ceiling glass stretched wide behind Julian, revealing a horizon bathed in golden light—glittering, serene, and utterly oblivious to the tempest gathering above it.

He stood in the middle of the room, surrounded by perfectly curated greenery—twisting vines and exotic blooms, each placed with surgical precision. A manufactured paradise. Beautiful in its sterility.

Like everything he controlled.

He savoured the quiet as a predator after the hunt—only the click of distant glass and the whisper of enchanted leaves around him.

At his feet, atop a pedestal of polished marble, rested a scrying bowl carved from nightstone. The water within lay motionless, void-black—dark enough to devour the room and everything in it. He extended his hand—not with urgency, but with purpose. This wasn't communication. It was invocation.

He touched the surface. "Brinnan."

It quivered.

For a moment—nothing.

A single ripple spread.

Darkness billowed—thick and hungry—unfurling in ribbons that twisted, swallowing distance and shape. A chill swept through the room as power surged along the unseen tether that linked them.

Brinnan's face emerged.

He sat in his study, candlelight casting long, stark shadows behind him. The space felt off-kilter, even through the scrying bowl—steeped in an oppressive stillness, as if the walls had witnessed something unspeakable and were caught in the vacuum that follows.

Julian allowed a slow smile.

"I have news."

Brinnan didn't speak. But Julian knew him. Knew that slight narrowing of the eyes meant he was listening.

"Seraphina has returned to the Enclave as predicted."

Brinnan remained motionless.

"And?"

"She didn't come alone."

The water shuddered.

Candles behind Brinnan flickered low, flames bending as though drawn to his silence.

Julian waited a beat longer before twisting the knife.

"She has children."

"You're certain?"

"Would I waste your time if I wasn't?"

"How many?"

Julian was all polished civility wrapped around malice.

"Twins."

The liquid in the bowl convulsed, as if the word had awakened something buried.

Brinnan's fingers curled against the wood of his desk, knuckles whitening.

A single heir was a threat. But twins?

Twins were prophecy—chaos forged in symmetry, poised to tip the scale.

"Tell me what you know about them." Not a request. An instruction he'd decided would be followed.

"The boy is volatile and unstable."

Julian let it breathe—he wanted Brinnan to sit with the implications.

"The girl?" His mouth curved—just enough to show he was already doing the math.

"She doesn't fear magic the way he does."

Brinnan marked it down in silence before answering.

"A liability and an opportunity."

"Exactly."

"And Seraphina?"

"Protective. Afraid." He let the word hang, heavy with implication.

Brinnan tapped a finger against the desk. "She knows she's at a disadvantage."

"Which makes her dangerous." Julian had no illusions about that truth.

"A mother guarding her offspring is predictable." Brinnan's mind was moving, calculating outcomes.

"If we move now, we strike before they understand what they are. Before they can use it." Julian didn't press the point. He didn't have to. The timing bled urgency.

"And your proposal?"

Julian approached the bowl with all the reverence of a man about to redraw the board.

"We remind Seraphina where true power lies."

Brinnan chuckled, the laugh rough with something cruel.

Julian knew that sound. The sound of a beast scenting blood.

Brinnan's fingers moved across the desk—not absent, not idle. Each mark was a sentence, and the intent behind it wasn't just tactical—it was personal.

"Let's breach the outer wards. See how strong her little sanctuary really is—and how well her children hold up when the walls collapse."

"Perfect. Let's see what cracks when we shake the foundation."

He severed the connection with a snap of his fingers.

The water stilled. The void returned.

Julian leaned back, a slow breath escaping as satisfaction curled at the corners of his mouth.

Brinnan wanted to wipe the twins out before they became a threat. Short-sighted. Predictable.

Boring.

Julian had other plans.

The prophecy had never been his to touch—never for the singular, only for the mirrored two. Twins were rare. Chosen. Destined.

He was none of those things.

But he didn't need to be written into fate to claim it.

Let the prophecy name its champions.

He would make them kneel to him all the same.

All he needed now… was for the boy to break.

Eleven

"I thought I'd sealed the door. But darkness doesn't wait behind walls. It breeds inside the ones who inherit it."
— Killian Graves

The Scriptorium was too quiet now.

Residual magic clung to the walls, dense with the tang of singed spellwork and something darker—something Sebastian refused to name. The wards lining the bookshelves had settled, no longer pulsing with alarm, but the aftermath hung in the air like smoke after a fire, not yet ready to disperse.

Killian, Seraphina, and Saffron had retreated to whatever clandestine meeting was happening in the study.

That left him, Sage, and Samthrax—with nothing but a heavy-arse tome of homework and the elephant in the room no one wanted to address.

Sebastian hadn't spoken since the training disaster.

He hadn't stopped shaking either. Not that anyone could tell—he was too proud for that. But beneath the silence, under the snark, something was splintering. Not fear exactly, but whatever came just before the scream.

Sage, predictably, was already nose-deep in the book, flipping pages with a degree of fervour that suggested she could will entire chapters into her bloodstream.

Sebastian, on the other hand, was doing his best to pretend the stupid thing didn't exist.

Samthrax—dramatically sprawled across a chair—was watching the twins with far too much amusement.

"So," he drawled, flashing a shit-eating grin, "are we taking bets on who snaps first? Because I've got five bucks on you, Seb."

Sebastian shot him a look, the message unmistakable: bite me.

Sage didn't look up. "I'm fine. Unlike others."

Sebastian rolled his shoulders, but the horror didn't move. It just sat there. "You weren't the one on the verge of cracking the damn universe in half."

Sage met her brother's stare, cool as glass. "On the verge. Keywords: not actually."

Samthrax threw himself back with a hand to his chest, like someone had shot him. "Oh, the tragedy! So close to cosmic doom… and yet, alas, still not even crispy. Onward and upward."

Sebastian's laugh stuck in his throat. What a goddamn joke. "Screw both of you."

Sage flexed her fingers until her knuckles popped, sharp and intentional. "Seb, I cannot stress this enough—get your shit together. Some of us are trying to learn while you're over there headlining your own teen melodrama."

Sebastian's fists balled so tight they stung. The familiar itch buzzing beneath his skin, begging for an outlet.

"You don't get it."

Sage turned to her brother. There was heat in her eyes now—but not the comforting kind.

"So, explain it to me."

But how? How was he meant to describe it? Like something was lodged way too deep—not his but hitching a ride. Not loud. Not obvious. Just… there. Breathing with him. Moving when he didn't.

He dragged a hand through his hair. "I can't."

Sage studied him for a long moment. She closed the book and leaned back.

"Alright, then don't. But being a pain in the arse doesn't excuse you from doing the work."

Sebastian let out something that could've passed for a laugh—dry, bitter, all edges.

"Right. Because reading that thing is definitely going to fix whatever the hell is happening to me."

The shift in Sage was instant. That easy warmth she always carried? Gone. In its place: the urge to slap her brother upside his stubborn head. Hard.

"It might actually help—if you stopped fighting everything and tried to understand it."

The comeback was right there, sharp and ready, burning the back of his throat. He bit it down. Barely.

Samthrax slid in with perfect timing, grinning like he'd bought front-row seats to the fallout. "Alright, alright—enough with the quarter-life crisis, young Seb."

He threw his arms out, all mock preacher about to testify. "We get it. You almost obliterated reality in a fit of magical teenage angst. Happens to the best of us."

Sebastian shot him a look that could've melted concrete. "Glad I could provide entertainment."

"Oh, you have no idea. But here's the thing—Sage is right."

Sebastian was knocked off balance, just for a second.

Samthrax leaned in, clawed finger raised like a lecture was incoming—but his tone? Pure bite. "You can't keep sulking about your little 'oops' moment. What you need to do is get a grip. Because I know darkness."

He didn't explain. The flicker behind his eyes said enough—and none of it was good. "And make no mistake: the thing inside you? It will rule you if you don't rule it first."

The words burned into Sebastian's mind, branding him with their truth.

Samthrax leaned back, stretching slow, already done with the drama. Settling into business-as-usual—annoying and impossible.

"Now, as a reformed hellspawn—I say that with no real conviction— I could absolutely enjoy watching you spiral into villainy. But I'm trying this whole 'personal growth' thing."

He tapped his claws together like a cartoon villain giving a TED Talk. "So! Slap on your magical Einstein hat, quit brooding, and start actually learning."

Sebastian let out a low, wounded sound—equal parts pain, defeat, and eternal suffering—and grabbed the book. "Fine. But if I explode again, I'm taking you both with me."

Samthrax lit up, a walking celebration of his own bad ideas. "That's the spirit!"

Sebastian sighed and opened it. Reality thinned—whispers bled through, calling his name. His hands moved like they belonged to someone else—someone who hadn't nearly lost control. But every turn of the page felt like prying open a wound that hadn't even scabbed yet. He was terrified.

But he kept that to himself.

***

The study was a veritable pressure chamber.

Killian went straight to the bar and poured two whiskeys, the tension thick enough to suffocate. He handed a glass to Seraphina and sank into a winged chesterfield near the wall.

This room had always been a favourite of his—so much so that his own mirrored it: old-world elegance, carved wood and quiet power.

The words crowded behind his eyes, pressing against the dam he'd built to keep them in.

Seraphina paced, downing the whiskey in a single gulp. It burned her throat and lit fire through her frayed nerves. She set the glass down and took the chair opposite him.

Saffron perched on the sofa—deceptively calm. Her gaze dissected Killian with clinical precision, every blink a slide under a microscope.

Their combined stares pinned him in place, but he didn't flinch.

"So," Seraphina dropped the word like a weapon. "Are you going to tell us what the hell happened in there? Because I'm pretty sure you weren't surprised."

His neck popped as he rolled his head side to side. His joints were screaming. Or maybe that was his composure. "You're right. I wasn't."

He lifted the whiskey to his lips and let it burn all the way down. It didn't help. "I was just hoping I was wrong."

Saffron's fingers tapped at the armrest—barely audible. She really did miss having a body. She could make so much more noise when the moment called for it.

"Well, you weren't. So, let's not dance around it, Killian. What are we dealing with?"

Killian set his glass down. The time for stalling was over—and the truth wasn't going to wait politely.

He leaned in, forearms braced on his knees. "Sebastian's magic isn't just powerful. It's ancient. It's something that's only surfaced a handful of times in my bloodline."

Every part of Seraphina had gone quiet in that lethal way—like her body was choosing whether to snap or strike.

"Your bloodline."

He nodded. "Always a male. Always a twin. The Graves are descended from the Original Dark One."

Seraphina was cartwheeling inside. What the actual hell? And how the fuck was she supposed to navigate that little nugget of life-altering truth—thank you very much.

Saffron wasn't doing any better. Intrigued, horrified. Equal parts both. Well. That explained the magical dumpster fire they'd just lived through.

"The Original Dark One? The one who made darkness a living thing? As in the first Warlock."

Killian nodded again.

Seraphina's breath was that sharp exhale before a body launched into violence. Her hand shot into her hair, fingers fisting at the roots.

"You're telling me our son is carrying power older than the devil himself?"

"Yes."

"He's not just dangerous," he went on. "He's carrying a fragment of something that predates time."

Her pulse hit a higher gear. The fear? Already gone. Burned off in a flash—pure ignition. "And you knew? You suspected this and didn't tell me?"

"I wasn't sure. Until today, it was only a theory."

Saffron looked as if someone had upended the laws of physics. "Well. Shit."

"The last warlock to wield this kind of power was my great-grandfather."

Killian's fingers tapped against his forearm—an old habit that never quite got exorcised.

"He's still missing. Presumed dead."

Her gaze didn't waver—and Killian felt every ounce of judgement behind them.

"Presumed?"

Killian's eyes went flat. "If he were dead, we'd know."

Saffron leaned forward. "Tell us. What happened to him?"

"He vanished. But not before half a city burned. Not before he killed his twin. Not before he tried to tear open the veil to something far worse."

Seraphina swore under her breath, jumped to her feet and started pacing, sparks flaring at her fingertips. She wouldn't say it aloud, but the truth clawed at her: if Sebastian lost himself to this ... could they bring him back?

"So, what you're saying—what you're actually telling us—is that our son has inherited the most cursed bloodline in existence and is walking around like an unexploded bomb?"

"That's the short version, yes."

Saffron let loose something in a language older than stone. The walls shivered.

Seraphina arched a single brow. "You're explaining that later."

Her lips barely shifted. Not a smile. Just stress leaking through the mask. "Maybe. If we make it that far."

Seraphina turned to Killian. Her body was still. Her inside? Not so much. Everything in her was ready to move, to fight, to burn down the bloody universe if she had to. "So, how do we stop it?"

"I don't know if we can."

Her magic flared—only to vanish under iron control. "Not an option."

"You think I want this for him? You think I'm unaware of what happens when this level of power goes unchecked?"

Seraphina's hands curled into fists at her sides. Not because she wanted to hit him—because if she didn't, she'd lose it. And now was not the time. Not when her son's life was on the line. Not when the scream pressing inside her was too close to the surface.

She took a breath she didn't need. Just something to hold onto before the fire in her chest became words.

"Then tell me what the hell we do. Because I swear on all I have left,

I will not let this consume our son."

Killian held her stare. No retreat in him. No softness either.

"That makes two of us."

Saffron cleared her throat. "Actually, it's three. That's my grandson, and I'll be damned if some fossilised arsehat with a god complex gets his claws into him."

She leaned back, folding her arms. "The estate has a network of underground tunnels with hidden chambers. You can train him there."

Seraphina didn't argue with the logic. She just wasn't ready to stop being furious.

"We don't even know if training will help."

Killian eyeballed her. "Would you rather we do nothing?"

Saffron leaned in. The edge in her stare needed no words. "From where I'm sitting, Killian's the most qualified. You carry the legacy too, don't you?"

Killian didn't answer. But Seraphina saw it in the way his posture changed. "You have it?" Everything in her went cold. Anyone close enough would've felt it in their bones.

"Not like Sebastian does. I was older when it surfaced. I barely controlled it—and I was disciplined. Sebastian's younger, angry and vulnerable. This can go either way."

"But… you're not a twin."

"I was."

Seraphina didn't speak at first. Her body registered it before her mind caught up—everything in her went rigid, toes to spine, like impact.

Why hadn't she known that?

"You never told me."

"It didn't seem relevant. He died in infancy. The bond never had time to form—but the power did."

Saffron's eyebrows shot to her hairline. That was the kind of truth that knocked the breath out of you.

"Bloody hell, Killian. That's not irrelevant."

Seraphina eased back. Her centre of gravity was gone. Like the ground no longer trusted her. "So, our son inherited a curse neither of us can stop—and a twin bond that might not be his alone."

Killian didn't argue. No point arguing with facts.

Seraphina's magic simmered beneath her skin. "I'll do whatever it takes to keep him safe."

"Good. Because I need full access to him."

"Come again?"

"I want to train him. Alone. No audience. Not even you."

Saffron tilted her head, one brow lifting. The corner of her mouth curled. "I'm basically ghost furniture. I'll haunt from a distance."

Seraphina wrapped her arms around herself. Every part of her wanted to hex them both into the floor.

But she wasn't blind. Sebastian pulsed with a darkness that didn't belong to this century. And Killian was the only bastard in the room ruthless enough to meet it head-on—and walk out breathing.

She didn't want to say it. But protecting Sebastian meant letting the devil take the wheel.

"Fine. You get him. But if he comes back with even one bruise—"

Killian made no effort to pretend. He knew exactly what she meant.

"You'll gut me without warning, wouldn't expect anything less."

Saffron floated out of the chair and circled it slow, like she was the ghost of drama past. "Excellent. We're threatening each other again. Everything's back to normal."

Seraphina cut her a look. The kind that said: not now, not ever. Then she turned to Killian.

"The sooner we get Seb sorted, the sooner we prep for the incoming shitstorm from the Tweedle-Twat Twins."

Killian's mouth twitched. That was the Closest he'd get to humour today.

"Tweedle-Twat Twins?"

"Julian and Brinnan."

Saffron poured the names like champagne—expensive, dangerous, about to explode. "Chaos in tailored suits."

Killian tossed back the last of his drink and set the glass down hard. "God help us."

"No God."

Seraphina wasn't being blasphemous. She was being honest.

"Just us."

***

The stone corridor narrowed the deeper they went, the cold pressing in as they moved forward. Runes etched into the walls sparked with soft blue fire, reacting to their presence—recognising the sorcery in their blood and parting as a sea would yield to command.

Sebastian trailed behind, jaw locked, shoulders strung so tight they felt wired to snap. Every step was a silent declaration: I'm holding it together. Barely.

He hadn't argued when Killian told him to come—not after the Scriptorium. Not with the shadows still lurking beneath his skin, begging to be let out.

Killian stopped before a vast iron door, its face fused seamlessly with the stone—as though the mountain itself had birthed it. Enchantments shimmered across the metal, a cascade of iridescent glyphs that moved with the grace of old, forgotten tongues. Power thrummed below, deep and contained.

"This room was built to contain magic that shouldn't exist."

He placed his palm on the door.

It responded with a sound torn from the bones of the earth—grating, slow, deliberate—as iron and rock wrenched apart.

Darkness waited within. Thick and absolute. A chamber that

repelled intrusion, where even time itself seemed reluctant to move. The walls bore carved sigils that smouldered with low light, arcane threads stitched into every seam—not inert, but alert.

Sebastian hesitated, one step from whatever was inside.

If this goes south, at least they'll have a dramatic origin story to put on my headstone.

"You coming?" Killian didn't bother turning. He already knew the answer.

Sebastian hitched up his emotional Kevlar and followed his father.

The door slammed shut behind them, the sound reverberating through the stone—a finality that rang with the gravity of a tomb sealing. He flinched.

Geezus, this place means business.

Killian moved into the heart of the circle etched in the floor. Though soundless, his approach disturbed the wards, setting them quivering with unseen energy.

Sebastian was all about containment—tight and locked down.

"Rule one."

A pause. Just enough to make it land.

"Your emotions are fuel. But that rage in the Scriptorium? That wasn't power."

He inclined his head slightly.

"That was chaos."

Sebastian's chest compressed. His lungs seemed too small. He folded his arms, not to defy—but to hide the tremor in his hands.

"I didn't mean to—"

"I know. That's why we're here. To make sure you never do it again."

Silence settled, the kind that follows oaths or executions.

"You either command your magic or it devours you from the inside out."

Sebastian swallowed. Felt it all stick in his throat.

I don't want to do this. But I'm done running from what's in me.

Killian was composed—like this wasn't a nuclear moment waiting to happen.

"Focus. You're the gate. Start small. Don't force it."

Sebastian closed his eyes and reached inward.

Past the hum in his blood. Past the cold knot in his stomach. Past the fear.

He found it.

This time, it rose as a tide might—slow, measured, cautious. Magic gathered at his fingertips, soft violet light curling upward, drifting like smoke from an old, long-burning fire. Wisps floated higher, aimless but harmless and controlled.

"Good. Now hold it. Don't grip too tight. You want to guide it, not strangle it."

Sweat beaded on Sebastian's brow. Suddenly—an explosion. The current itself fractured. The runes along the chamber walls jolted violently—once, twice—flaring in warning. The magic twisted.

It slithered down his arms—no longer smoke, but tar: thick and clinging.

Sebastian went rigid, a sudden pressure closing in from within.

This wasn't his.

His power was violet. Wild, yes, but rhythmic—vital. This… this was something else. Something heavier. Older. Corrupt.

The colour drained. That brightness—gone, swallowed whole.

In its place, oily tendrils of black crawled up his arms, spreading across his skin. His heartbeat spiked so fast it no longer felt like rhythm—just static. Symbols sparked and vanished—jagged, angular, unfamiliar. They flickered in and out, ghosts of a language never meant to be spoken aloud, let alone worn in flesh.

"What's happening?"

Sebastian's words rang out—too loud in the crushing stillness.

The shadows climbed higher. Up his forearms. The noise in his head rose—deafening, rhythmless, relentless.

A voice spoke right beside him.

"At last. My blood. My bones. My echo."

Sebastian dropped to his knees, hands over his ears.

"Get out—get out—get out!"

But it kept coming.

The images hit him like a freight train—flames eating through streets, a mirror unravelling itself in slow-motion reverse, and a stranger's hand—his, but not. Shaping magic that shouldn't exist.

"I've waited so long."

Across the chamber, Killian froze.

His stomach twisted in ways he didn't even know it could.

That voice—he had never heard it before, not with his ears. But his blood knew. His powers responded with the jolt of an ancestral memory tearing itself loose from the dark.

It lived in family warnings. In dead pages. In nightmares.

No body. No grave. No farewell. The one who never came back.

His great-grandfather.

Killian's instincts screamed. Don't let it finish. Don't let it through.

He moved.

Both palms slammed against the floor. Wards detonated across the chamber in a wave of searing blue light. A scream—inhuman, furious—ripped through the space. The darkness writhed. Shrieked. Then vanished.

But the chill it left behind? That lingered.

Sebastian's breath tore from his lungs in a broken surge. Sweat soaked his skin. His fingers clawed at the stone floor, nails scraping deep, trying to anchor himself to reality through sheer force of will.

Killian crossed the room in slow, deliberate steps. Inside, adrenaline surged, but his face gave nothing away.

Sebastian's head jerked up. Eyes blown wide. "What—what was that?"

Killian knelt beside him. "That was something that doesn't belong here."

"I felt it inside me. Like it was trying to get out." Sebastian was pretty sure he'd just shit himself. Not that he was going to check.

Killian didn't respond right away. He couldn't.

He'd spent years convincing himself the darkness had stopped with him. That the thing in his bloodline was controlled and contained.

But seeing Sebastian come apart—seeing those shadows twist and hunger—he now realised it was not.

It had tried to claim him once, too.

He remembered the nightmares. The blackouts. The whispers. He'd buried them deep and called it strength. But it had been testing him. Probing for weakness.

He had shut the door.

Now it had found another crack to slip through.

His son.

But he couldn't say that. Not yet.

So instead, "It's trying to use you. That's why we're here. You will get through this, Sebastian. But only if you embrace discipline."

"Everyone's looking at me like I'm a walking bomb."

"Then let them."

Something cracked under Sebastian's ribs. Might've been courage.

Killian leaned in. "You're not broken. You're dangerous. And danger? It doesn't apologise. It learns control—or it gets used."

Heavy silence stretched between them.

Sebastian hated the idea of being used. But whatever lived inside him? It probably didn't give a damn.

Killian ruffled his hair.

He didn't react. Too stunned—or maybe too tired—to swat his

father's hand away.

"Good work, kid. You're still in one piece."

"Give it time." Sebastian could feel the countdown ticking.

Killian pushed to his feet and offered him a hand. "Come on. That's enough for today."

Sebastian took it.

As they walked toward the exit, the runes stirred in their stone skins—soft and slow. Bound intelligences and half-asleep witnesses. And deeper still—something old turned its attention upward.

After all, blood always answers when called.

Twelve

*"If your family tree has more cursed roots than leaves, maybe don't be
surprised when the branches start screaming."*
— Samthrax, during an exorcism, probably

Sage sat curled in a high-backed overstuffed leather chair, legs tucked beneath her, the book spread wide across her lap. Dust motes floated lazily in the shafts of golden light spilling from the floating candelabras overhead. Silhouettes moved with a rhythm that didn't quite belong to the flames—off-tempo, deliberate, as if following orders no one had given.

She hadn't meant to stay this long.

The almanac had practically called to her—wedged behind a false row of books on the topmost shelf, hidden not just from sight, but intention itself. When she touched the spine, it thrummed beneath her skin—almost eager. The moment it landed in her lap, it fanned open on its own.

She should've been uneasy. But instead, curiosity stirred within her.

The pages were brittle but warm, the ink glinting faintly gold. A line stopped her cold. She traced it, then read aloud, her voice a whisper laced with awe and unease:

"When the shadow and the flame are born as two, the world shall kneel or burn."

136

Her brow furrowed, the words searing themselves into her thoughts.

Born as two.

Twins.

The meaning landed like a stone dropped into still water.

Sebastian and her.

Her magic danced—sunlight threading through storm clouds—brilliant, wild, alive. But Sebastian's… his was older, heavier. It didn't flow—it uncoiled, thick and relentless, rising from him in dark tendrils carrying the echo of wars no one dared name, and promises bound in oath and sacrifice. It carried the burden of something buried deep in his very fibre, a secret carved into the bloodline itself, waiting centuries for this moment to surface. When it stirred, the shadows didn't just shift—they gathered. Ravenous. Reverent. Answering a summons of timeless rites.

Shadow and flame.

Her body started to react. Negatively.

Kneel or burn. Those weren't metaphors. They were choices. And neither felt survivable.

She flipped the page, the parchment rasping through the quiet. Another passage stared up at her, handwritten in a jagged scrawl that burned more than it bled:

Balance must be chosen.

If not, one will consume the other.

Only through unity may the power remain stable.

Otherwise… devastation.

One twin must fall for the other to ascend.

Her vision tunnelled. The words consumed everything else.

One must fall.

Her heart slammed against her ribs like it wanted out. Like it didn't want to be part of this body, this prophecy, this screwed-up fate. The parchment might as well have screamed. Choose. Or be chosen.

Her mouth went dry. Her hands trembled slightly over the paper. She reread it once. Twice. Please let this mean something else.

But the meaning was clear and blunt.

This wasn't some old riddle. It was a verdict.

Is this what Killian meant when he talked about control?

She sat still, her heartbeat threatening to choke her.

What if this was the real reason their mother had bound their powers and removed them from magic? What if she wasn't just protecting them from the world—but from each other?

Was that why Sebastian looked so scared all the time? Did he feel it too?

Does he think he's the threat… or do they?

She sucked in a breath. And what if they're wrong? What if I'm the dangerous one? What if I'm the one who has to choose?

Would she be strong enough?

Would she be willing?

Could she destroy him to save the world?

That was a hard no, she didn't care if she was the fire and Seb the shadow. If the world expected either of them to die on cue? Screw that. The whole damn planet could burn before she'd pick. Sage was about to turn the page when unease slipped into the room. It was subtle at first—a creeping distortion, as if the walls themselves had begun to tilt imperceptibly off balance. The pressure came next, a low vibration pressing against her skin. The candle flames wavered; one snuffed out with a hiss. Another guttered and died. A brittle crack echoed from deeper within the estate.

Sage was on her feet instantly, the book clutched tight against her chest, her eyes locked on the arched doorway.

The silence was no longer peaceful.

It had teeth.

A whisper followed—low and gentle.

"Sage…"

Her mother's voice. But no footsteps, no presence. No warmth.

Just the voice.

Coming from the hallway cloaked in shadow.

A chill licked up her spine. Every instinct screamed at her that something was wrong.

That wasn't her mother.

She edged backward, candlelight pooling around her as if reluctant to leave her. Her gaze darted to the book in her arms.

The words on the page seemed to quicken, charged with fresh urgency.

One twin must fall.

Another whisper, closer now.

"Sage…"

She took another step back.

And this time, she didn't say no.

She ran.

***

Outside, the chill air bit at Sebastian's cheeks as he wandered the manicured garden path, crunching dead leaves underfoot like brittle promises long since broken. His hands were buried in the pockets of his hoodie, shoulders hunched, thoughts chewing on themselves.

Samthrax danced around him in slow, lazy circles—part demon, part chaos sprite—flicking a conjured coin between his fingers. A red sheen skated across its surface, humming an eldritch melody that only he seemed to enjoy.

"So."

A pause. Long enough for the sarcasm to breathe.

"On a scale of one to 'well, shit,' how are we feeling about the whole unstoppable death-magic that might eat your soul thing?"

As if this was a joke. As if any of it was funny.

"Personally, I'm rooting for 'flaming catastrophe with a redemption arc.' It reeks exponential growth."

Sebastian didn't take the bait. "You were a demon, right? Before this advisor schtick?"

"Still am, sunshine." Samthrax threw his arms out, like the second coming of self-aware menace.

"I've just upgraded from 'apocalyptic murder-lizard' to 'charming emotional support sociopath.'"

Sebastian huffed a laugh.

Something inside him had been torn from the root. That voice—his voice—still rattled in his head, taking up space it had no right to.

It knew him. It didn't just speak to him. It spoke through him. And it had been riding shotgun in his bloodstream this whole damn time.

He didn't like what that meant.

Samthrax seemed to notice the way the moment dragged, and for once, he toned down the theatrics. "I get it, kid. Legacy magic's a bitch. Mine was less 'inherit a cursed power' and more 'get summoned by warlocks too arrogant to read the fine print.' But same vibes."

Sebastian stopped mid-step. His gaze snagged on a rosebush, petals flared open, torn and lush, a strange mix of beauty and hurt.

"What was it like being imprisoned?"

The coin flashed — caught without effort, gone just as fast.

Samthrax's usual flair vanished.

That alone was a warning.

"Picture this."

He didn't look at him. The shift was internal, a veritable storm rolling under skin.

"You're stuck in a circle drawn by Bellarose ancestors and their cult of magical micromanagers."

A twitch at the corner of his mouth. Not humour. Not even humour-adjacent.

"Listening to a portal recite your worst regrets like it's gunning for host of the world's saddest podcast."

He tilted his head back, eyes half-lidded, the memory playing on the backs of his eyelids. "Endless reruns. No off switch."

Something flickered there — the break between lines wasn't just for dramatic effect.

It was control. The kind you white-knuckle.

"And the bonus prize? Company. Every being my family ever pissed off. Commentary included. Like a demonic book club with vengeance issues."

Sebastian looked over.

For once, the wall behind his eyes wasn't bulletproof. Just… thin.

"So why didn't it destroy you?"

Samthrax reached back into the moment it happened and let it rise in his throat before answering.

"Oh, it did. Splinters, shards, the whole piñata."

He didn't look hurt. He looked like someone who'd been through it and come out wearing the t-shirt.

"But at some point, I got bored of breaking. Started paying attention. Stopped screaming. Laughed once by accident—kept going. Turns out sarcasm's cheaper than therapy, and you don't have to tip your therapist."

"I'm not scared of the magic." Sebastian didn't even want to say it. But there it was, burning a hole in his teeth.

"I'm scared it's just the beginning. That it's not what breaks me… it's what finally lets out what's always been broken."

Samthrax tilted his head.

He wasn't about to wax poetic. That wasn't his brand.

But the kid looked cracked open in all the places that mattered. And yeah—maybe he knew something about that.

"All of us carry some version of broken," he said. "You don't get out of life without scars, Seb. The question isn't whether you're damaged. It's what survives. Who you become because of it."

He let the words do the heavy lifting.

No jokes this time. Just truth.

"And yeah—it came out ugly. Most real things do."

He let that settle. Let it hit.

"But that doesn't mean you're the monster. It just means you've met him."

He let that settle too.

"Now figure out how to make him your weapon."

Damn, that almost sounded wise.

It unsettled Sebastian more than he wanted to admit.

He glanced away, about to reply—then stopped.

The atmosphere shifted.

It wasn't just cold. It was off-kilter.

All heavy and electric. As if something had taken a bite out of reality and was licking its teeth clean.

Sebastian raised his head, looking around him, trying to see what he could sense.

Samthrax stopped mid-hover, mentor mode—on hold.

Whatever came next wasn't about guidance.

"You feel that?" Everything convulsed. A shatter-line of power ripped the sky and heaved the ground beneath their feet. The wards circling the estate blazed—bright, violent, panicked—and burst apart in a thunderclap. Like glass exploding under pressure. Silence swallowed everything for a heartbeat.

"Shit."

Samthrax grabbed Sebastian's sleeve with surprising strength.

"Run. Now. Whatever that is, it ain't a social visit."

Sebastian didn't argue.

They tore across the garden toward the house. The sky overhead buckled under unnatural energy. Shadows twisted as if rejecting the laws of light altogether. From somewhere behind, shrieks—too shrill, too distorted—mimicked the death cries of forgotten things.

Sebastian's body was already quitting. He didn't blame it.

"We're not going to make it."

Samthrax spun mid-stride and slammed his palm against the earth. A wall of black flame erupted in their wake, sizzling as it consumed the unnatural beasts chasing them.

Sebastian tripped, caught himself. "What the hell was that?"

Samthrax was breathing hard. Not that he'd admit it. "Emergency demon protocol."

He didn't slow down, didn't look back. "Also known as: I don't lose kids I've been assigned to corrupt, thank you very much."

The front doors loomed ahead, glowing faintly with whatever protective enchantments hadn't been annihilated. More figures crept from the shadows—inhuman shapes, clawed and hungry.

Sebastian's legs gave out. Muscles shorted like a blown power grid— every signal screaming shutdown.

Samthrax caught him and hurled a dagger made of void-stuff. It struck a creature mid-lunge—it screamed, exploding into dust.

"Move your arse, Seb!"

They burst through the front doors just as a blast of magic detonated behind them, slamming it closed with a force that felt final, not protective.

Sage stood in the foyer, breath ragged, the almanac still clutched like a lifeline.

"Sage!" The word tore out of Sebastian before he even knew he was yelling it.

She turned as the walls shook.

From the west wing, a wave of darkness erupted—smoke and talons and grinding bone, a monstrous tide slithering through torn wards, glyphs searing along its sides.

"Get down!"

Samthrax didn't wait—he grabbed the twins and yanked them toward the stairs, hands blazing hot enough to burn.

One guttural word—no language known to this world—then his fingers snapped together.

The air blew outward, and suddenly they were wrapped in it: a dome of red-black power, pulsing like a heartbeat with teeth.

"Stay inside the bubble!"

No room for argument. No room for out.

Saffy joined the twins, looking thoroughly pissed off. "Really not happy about being dead and magicless right now."

The demon turned and threw himself into the battle as Seraphina and Killian stormed into view—a collision of light and dark, shrouded in war.

Seraphina blazed like a supernova. Her arms wreathed in living flame, the energy danced in cascading ribbons of gold that wrapped around her body, forming into weapons of burning fury.

With a twist of her wrist, she hurled fire that detonated through a cluster of wraithspawn, turning them to cinders mid-scream.

Beside her, Killian was silence personified. His magic unfurled in ripples of oil-black shadow, sliding across the floor and rising in serpentine coils.

Where Seraphina incinerated, he unmade.

Together, they moved with a terrifying symmetry—creation and oblivion in perfect tandem.

Samthrax dove into the mess, claws lit up like forged steel.

He spun mid-air, launched a bolt of abyssal magic—

—and laughed when the thing took it mid-leap and exploded backward, all limbs and wrong angles.

"Now this is my kind of reunion."

Seraphina didn't even look his way.

"Protect the children."

"You wound me, Mumma Bear. They're safely bubble-wrapped."

The battle roared on.

The manor groaned beneath the strain—stone fracturing, enchantments faltering.

Magic tore through the space in blinding bursts.

Light. Dark. Fire. Shadow.

War in every colour—and none that belonged to peace.

Inside the shield, the twins didn't move.

Like the story had skipped them, and no one gave them a pen.

Sage clutched the almanac tight, knuckles white.

If this is what 'protected' feels like, She'd rather take her chances outside. Beside her, Sebastian was all locked muscle and fury.

Power pressed against his skin begging to be let out.

If he didn't move soon, he was going to explode—and not in the cool, heroic way.

"We should help—" he started.

"No." Saffron couldn't believe what she was hearing. "Neither of you are ready yet."

Another surge of monsters poured in from the broken wards.

Seraphina shouted—words no one could understand, only feel. The hall lit up in fire and fury, white-hot and absolute.

Killian's command cut through it all.

"Enough."

He raised his head.

Threw both arms wide. Like he was about to part the world in two.

Sigils ripped up from the ground around him—ancient and pissed off, drawn from dead languages that hadn't been spoken since the first warlock burned the sky. They didn't float. They shredded the air, spinning so fast they carved rings of raw power into the room, the kind that remembered blood and demanded more.

Then the darkness came.

This was the end. No ceremony. No closure. Only an execution written in shadow.

The last wave of creatures turned to ash mid-scream. One second they were rage and ruin. The next? Dust molded by regret.

And then—the chaos cracked.

Smoke didn't drift. It coiled, as if it knew what it was summoning. It thickened in the centre of the wreckage, pulling itself together with the arrogance of something that had never been stopped—because it never had to run.

And then he was there.

Brinnan.

Cloaked in blood-red, eyes lit with the kind of cold calculation that killed without needing heat.

He stood with the menace of a man who never had to raise his voice to be obeyed.

"I thought it was the Shadowkeep's power I wanted." The words slid out easy. But there was nothing soft about them.

His eyes moved past Killian.

Past Seraphina.

To the bubble.

"I see now... There's more to have." The shadows at his feet shifted sharply along the floor—hunger-honed, tuned to his wanting. Killian's stare didn't waver.

"There's nothing here for you, or your son. You're the kind of rot that begs for a knife."

"Sanctimonious as always Killian."

Brinnan's eyes slid to Sebastian—full of intention.

"I see that your legacy didn't fall far from the tree."

The boy practically hummed with potential. Breakable in all the right ways.

"I look forward to collecting one way or another."

That was it. Samthrax's daily quota for arsehat? Officially maxed.

"Collect this, Ash-Breath."

A searing bolt of red-black magic tore across the room and slammed into Brinnan's chest.

The warlock staggered.

Surprised.

Samthrax hurled another. "Take this as an official eviction notice—effective immediately."

Brinnan spat a curse and vanished into smoke.

The wards flickered—then ignited, renewed.

Silence.

Killian turned to Samthrax. There was a hint of something in his expression—approval, maybe. Or just surprise with better posture.

"I'm impressed. You got a direct hit—even while he was in shadow-form."

Seraphina made a note of it. The demon had value. "How?"

Samthrax gave a shrug that could've taken all day. "I'm a demon. He tried to wield power forged in damnation. Honestly, he torched his own house and then blamed the matchstick."

Saffron inhaled out of habit. It didn't help. Being dead did that. "We need a new plan. Fast."

Killian didn't answer.

His eyes were fixed on the space where Brinnan had stood.

Because the war had just begun.

***

The doors of the Scriptorium slammed shut behind them, sealing with a sound that rang

like final judgement. Outside, the world ceased to exist—cut off, muted as if a curtain had been drawn across reality itself.

Killian raised one hand, muttering a phrase in a tongue so old that even Saffron tilted her head to catch the cadence.

The magic it summoned answered in silence. One by one, seals ignited along the stone—curse-script, etched in Graves discipline layered beneath the Bellarose glyphs, as if blood had soaked into the spellwork itself.

The books whispered in their sleep, murmuring in dead languages.

Candles flared—then steadied, their flames rigid—small, obedient mouths gone soundless.

Killian stood at the center of the chamber, spine straight, energy drawn tight around him like wire.

He extended two fingers in command—and the runes surged to life. Onyx and gold. Old and binding.

Pressure crawled through the warded space.

Security and secrecy.

"Panic room mode: engaged."

Samthrax lounged across the bookshelf like a gargoyle with an attitude problem.

"In case of magical apocalypse, please secure all limbs, curses, and emotionally shattered loved ones. Remain inside the dome. No refunds."

No one laughed.

The tension was razor-fine and humming with the threat of collapse.

Seraphina stood near the middle table, arms folded, jaw locked as if she'd bitten down on a promise she couldn't afford to spit out.

Saffron hovered nearby, her usual sass softened into something haunted.

Sage still clutched the almanac like a shield. Sebastian slouched in silence, hands in his pockets, gaze on the floor, every inch of him shut down.

Seraphina was the first to speak.

"You both deserve to know the truth about Brinnan. And Julian."

Sage's head snapped up.

Sebastian lifted his eyes, wary.

"He's my half-brother." Saffron hoped he died ugly. Preferably slow.

"Vander Bellarose—your great-grandfather—had an affair with another witch. Brinnan was the result."

Ice swept through Sage.

Her family tree was starting to resemble a dysfunctional labyrinth.

"His mother passed under mysterious circumstances." Saffron looked at each of them in turn. If that bastard caught a curse that peeled him from the inside out, she'd call it balance.

"I always suspected my father was responsible." She gave that a moment. "So does Brinnan."

Sebastian's gut twisted.

"Vander took Brinnan in. Raised him. But never as family." She hadn't seen him as family either. Not really.

"Turns out, he never wanted a place at the table. He wanted the kingdom. Which includes the Shadowkeep."

Saffron stopped. Not because she didn't know what to say next—but because she needed to see how they were dealing with it.

Sage sat there with that stock-standard curiosity of hers, the kind that didn't flinch even when the story turned unpalatable.

Sebastian?

He looked like he'd rather be on the moon than anywhere near this train smash.

"The Shadowkeep. It's a vault. A prison. A sealed hell under this estate."

Her eyes didn't leave them.

"For centuries, our bloodline's locked away the worst kinds of magic. Cursed relics. Dark souls. Living spells that shouldn't exist."

Saffron let it hang there.

Not to be dramatic.

Just because it needed to be digested.

"The Keep holds them still. I performed a sealing rite when I inherited it—made sure only a direct matriarchal heir could access it. I knew Brinnan would come eventually. And if he ever opened those doors—"

She stalled, as if even speech might give power to the nightmare.

"The world wouldn't unravel slowly. It would explode."

Sage didn't want any of this to be true. But the way Gram's said it, left no room for doubt. This was prophecy wrapped in her family's unfinished sentence. "That's... a lot."

"You've no idea, then Brinnan sent Julian to kill me." Saffron was looking straight at them—like they needed to see her face to believe any of this.

Seraphina's stomach cramped as her mother's lifeless body rose up from memory.

"And Julian obeyed."

"Without blinking." Saffron went inward.

The dagger had gone in clean.

It was the leaving that did the damage.

"He thought the Keep would be his." For just a second, Seraphina saw herself sending them both to hell. "But instead, it passed to me."

Her gaze flicked toward the twins—lingering on Sebastian. The weight behind it was unmistakable.

"And now they're both furious."

"Tonight wasn't an ambush," she continued. "It was a test. A warning shot. Now that Brinnan knows Killian is your father—and that he stands with us—he'll change tactics."

She paused, lips pressing into a line. "Your father has a reputation. And Brinnan's smart enough to fear it."

Sebastian took a half-step back—not in retreat, but in recalibration.

Everything grew suddenly thinner. The edges. His balance. Whatever held him together.

Is this what it feels like when the ground shifts and forgets to warn you?

"Is that why you took us away?"

Seraphina nodded. Slowly.

"There were reasons. Magical. Political. But mostly?"

She looked at them—really looked at them.

"I wanted peace. I wanted you to grow up with laughter and bad school lunches and late-night movies. I didn't want you raised as heirs to war. I wanted us to be safe. Ordinary."

The distance between them tightened, laced with emotion.

Sebastian was so damn tired. A tired that went so much deeper than his physical body.

"I get it. I really do. I just… miss it. I miss home. I miss ramen nights. I miss my friends."

That broke something open in Seraphina.

She closed the gap in a heartbeat and wrapped both of them in her arms. Fierce. Unapologetic.

Sage melted into the hug, her fingers curling tight into her mother's sleeve. Sebastian stood still at first, then his head fell forward, forehead against her shoulder, eyes shut.

"I'm sorry. That everything you thought was real… wasn't."

Seraphina leaned in, inhaled the scent of her children—like she used to when they were fresh-washed and safe and hers.

God, the guilt was a blade in her throat.

She was bloody terrified. She pulled back enough to look them both in the eyes. Her hands cupped their faces, wishing she could anchor them to this place in time.

"You have every right to be angry. But I have never been prouder of you than I am right now."

For a second, it was only them. Mother and children.

Killian didn't want to break the moment. But the world didn't care.

"We need to be practical. He's not just after the Keep anymore."

Killian's gaze zeroed in on Sebastian, already knowing it wouldn't land gently.

"Brinnan sensed your origins during the attack."

Sebastian had seen Brinnan's reaction to him. To the thing within him.

"What did he see?" The question was like reaching into a fire—not to find warmth, but to confirm the burn was real.

Killian's eyes darkened.

"Something older than the Keep."

The room went still.

"He sensed what I've felt since your power unbound."

Sage moved closer, shoulder brushing Sebastian's, instinctively protective even as her heart slammed in her chest.

"What does that mean? What the hell is inside me?"

Killian didn't soften.

"The Graves bloodline descends directly from the Original Dark One."

Sage looked at her brother, her expression said it all: immediate concern.

Sebastian kept his eyes on his father.

His attention was locked, and that—more than anything—told her he already knew.

Killian went on. Every word chosen like it might explode.

"He was the first warlock to fracture the balance of light and dark magic. He didn't fall to darkness—he became it. Turned shadow into force. His name is gone from the records. Erased. Because even speaking it was said to summon remnants of his power."

He paused, letting that sink in.

"Every generation, a fragment of that legacy resurfaces. Always in a male. Always in a twin."

Sebastian staggered as the ground shifted beneath him. He couldn't breathe properly—not from fear, exactly, but from the sense that something old and nameless had taken up residence inside him, whispering, you already knew.

"So that voice—"

Killian nodded once. "Wasn't foreign. It was blood calling to blood."

Sage turned toward her brother, face pale, the book resting against her—a promise she couldn't yet let go of.

"But... you're not him, Seb. You're not some monster just because of our bloodline."

"No."

Killian squashed the primal instinct to bubble-wrap his children and bury the Keep in six feet of concrete.

"He's not. But Brinnan doesn't care who Sebastian is. He only sees what he could become—and what that power would be worth if stolen."

Sage hesitated for half a second—then pulled the almanac out.

"Before the attack... I found something in this."

She opened it slowly. Not because the book was fragile—because what was inside might be.

"I didn't understand it then. Not really. But now..."

Her eyes lifted to Killian.

"Now I need you to explain this."

She turned the page.

The prophecy stared up at them in ink that looked half-burned yet half-alive:

"When shadow and flame are born as two, the world shall kneel or burn. Balance must be chosen. If not, one will consume the other. Only through unity may the power remain stable. Otherwise..."

devastation. One twin must fall for the other to ascend."

Sebastian read it. "So that's it. We're not part of this war. We are it."

Killian nodded. "You are the fulcrum now."

He looked between them.

"You are shadow and flame. Two halves of a prophecy written in fire and blood. And if you fracture—"

"One of us dies." Sage's brain short-circuited. Seriously—could this get any more complicated?

"And the other ascends." Sebastian was about five seconds from relocating to another continent.

Seraphina stepped forward, driven to move, her magic condensing at her fingertips.

"Not while I'm still breathing. This prophecy doesn't get to decide who you are. You do."

Killian had whiplash from the number of threats coming at them. But he'd be damned if he showed it.

They needed strength. That meant him.

"You don't win this by pretending the danger isn't real. You win it by facing it together."

Sebastian looked at his sister. She looked back.

And in that shared silence, something locked into place.

Not fear. Not resignation.

A vow. Unspoken. Unbreakable.

Samthrax, who had been uncharacteristically silent, suddenly sat up straighter on the edge of a shelf, tail swishing like an amused cat watching mortals play chess with dragons.

"Okay, wow. All of that was deeply traumatic, and I say that as a literal demon. Can we just underline 'kill Brinnan' and make it item one on the group project list?"

Sage's hand reached for Sebastian's.

He took it.

TWELVE

And for the first time since their world fell apart—they stood steady.
Together.

Thirteen

"Some loves don't die. They calcify. And when you touch them again—gods help you. Because nothing bleeds like stone breaking open."
— The Graves Testament, Verse III, Redacted

The others had gone to bed.

The Scriptorium, usually too full of movement and flame, had fallen into a quiet so deep even the stone exhaled. Glyphs of light shimmered above the candles—fragments of forgotten invocations, unwilling to fade. Below, protective sigils flickered under the floorboards, pulsing with watchful intent.

Seraphina sat with one leg tucked beneath her, a glass of wine balanced between two fingers. She stared into the fire, studying the embers as they rearranged themselves into dying patterns. Her hair had come loose from its braid—wild from wind, magic, and the aftermath of battle. She hadn't bothered to fix it.

Across from her, Killian leaned against a bookshelf, arms folded, shadows crouched at his boots.

They hadn't spoken for several minutes.

They'd opened with strategy—reinforcing the west wing, reinforcing the wards, interrogating what Brinnan's next move might be. But like everything between them, the conversation splintered—drifting in circles without ever landing.

Killian broke the stalemate first.

"Why didn't you marry?"

Seraphina nearly laughed at the absurdity.

Of all the things he could've asked, like—why she'd hidden the twins, why she'd never reached out, why she'd stayed in the Mundanii world—he chose that.

"That's where you go first?"

"You had what you wanted. A quiet life. A safe one. Maybe someone could've made it last."

She took a sip of the merlot, letting it sit on her tongue. Hell yes—this was survival in a glass.

"I didn't want more than that."

His eyes clung to her, tracking every move. Lucky wineglass. "There was a time you wanted me."

The words weren't gentle. Not cruel either. Just stripped-down truth—and undeniable.

"I wanted the version of you who might've stayed. But that version didn't exist long enough to matter."

"You think I left because I didn't love you?"

"I think." Her eyes remained on him. "That you loved me in a way that was always going to break me. And I couldn't afford to be broken. Not with them on the way."

He crossed the distance between them, footsteps whispering against the worn stone. When he stopped, it was close enough for her to smell the clinging smoke on his shirt, the scent of steel and shadow and him.

She didn't move away.

"You should've told me about the twins."

"You should've been someone I could tell."

Guilt hit Killian hard. She was right. He hadn't been that man.

"I had to choose—between telling you and protecting them."

She stopped for a moment.

"And if I were standing there again… I'd still choose them."

The fire gave a sharp, dry pop.

She continued to hold his gaze, and for once, there was no fury behind her stare. No shields. No war. Just grief. And exhaustion. And something rawer than regret.

"I didn't marry. Because no one after you ever stood a chance."

It shouldn't have cut. But it did.

Killian sat beside her. Not touching. Not crowding. Simply there, shoulder-to-shoulder, heat brushing heat.

"They were my reason for all of it. But you—"

"I was your ruin." He felt it again—that ache of what he'd cost her. She didn't argue.

The moment stretched—full of old love, old pain, and everything they used to be.

She thought it would've healed by now. It hadn't. "But you were also the only thing that ever made me feel alive."

His hand found hers.

Not rushed. Not forced. Just inevitable—like a storm gathering slowly, until the sky split wide open.

When he turned toward her, she met him halfway.

Their mouths didn't crash. They collided with something more dangerous—recognition. All the unspoken years poured into the space between their teeth, their breaths, their hearts.

She twisted onto his lap, fingers buried in his shirt. His hands travelled her spine, steady and sure.

Didn't matter how much time had passed. She still undid him. "I want you. Even if I shouldn't."

Her reply was a kiss—deliberate, anchoring, meant to erase any doubt.

His mouth found the place beneath her jaw. Her whole body answered.

Then came his hands mapping her thoroughly, each touch a reclamation. He didn't move with haste—he moved with certainty, as if her body were a language he'd once memorised in the dark and was finally reciting aloud.

Her legs tightened around his waist as she pulled him closer, not with desperation—but with possession.

She didn't want comfort. She wanted to own this. "You left. And I hated you for it."

"I know."

"I wished you dead."

"I know that too."

"But I never stopped wanting this."

She undid the buttons on his shirt, hands shaking—not from nerves, but from the way her body remembered his. Every part of him was harder now. Cut from war. Forged in discipline. Scarred where she hadn't touched.

Still him. Still hers.

Killian slipped his hands under her top. Palms dragging up, slow as sin. Careful, reverent—like touching her too hard would snap something they couldn't fix. His thumbs found her nipples, already tight under the lace. She arched into him. Couldn't help it. Didn't want to.

A sound broke out of him—low, guttural—and then he was on her, mouth crushing hers, because waiting wasn't in him anymore. He'd had this in his head a thousand times. But not like this. Not with her skin this warm. Not with her breath panting into his mouth.

"I dreamed of this."

Her teeth grazed his jaw. She didn't even try to pull away. "Then stop dreaming. Take me."

He didn't hesitate.

He stood, lifting her in one clean motion. She didn't just hold on—

she fit. Like everything had always led back to this.

They hit the floor hard. Her spine thudded onto the rug, dust rising, the air shifting around them. The shelves shivered behind them. Nothing else touched the moment.

He hovered above her, eyes on her chest, her stomach, the curve of her hips. Everything his. And his brain shut down.

She didn't ease his shirt off. Just shoved the thing down his arms and out of the way.

Her top came off next. The bra? Gone in a flick of practiced fingers.

Her skin flushed under the sudden air. Breasts fuller than they once were. Softer. Changed in ways that never fully returned—not after the kids.

She felt it all. The weight. The stretch. The gravity of time and motherhood stamped on skin that had been tighter, higher, smoother.

He was looking at her as if none of that mattered. Or maybe it did—and he welcomed it.

Her arms stayed down. She made no move to cover herself.

"You're even more dangerous now."

"So are you."

Their mouths crashed again—messy, frantic. Her nails scored his chest. Then her teeth caught his lip, and he felt the dare in it. The challenge. She wasn't backing off, and they both knew he wasn't stopping.

He tore at her jeans, got them down and gone. His own followed. Clothes hit the floor like it didn't matter. Because it didn't.

Skin to skin, heat to heat. Memory bleeding into now.

He slid his hand between her thighs.

Wet. Jesus.

That sound she made—soft, raw—slammed into him. He hadn't even touched her right—and she was already there for him.

"I want to taste you."

She grabbed his wrist, dragged him back up, and kissed him—shutting him down with her mouth.

"Later. I need you. Now."

He gave her exactly that.

He pushed in—slow, deep, unrelenting. Buried inside her like that was the only place he'd ever belonged. Their eyes stayed locked. Daring. Needing. Not letting go.

This was more than want. It was forgiveness. And it wrecked him.

She arched beneath him, hips meeting his in a way that stole every thought. Muscles clenching tight, pulling him in, holding him there.

"God, Sera…"

She held his face, steady and fierce, as if loosening her grip would undo everything they'd just found again. He moved—slow at first. Each thrust a reclaiming. A punishment. A prayer. Her legs wrapped around his waist, dragging him in deeper, her nails leaving red down his back.

Her head tipped away. The burn of it—his body, the years in between—hit all at once. He still wanted her. Still felt her. And that undid something she thought she'd buried for good.

"You feel the same. Tighter. Hotter. But the same."

She didn't answer. Didn't need to. Her body knew what it wanted—and it was him.

They moved faster. Harder. Her moans tore free. Gasps, then cries. He kissed down her throat, across her collarbone. Bit her shoulder just enough to leave a mark.

She started to come apart. He felt it in the way her legs locked around him, the way her body stopped chasing rhythm and just held on. And didn't that make him lose his ever-loving mind.

"I hate how much I still need this."

He didn't look away. Couldn't. "I don't. I'd never survive losing it again."

She shattered beneath him with a sound he'd never forget. A cry full of years. Of fury. Of love.

And in that second, she stopped fighting the truth. It was always him. Always would be.

He followed—one final thrust, rough and raw—spilling into her as her name tore from his throat.

He didn't even try to hold it back. It wasn't only release. It was everything he couldn't say. Everything he still longed for.

Afterward, they didn't move.

Just lay there, skin to skin, breath ragged, pulse wild. Her heart beating under his hand. His face buried in her neck.

What they gave, what they took—it lingered, alive between them. And for once, no one was running.

For a long time, neither of them spoke.

The fire burned low. The world for now didn't ask anything of them.

And what followed wasn't emptiness.

He didn't say, "I still love you." He didn't have to. That kind of love never died. It just waited to be asked if it was still willing to burn.

As Seraphina slipped deeper into the life she'd once left behind, someone else was wondering where she had gone. The question moved through the edges of thought, unsettled, unfinished, refusing to dissolve.

***

The rain had stopped an hour ago, but wet asphalt still clung to the night. Zinnia Hart hovered at the foot of Seraphina's front steps, keys in hand, her insides keeping time with something she didn't name. The porch light was off. No movement behind the windows. The house looked asleep—or worse, intentionally abandoned.

It had been two days since she'd heard from her best friend. Tuesday morning, Seraphina had missed their 6:00 a.m. spin class—no text, no call, not even a cryptic emoji. And that wasn't like her.

Seraphina was many things—chaotic, brilliant, always five minutes late with a smoothie in hand—but she had never disappeared.

Zinnia pushed the key into the lock and turned it. The familiar click sounded louder than it should have.

She opened the door.

Cool, stale air met her—tinged with lavender and the fading trace of sandalwood—the scent of Seraphina's diffuser, long since shut off. Zinnia stepped inside slowly, the wooden floor creaking beneath her trainers. The door sealed behind her with a soft thud.

"Sera?"

She moved through the entry hall, eyes scanning automatically. Mail sat untouched on the side table. The kitchen was spotless. The fruit bowl had started to turn. A single banana had gone black, and the sink was empty.

Something was definitely not right.

Zinnia was fit, fast—muscle and instinct refined by sport and tempered by discipline.

She was also the friend Seraphina had once called at two in the morning because the moon "felt weird," and they'd spent an hour sitting on the roof in silence. She was the one who made protein pancakes while Seraphina cursed astrology in her pyjamas.

Their friendship didn't always make sense. But it was real. Solid. Earned.

And Seraphina didn't vanish without telling her.

Something itched at the back of her mind. A hunch. Zinnia turned and walked toward the hallway, pausing at the foot of the staircase.

The whole house was untouched. Not deserted in panic but left behind by someone who knew they wouldn't be returning. It wasn't chaos. Or crime-scene cold. Just... emptied of life.

She took the stairs two at a time, heart drumming harder now, and checked the master bedroom first.

The closet doors stood open.

Inside—nothing.

No jackets. No scarves. Not a single pair of those ridiculous heels Seraphina never wore but kept "just in case."

Zinnia moved to the kids' room next. Same story. Clothes gone. Drawers empty.

She stepped back slowly, breath catching.

This wasn't a sudden emergency. It was a deliberate departure.

She grabbed her phone from her jacket pocket and checked it again. Still no response. She opened the call log. Redialed.

Straight to voicemail.

She hung up without leaving a message and sat on the arm of the couch, staring at the empty air. The house pressed inward—not with silence, but with absence.

Something pricked against the base of her neck.

Zinnia reached back, fingers brushing the soft flesh just beneath her hairline. Her fingertips paused on the familiar crescent-shaped birthmark there—a perfect sliver of moon, pale against her nape. But now... it was warm.

Not hot. Not painful. But unmistakably responsive.

Her brow furrowed. She pressed it gently, half-expecting it to ease. It didn't.

She stood slowly and turned in a circle, eyes flicking over the house again. Nothing had changed. And yet—a current stirred in her blood. Not panic. Not fear. Something stranger.

She lowered her hand and exhaled through her nose. Then she scrolled through her contacts until she reached a name she'd nearly forgotten saving.

Sage.

She tapped it.

The phone rang once.

Twice.

"Hello?"

Zinnia stood up straighter. "Sage—thank God. It's Zinnia. I've been trying to reach your mum." Paper rustled in the background, and a wind that didn't sound like it came from the weather.

"Zinnia?" "Yeah, it's me. I'm at the house. Where are you guys?"

Silence.

"I'll get her to call you. I promise."

"Wait—what? Can you at least tell me—"

"Not right now. But she's okay. We're okay. There's… a lot going on."

A tremor of something passed through Zinnia—confusion first, followed by a slow twist of dread. "What does that mean?"

Zinnia's heart was thudding hard, not with panic. Not yet. But getting bloody close.

"She'll call you."

Sage's thumb hit the screen. Done. And yeah, it felt like crap.

She knew Zinnia wasn't letting this go. She hated not being able to tell her the truth.

Her mom? Was gonna dodge this faster than a bullet.

And against Zinnia? She didn't stand a chance in hell.

Zinnia stared at the phone in her hand, her jaw locked. She didn't even realise how hard until her molars started aching.

The house was quiet again.

She remained there, unmoving.

The warmth at the back of her neck still hadn't cooled.

***

Rain clawed at the windows, a whispering percussion that filled the otherwise soundless penthouse. Brinnan's study—high above the city's oblivious sprawl—was a cathedral of control: steel, blackwood, and glass arranged with precision. No clutter. No warmth. Every detail curated. Every corner wielded with the same cold authority as its owner.

Brinnan stood just beyond the light, staring over the glittering skyline. In his hand, a stemmed glass of wine swirled, untouched.

At his back, Julian lounged in a leather chair, immaculately composed. One leg crossed, cufflinks gleaming in the ambient glow. On the other side of the room, Malrik leaned against the side of a credenza, dripping water onto the polished floor, unbothered by the small puddles gathering at his feet. The moment drew tight, stretched thin as wire—until the stone set into Brinnan's ring flared once. Subtle, but unmistakable. The flame inside the nearby lantern stuttered. A shift moved through the room—fine as static, skimming along nerves before vanishing.

Brinnan turned slightly, gaze narrowing.

Malrik's spine went rigid. "You felt that too?"

Julian lifted his head. The hairs on his arms stood up.

"Something just woke up." Brinnan knew that energy. Not theirs. Not hers. But familiar.

"It wasn't ours. And it wasn't Seraphina."

"Then who?" Malrik peeled off his soaked jacket and flung it over a chair. "The estate's locked tighter than a hex vault. Nothing should be moving."

Brinnan didn't answer at first. He crossed the room to a small cabinet and opened it, revealing a stack of ancient vellum and runes scribed in black wax. He pulled one free and spread it across the table. The parchment had gone brittle with age, but the spells embedded in it still hummed like sleeping snakes.

A map of bloodlines.

The sigils flared where magic bled through.

Tonight, a new one emerged—faint, hesitant—but real.

Julian rose, eyes locked on the map. "That's not a Graves or a Bellarose."

"No," Brinnan didn't look away. "That's much older."

He tapped the mark that hadn't been there yesterday.

There, far from the estate, further still from the known heirs, a dormant line had flickered awake. Unclaimed. Unacknowledged. Impossible.

"Les Revenantes," Brinnan's blood spiked. This was old power—and now, new possibility.

Malrik's gut tightened. That name didn't belong in the present. "They're extinct."

Brinnan adjusted his cuff. "They were meant to be."

The pause that followed held the room in its grip.

"You think it's an heir?" Julian put it out there. Whatever this was, it wasn't part of the plan.

"I think it's a complication." Brinnan let that land. "One we didn't account for."

Malrik came in closer, boots heavy on the stone. "That coven was wiped out centuries ago."

Brinnan stared at the sigil. Nothing gave him away. And that was where the danger lived. "Which means someone was hidden. Buried so deep even the Council missed it."

Julian had learned his father's tells the hard way. Brinnan was already ten steps ahead.

"Or someone made sure she stayed that way. Deliberately. Tucked into the Mundanii world—where no one would think to look."

Brinnan traced the pulsing mark with a finger. "She's untrained. That much is certain. The signature is raw. Clumsy."

"But awakening," Julian knew enough to start drawing lines. "Which means it won't stay lost for long."

Malrik didn't dress it up. "Once she wakes up, we're going to need a leash on her. You think she can open the Keep?"

Brinnan didn't give them room to speculate. "No. The Keep answers to one key—and we already know who holds it."

Julian got his footing back. "So, at this stage, you're saying she's simply noise."

Brinnan gave a nod. But inside, a spark had caught flame.

The Veil…

He didn't give them anything. Just steepled his fingers and waited. Let them circle the surface while he mapped the abyss beneath.

Les Revenantes were guardians of the gateway, not vaults. Their gift was never containment—it was passage.

The girl was a fracture line. A tear in the seal. A door to something older. Something locked away by force.

The Veilborn.

The word itself hissed through his thoughts like smoke worming through a ruin-veined monolith.

Julian didn't understand the magnitude.

And Malrik—useful as he was—didn't have the imagination for what was buried on the far side of the Veil. He saw leverage and revenge. Not legacy.

Brinnan felt the corner of his mouth lift. Control tasted better than curiosity. "She's an anomaly. We don't know what leaks through when a line like that stirs."

Julian tilted his head. No surprise there. Just strategy. "So, we contain her before someone else makes use of her."

Brinnan didn't blink. "Exactly. Let's not lose hold of such a perfectly placed advantage."

***

The fire in Seraphina's bedroom had burned down to embers. The sheets were tangled, her limbs still heavy from sleep and the residual heat of Killian's body wrapped around hers. His breath stirred the curve of her shoulder. For a moment, there was nothing but contentment.

Her phone vibrated.

Killian made a noise of protest. "Ignore it."

She reached for the nightstand anyway. The screen lit up with a message from Sage.

Zinnia's called a bunch. She's worried. Said it's urgent. I told her you'd call her back.

Her stomach flip-flopped. Seven missed calls. Multiple voicemails.

The guilt hit low—shit, shit, shit.

Killian shifted behind her. "Someone important?"

"Zinnia. My best friend. She's… outside of all this. She doesn't know anything."

Killian didn't reply, but she felt the change in him—the way his body tensed.

Seraphina opened the most recent voicemail and pressed it to her ear.

"Sera, it's been two days. You missed spin class. You never miss spin. I've called. Texted. I went to the house. All your clothes, the twins' stuff—gone. It's like you left in a hurry. What the hell is going on? Call me."

Seraphina didn't wait. She hit Call Back.

The line connected on the first ring.

"Sera?" It came out rough—too much in her to get it clean. Relief. Fury. Panic. All of it jammed together in one breath. "Where the hell have you been?"

"Zinnia—"

"No. You don't get to start with that. I've been losing my mind. You vanish. No warning. No explanation. I go to your house, and it's half-empty. It looked like you grabbed the kids and bolted."

Seraphina drew a breath, her hand clamped around the phone.

"I had to leave. I didn't have time."

"That's not good enough. Are you guys in danger? You need to tell me what's going on."

"We're safe. But I can't tell you everything. Not yet." Her chest ached with what she couldn't say. But survival came first. Even if it meant lying to the one person who deserved better.

"Don't pull that on me. I know you, Seraphina. You wouldn't run unless someone was chasing you."

Seraphina kept her grip on the phone. Tighter than she intended.

"I didn't want to put you at risk."

"I'm already at risk." Zinnia didn't give her room. "You disappeared. I thought someone had taken you. I've been walking around with a thousand worst-case scenarios in my head."

The pause stretched, full of everything neither of them would touch.

"We've been through a lot. And you won't even tell me why you're gone?"

Seraphina opened her mouth—struggling to find the words.

"I'm sorry, Zin. If I could tell you more, I would. But this… it's not something I can explain right now."

Zinnia's gut took the hit. Something was off, like roadkill cooked on hot pavement.

"Are you coming back?"

"I don't know yet."

"You better. Because if you don't, I will find you. And I will beat the truth out of you over overpriced coffee."

Seraphina's mouth pulled at the edges—could've been a smile, could've been guilt trying to find a way out. "You'd make a terrible interrogator."

"I'm persistent. You should realise that by now."

"I do."

"Tomorrow. Eleven. Our place. You miss it, I swear to God I'll show up at your funeral and drag your ghost to the table."

"I'll be there."

"Good. And Sera?"

"Yeah?"

"I don't care how weird things are. You're still my person. Don't forget that."

"I haven't, and Zin, you're mine too."

Seraphina hung up, staring at the screen.

Killian took the phone from her. He didn't say anything at first. Just gave her something to come back to.

"That sounded… intense."

"I think I just made her part of this crapfest."

The truth hit harder than Zinnia's voice: she'd dragged her into this war without lifting a hand.

Killian rested his chin on her shoulder. "Then we watch her back. Like we watch each other's."

Seraphina didn't answer right away.

Because in her heart of hearts, she knew tomorrow wouldn't be just coffee.

***

The kettle screamed.

Zinnia didn't move.

She sat on the hardwood, spine braced against the kitchen cabinets, legs folded beneath her. The throw blanket around her waist tangled in a knot she hadn't bothered to fix. One hand holding her phone, the other resting at the back of her neck, where the crescent-shaped birthmark throbbed.

Her screen lit up again. A text from Seraphina.

Sera: "Tomorrow, 11AM. Same place. ♥."

Zinnia stared at the message until the light dimmed and disappeared.

She didn't buy the calm voice on the phone earlier. Seraphina had sounded… contained. Measured. That tone—too warm, too smoothed-over.

Zinnia stood. Her legs ached from the floor's bite, but she didn't care. She clicked the kettle off mid-scream and poured boiling water over the mint leaves waiting in her chipped mug. The scent hit her—crisp, green, grounding. She leaned on the counter with both hands, staring down the tea like it owed her answers.

She and Seraphina had met fourteen years ago. Same gym, same spin session, same instant, mutual you're-my-people recognition. Seraphina had invited her for smoothies afterward. By the end of the week, they were sharing playlists, swapping protein shake recipes, and watching out for each other.

A year later, Zinnia's boyfriend shattered her jaw and her last illusion. Seraphina was the one who found her. Took her in. Cleaned her blood off the tiles, packed the go-bag, stood between her and the door when he came searching. She never asked why Zinnia stayed so long. She only made sure she never went back.

Zinnia owed her life to that woman. But this silence? This wasn't protection. This was being shut out.

And it wasn't about missed classes anymore.

She brought the mug to her lips, held it there, but didn't drink. The heat against her skin barely registered. The mark on her neck burned inward—deeper now, burrowing under flesh.

She turned toward the rain-slicked window. City lights bled against the glass in fractured gold. In the reflection, her own face stared back—short black hair clinging to damp temples, jaw set, dark eyes hollow from too little sleep and too much wondering. The tattoo sleeve down her left arm curled into shadow.

She rubbed the nape of her neck again, breath catching.

Heat radiated outward now, no longer a warning. It was a summons.

And she was done waiting for permission.

She needed to know where Seraphina had gone. Why she'd vanished without a word. Why the house looked evacuated. Why the voice on the phone had stopped sounding like home.

She turned away from the window.

Walked back to the counter tipping the tea into the sink and watched the steam evaporate.

She didn't need soothing.

She needed truth.

And if Seraphina couldn't give it to her willingly—she'd drag it into the light herself.

Fourteen

The soft filament of rain had faded sometime before dawn, leaving the world rinsed clean. Pale light filtered through gauzy curtains, casting silver across the tangle of sheets. In the quiet, the only sound was the even rhythm of two breaths, drawn in sync.

Killian lay behind her, one arm draped possessively around her waist. His fingers moved lazily, drawing idle circles against her skin.

"Morning, sunshine," he rumbled, his mouth brushing her shoulder, voice gravel-thick with sleep. His hand drifted lower, tracing the curve of her hip. "If I had my way, we wouldn't be getting out of this bed for a week."

She let her eyes flutter open, her body instinctively leaning back into the heat of his. The moment she shifted, she felt the clear response of his arousal against her.

"Mmm. Morning." A smug smile pulled at her mouth—because she knew exactly what he was feeling.

He kissed the side of her neck—deliberately, leisurely—his teeth grazing the sensitive spot beneath her ear. His hand moved to her breast, teasing the nipple between his fingers. Pleasure sparked—hot, immediate, and entirely inconvenient. Which was what happened when your dry spell had its own birth certificate.

It would be so easy to surrender to it, to let the morning stretch into something far less responsible.

"Unfortunately." She didn't look at him when she spoke. If she did, she wasn't getting out of this bed. "We both have commitments that won't wait."

Killian groaned in protest. "I'm happy to continue this later." He wanted her under him again. Now. Every inch of him was still keyed up, ready to go, and walking away from her felt like peeling his own skin off.

She chuckled, though the sound came out a little breathless. Her body burned with memory—and his hands hadn't exactly helped douse the flame.

"We should talk about what this is. What we are." He didn't circle it, didn't pad it. Just laid the truth down between them and waited, knowing full well it might stay there, untouched.

She shifted to face him fully. He caught her mouth—part of him knew he was stalling her answer. The rest wanted the taste of her again. Their tongues met in a clash of need and heat, passion igniting in her like dry tinder. Her desire for him hadn't waned. If anything, it had fermented—volatile now, ripe for combustion.

His hand slid down the dip of her spine, gripping her hip with the kind of restraint that made her itch to unravel it. He pulled her closer, deepening the kiss, his control fraying at the edges.

"You still want me." His mouth brushed hers. "I can feel it."

She arched against him. His thumb swept across her nipple again, making her want to throw caution to the wind.

"We shouldn't." Her body straddled the line between sense and surrender.

"Yes." His hand slipped between her legs, fingers finding slick heat. "We should." Seraphina caught his wrist. It cost her—God, did it cost her. Every nerve was screaming for more. But now wasn't the time. She needed to say this while she still could. "I do want this. I want you. But I'm not ready to parade it through my mother's kitchen or wave it in front of two temperamental teenagers."

He looked damn pleased with himself. "So, we're hiding our scandalous tryst from the children."

She sat up, the sheet slipping off her shoulder. "We're not hiding. We're… pacing."

And maybe it was naïve to think they could pace anything when their lives were sprinting toward ruin. But for now, they could pretend it wasn't just avoidance. That it was hope, wearing a disguise.

Killian leaned back, lacing his fingers behind his neck, watching her with that maddening calm that made her want to both kiss him and throw a pillow at his head. "Very noble of us."

She gave him a dry look, but something warm curled in her chest.

She'd missed this. His ease. His gravity. The way he grounded everything, even when the world tipped sideways.

"I'm here, Sera. I'm not walking away again."

She met his gaze and held it.

"I believe you." The words landed before she could question them. "But right now… I need to handle the Zinnia situation."

He nodded, brushing a kiss against her temple before reluctantly drawing back. "You said she's your closest friend."

"For fourteen years. She's tough. Loyal. Scarily good at deadlifting." And not exactly someone she could bullshit.

"So, I'm going to lie to her face while trying not to lie at all."

Killian sat up, hair tousled, the early light slipping over the sharp lines of his profile.

"If she's as close to you as you've said… this isn't going to stay simple."

Seraphina turned, drawing the sheet tighter around her.

"She doesn't know who I really am, Killian. To her, I'm a single mum with the usual problems—bills, bad coffee, bad hair days."

What she didn't say aloud was that she missed pretending to be ordinary. Killian saw it anyway. Like always. He didn't push. Didn't press. He just backed her, like he always did.

"Then she's already in this, Sera. Whether you tell her or not. The only question is when."

***

The sun had risen high enough to warm the frost-laced glass as Seraphina stepped into the Scriptorium. An emerald mohair jumper and her favourite jeans hugged her frame; her hair was twisted into a loose knot, still faintly scented with lavender soap and woodsmoke.

Sage sat cross-legged on a deep couch, surrounded by a fortress of open books, highlighters wedged behind both ears like enchanted tools of scholarly warfare. She glanced up from her notes, brows lifting.

Sebastian lounged nearby, a half-filled notebook balanced precariously on his thigh, one hand wrapped around a mug of hot chocolate that steamed faintly in the cool air. He looked more alert than usual—still exhausted, but focused, a line of tension drawn across his shoulders.

Seraphina paused on the threshold, caught between the faint comfort of routine and the disquiet clawing at her insides.

She cleared her throat. "I'm heading into town for a few hours."

Sage tilted her head. "Zinnia?"

Seraphina gave a small nod. "She's worried, and she deserves some answers."

Her voice held its usual composure, but guilt rested behind her eyes. How much could she afford to say without making things worse?

Sebastian lowered his mug. "Are you going to tell her everything?"

"Not yet. Some things need better timing."

A rustling sound followed—parchment and muttered profanity—as Samthrax emerged from the far side of a scroll stack, where he'd been hiding with all the enthusiasm of a gremlin in a hoard.

"I volunteer as tribute to guard the young and magically explosive." He adjusted an imaginary crown. "Unless you'd prefer, I install a blackjack table and teach the kids to hustle with minor hexes and statistically improbable luck."

Killian strode in, his dark coat amplifying a presence that, as always, steadied the room—quiet authority threaded with something more intimate, his gaze lingering on Seraphina.

"I'm heading into the Enclave for a council check-in. Shouldn't take more than a few hours." He angled a look at Samthrax "No blackjack. And absolutely no hexes."

Samthrax clutched his chest like he'd been mortally offended. "Fine. Then, we'll start an illicit potions operation. Very boutique. Limited edition curses only."

Sage rolled her eyes. "He's probably not joking."

"Definitely not." Sebastian was sure of it.

Saffron floated through the doorway, elegant and amused, her expression far too pleased to be innocent. "Well, well. Off to slay dragons and dodge awkward conversations?"

She tilted her head, eyeing Seraphina, then Killian, brow arched. "Don't do anything I wouldn't do."

Seraphina wondered if it was possible to slap a ghost. "That leaves very little off the table."

"Exactly."

Saffron threw her a wink, then looked to the twins. "I'll keep them busy. They've got enough magical theory to survive a decade of exams."

Samthrax, now suspended upside down in a levitating chair, gave Seraphina a toothy grin. "Tell Zinnia I'm available for brunch. I'm a delight, truly. I only possess people on full moons, and only the boring ones."

It took Seraphina effort not to laugh. "I'll pass that on but no promises."

She crossed the room. As she reached the far archway, Killian stepped into her path, his hand brushing hers—brief and intentional.

"Be careful." He could've said more. God, he wanted to. But this— this was all she'd let him give her.

She leaned in. "I always am."

***

The café, nestled just beyond the heart of the Quarter, brimmed with quiet life—lush greenery curling from wrought-iron planters, vines draped from mismatched chandeliers like silk in motion. The warmth of chicory coffee mingled with pralines and burnt sugar, steeping the room in nostalgia and sweetness. Plush booths upholstered in deep garnet velvet lined the walls, each table adorned with tiny oil lamps and weathered calaveras tucked between stacks of tarot cards and overgrown succulents.

Day of the Dead murals stretched ceiling to floor, all painted in warm ochres and bruised indigos, the sockets of every skull lit from within, glowed with mischief.

Zinnia sat in the far booth, nursing a café au lait that had been cooling untouched for ten minutes. Her dark eyes darting to the doorway again, jaw tight beneath the clean lines of her cropped black cut. The tattoo sleeve on her arm flexed as she drummed against her thigh.

The door opened, and Seraphina stepped in.

Worn jeans and a jumper. Hair twisted loosely up. Her face unreadable—until her glance found Zinnia's, and something softened.

Zinnia was up in an instant. "Geezus. Sera."

They embraced before either could second-guess it. A hug built from habit and worst-case-scenario worry.

They slid into the booth in silence.

Zinnia broke it first. "You okay?"

Seraphina gave that a brief thought. Was she okay? Fuck no. "I'm managing."

Zinnia didn't buy it. "That's not an answer."

"It's the best I've got right now."

Zinnia didn't push—not yet. She took her time, looking Seraphina over. "You look exhausted."

"Nothing a century of sleep wouldn't fix."

Zinnia exhaled. "I didn't come here to yell. You already got my full freak-out on the phone. This… this is me worried. I'm trying to make sense of whatever the hell is happening." Seraphina wrapped her hands around the mug Zinnia had bought her. "I didn't mean for you to get caught up in this."

"You mean the vanishing act? Or the part where I walked into your house and it looked like you'd been abducted in the night?"

Seraphina winced. She deserved that. "It wasn't safe. For me. Or for kids. And it still isn't."

Zinnia's expression didn't shift. "Why?"

"It's not simple."

"Try complicated. I don't care. You're my best friend. If you're in danger, if the twins are in danger—I want in."

"I know you do. But it's not something I can explain in a sentence. Or even ten."

Zinnia leaned back. "So, explain it in twenty."

Seraphina's mouth lifted, then flattened just as fast. She'd once explained contractions to Sage using a stuffed bear and a slushie cup. She didn't have a script for: 'Hey, I'm a witch and the world's ending.'

Silence wandered in and stayed, the ripcord hanging there—waiting.

"Is someone after you?"

"Yes."

"Are you in danger?"

"Yes."

"Is it legal danger or…" She gestured vaguely. "Some other kind?"

Seraphina's brain was on the verge of short-circuiting. Sweet baby Jesus, this was an interrogation—one she wasn't built to survive.

Not because she couldn't. Because she didn't want to.

She wanted to sing like the proverbial canary.

Zinnia had no intention of backing off. "Don't go full FBI-blackout on me. I've known you for fourteen years. We've survived all kinds of hell together. You helped me leave mine. Now let me help you."

The memory of blood-soaked tiles, blackened face, and the post-survival emotional roller coaster made Seraphina flinch.

"I remember."

"Then give me the truth."

She fixed her eyes on the swirling surface of the drink. Her hands gripped the warm ceramic.

"I never lied to you. But I didn't tell you everything either."

Zinnia stared, hard. "Are you in a cult?"

The laugh escaped before she could stop it. "No. God, no."

"Then what the hell is it?"

Seraphina scanned the café. No one was paying attention. The barista was fussing with the milk steamer. A couple were laughing quietly over tarot cards near the window.

She reached across the table. "Watch."

She wrapped her hands around Zinnia's coffee.

The surface quivered and rolled. The centre turned molten, heat spiralling in perfect geometric patterns. Steam rose—not in chaotic curls, but deliberate spirals.

Zinnia jerked. "What the—?"

"This is what I've been hiding and why we had to go."

Zinnia leaned forward. "Are you saying what I think you're saying?"

"I'm saying I'm a witch. And there are forces moving now that I can't control alone."

Zinnia just stared. What she'd seen—there was no explaining that. No faking it. And Seraphina? She was a straight shooter. If she said something, it was because she believed it—every damn word.

"So, what—Harry Potter? Coven rituals in the woods? Pentagrams in your basement?"

"No—more like shit that kills when you're not looking."

Zinnia swallowed. "This is straight-up, balls-out insane."

"I know."

Zinnia looked at the mug, then at her. Her brain said no. Her gut said yes. And Seraphina had never looked more certain.

"I wouldn't lie to you."

"Apparently you already did. For years."

Seraphina nodded once. "I hid things. But I never lied about what we are."

"And what are we?"

Seraphina reached for her hand. "Still best friends. If you want to be."

Zinnia stared at her for a long moment, but didn't pull away.

She sucked in a breath through her teeth, hand flying to her neck. "What's wrong?"

"My birthmark. It's been burning for hours."

"Let me see."

Zinnia pulled the collar of her shirt aside. The crescent shape gleamed faintly in the morning light, the skin around it reddened and raised.

Seraphina's stomach left the room.

That mark wasn't random.

"How long has it been like this?"

"A couple days."

Seraphina could feel it now—vibrating, tuned to her magic.

Oh yeah. This was a spanner in the works. And nothing was coming out the other side the same.

Looks like Zinnia has a secret of her own.

"Zin, you need to come with me. Back to the manor."

"You mean your mum's haunted castle?"

"It's not haunted."

Zinnia didn't bother hiding the doubt.

"Okay, it's a little haunted."

Zinnia didn't ask if she should be worried. She already knew. Her life was about to change—and there was no unringing that bell. "What am I walking into?"

Seraphina let the truth show. "Honestly? I don't know. But I'd rather you walk into it with me than risk leaving you in the dark."

Zinnia ran a hand through her hair. "Okay. Let's figure out why my neck is trying to cook itself."

Seraphina sent up a heartfelt halle-fucking-lujah to the powers that be. "Thanks, Zin."

Zinnia drained her coffee and got up. "For the record? This is not how I thought brunch would go."

Seraphina rose beside her. "Me either."

Across the street, deep in the mouth of a shuttered bookstore, Malrik stood shrouded in shadow. His coat hung from his shoulders like a second skin, blending into the dark beneath a canopy of splinterlit signage and neon dust.

He neither blinked nor moved.

He'd seen her.

Not Seraphina. The other one.

The girl with the mark.

She didn't know what she was. But she would soon. The crescent burned brighter now—shining with waking power, old as stone and sacrifice.

Les Revenantes.

His lips curled into a slow, satisfied sneer. Brinnan was in the dark. And that was fine. For now.

This knowledge was currency.

She could open the door to The Veilborn.

The chained force locked away by rites, sinew, and forgotten gods..

The one Brinnan would never control.

But Malrik?

He had vision.

Now he had a face.

A name would come next.

After that, a plan.

He stepped back into the shadows, magic folding around him like a serpent lying in wait.

When the time came, he would not ask permission.

He would take what was always meant for him.

***

The city thinned as they drove—oak-lined streets giving way to narrow backroads that twisted toward the forgotten edge of New Orleans.

Zinnia sat in the passenger seat of Saffron's sleek black Mercedes, her fingers tapping a restless rhythm against the door. Her jaw ached from how hard she was clenching it, but she couldn't stop. Every mile dragged her further from the world she thought she knew, and closer to something her soul clearly hadn't forgotten.

The moment they turned off the main road, her neck flared.

The mark surged hot, vibrating with an unseen frequency beneath her skin.

"Shit." She pressed her fingers to it, like that would shut it up.

Seraphina glanced over, her knuckles white on the wheel. "It's reacting."

"Yeah, no kidding. What the hell is out here?"

Seraphina didn't answer. They rounded a bend—and the world changed.

Zinnia's breath caught.

The road dead-ended at a stretch of ornate black fencing. Iron-spined, spear-tipped bars veiled in ivy and fog. Abandoned. Forgotten.

Until it wasn't.

As they approached, the illusion melted away. Faint sigils shimmered over the metal—etching pale fire along its surface before vanishing into the mist.

A quiet voltage tingled through Zinnia's skin, as if her body remembered this place before her mind did. "I've driven this road before, but I have never seen this."

"It only shows itself to those with the blood."

She glanced at Zinnia's neck. Nothing more needed saying.

The gates parted in silence, drawn back by invisible hands. Not forced—invited.

Zinnia's mark burned brighter now, with longing. A pull deep in her being, as if the divine itself had finally seen her.

A sensation twisted low in her gut. Not rejection—more like déjà vu ripped open. A feeling that didn't belong in this moment, or in any moment she could name.

"Am I even supposed to see this?"

"Yes. You are."

The car passed through, and the world behind them fell away like a dream shaking loose.

Noise vanished.

The sky shifted—paler, gold-veined with violet. Time bent at the edges.

The Enclave didn't appear. It unfolded.

Five minutes later, they turned up a long gravel drive. And Zinnia saw it—Maison Bellarose.

A low curse slipped out before she could stop it.

Not for its size—though it sprawled across the land, seeming to rise from the bedrock itself—but for its presence. A grand stone manor dressed in vines and shadow. Tall windows framed in wrought iron. Balconies gleaming pale as moon-silver. The surrounding air whispered of secrets.

The gardens curled with sculpted precision. Wind chimes sang faintly, though no breeze stirred. A raven perched above the tallest spire, still and too knowing.

The birthmark maintained its rhythm—steady, consistent, and intent.

"This isn't a house." Zinnia couldn't take her eyes off it.

"No."

Seraphina said it like the word meant more than it should.

"It's more of a threshold."

And with that, Zinnia realised something visceral and awful.

The woman who'd helped her escape her ex. Who spotted her on deadlifts. Who dragged her out of the dark when she'd nearly drowned in it—

Clashed hard against the reality in front of her.

Seraphina hadn't come from a one-bedroom apartment with a leaky faucet and a yoga mat in the corner.

She came from this.

"So…" Zinnia cleared her throat. "Is this prep school for magical aristocrats, or a private cult with excellent landscaping?"

Seraphina let a tired smile slip free. "Depends on the semester."

She guided the car around a fountain that reflected the sky like starlight poured into stone and stopped at the base of the main steps.

Before Zinnia could take a full breath, the double doors swung open, and a blur of flannel and braid came leaping from the doorway.

"Sage?"

"Zinnnnn!" The girl hurled herself across the gravel with zero regard for decorum.

Zinnia scrambled to get out of the car just as the teenager tackled her in a whirlwind of limbs and half-sobs.

"Oh my God, I thought we were never gonna see you again." Sage was laughing and somehow crying at the same time. "You smell like coffee and stress. It's perfect."

Zinnia hugged her fiercely. "You feral little thing. Still not wearing shoes, I see."

"Why would I?" Sage swiped at her face. "We live in a magical manor now. Footwear is tyranny."

Zinnia's laugh came out broken, but it was there. Sage stepped back, beaming.

"Welcome to the insanity. You ready for the tour?"

Before Zinnia could answer, Sebastian appeared in the doorway, hands in his pockets, leaning like someone trying not to look nervous.

"Hey, Z."

"Hey, Seb. Pretty surreal situation, aye."

"You're not wrong." He nodded toward the open door. "Enter at your own risk."

"Not helping." Seraphina steered Zinnia forward with a hand at her back.

The doors closed behind them with a deep, thundering boom. Heat settled around them—denser now, tinged with citrus, old books, and something older still. A black cat sat on the banister, eyes molten gold, fixed and unblinking.

"Okay." Zinnia stared at it. "That thing's not normal."

"Well," came a voice smooth as silk and smoke. "Either someone ordered a hot, tattooed mortal, or the scrying mirror finally got my wish list."

Zinnia turned—a demon lounged on the stairs, all high-waisted trousers, velvet smoking jacket, and a monocle. Horns curled back from his head, blackened and glossy as forged hellstone, his black hair an unruly mop. His grin was wicked and delighted.

"What in hell is that?" She didn't even try to hide her shock.

"Language." The demon pressed a hand to his chest, eyes wide with fake offense. "There are children present."

"Yee gods, what are you wearing?" Seraphina actually looked pained.

"A cultural statement." Samthrax moved forward with predatory elegance. "Samthrax. Resident chaos demon, certified trauma connoisseur, and fashion risk-taker. You must be Zinnia. Love the ink. Terribly underutilised in blood rituals, by the way."

Zinnia blinked. "You have horns."

"And you have excellent taste in eyeliner. I'd call it even."

Sage popped up beside her. "That's Sam. He's our emotional support demon."

"You're all serious right now?"

"Unfortunately." Sebastian didn't even try to sound sorry. "He's contractually bound."

"Ex-cuse me." Samthrax straightened, affronted. "I am also a refined agent of infernal charm and legally sanctioned mischief. I have credentials."

"In crayon," Sage added.

Eyes wide, Zinnia turned to Seraphina. "You were going to explain this at some point?"

"We're getting there." A smile tugged at her mouth. "Come on. We'll talk in the Scriptorium."

"The what now?"

"Library." Sage translated. "With extra drama."

As they passed beneath a carved arch, Zinnia spoke under her breath. "Okay, I'm trying not to lose it, but you've got witches, demons, a possessed cat—"

"And that's just the foyer." Sebastian sounded bored, which was impressive.

"God, I need more caffeine."

They stepped into the Scriptorium.

Zinnia stopped dead in her tracks.

"Holy shitballs."

Behind her, Samthrax leaned in, voice smooth as honey over brimstone.

"Welcome to the deep end," he purred. "Hope you brought floaties."

Zinnia didn't answer. She was too busy wondering if the deep end was where she'd drown—or finally figure out what she was made of.

Fifteen

"When the Veil stirs, it does not knock. It remembers. And what it remembers, it summons."
— *Les Revenantes Codex, Fragment 17a*

The Scriptorium breathed around them, thick with candlelight and old power.

Zinnia stood beside Seraphina. A slow, heavy rhythm threaded through the room. Her body caught it—already strung tight as a bow. Her shirt clung damp to her back with anxious sweat. The air carried the scent of beeswax, mingled herbs, and something else—something that buzzed at the base of her skull.

She crossed her arms over her chest, eyes scanning the chamber as if someone—anyone—might jump out and yell gotcha. Some part of her still hoped that this was all a prank. Hidden cameras. Ashton Kutcher. Cue dramatic reveal.

But no one was laughing.

She turned—and froze.

Saffron Bellarose stood near the tall, arched windows, the sunlight bleeding through her. Not across her. Through her.

Zinnia blinked. Once. Twice. Her brain scrambling to make sense of it—but her gut already knew.

There was no shadow, no warmth. Just radiance drifting through her like Saffron was made of mist.

"Oh, shit."

Tears blurred her vision. Surely this couldn't be real.

"Zin—"

Seraphina swore under her breath. She hadn't told her. And this? This was a shitty way to find out.

"Sera, what happened to your mother?"

Zinnia was proud of herself—so far, no screaming. No bolting.

Saffron turned with the grace of someone unbound by time. Her face—composed. And her eyes held that sheen of grief too old to cry anymore.

"Why is she—" Zinnia's throat locked. The words shoved their way out anyway.

"She's passed over."

The floor inside Zinnia gave out.

She staggered back, heel catching the edge of a velvet ottoman. Her hand shot out, bracing on a high-backed chair, fingers sinking into the cushioning.

She didn't look away from Saffron.

"Why didn't you tell me?"

"She didn't want anyone outside the family to know."

Seraphina kept her eyes on Zinnia. She wanted to close the space between them, pull her in—but Zin didn't do comfort. Not when she was cracking.

"Then everything else… fell apart."

Zinnia turned back to Saffron.

"I'm so sorry, Saffy." The name felt raw in her mouth.

Saffron glided forward.

"As am I. I'm also sorry you've been pulled into this mess."

She gave her a small smile. The kind that said she wished it could be different.

"You've always stood beside my daughter and my grandchildren. I wouldn't expect anything less now."

A tremor hit low in Zinnia's gut. No breathing through this one.

"And Seraphina's always stood with me."

Her hand clenched at her side, nails biting into skin. Pressure helped. A little.

"But seriously—you shouldn't be here. How is this even possible?"

"No, I shouldn't."

Saffron didn't look away. Just let Zinnia see her—really see her.

"But I had unfinished business."

Zinnia pressed her palms to her eyes, fighting the spin behind them. "Ghosts. Demons. Magic. My birthmark's not a birthmark. And you're… not alive, but here. I'm one broomstick away from burning my sanity in a bonfire."

Boot steps filled the corridor, each strike purposeful, echoing off the stone with intent.

The chandelier flickered.

A cold draft swept through the room as Killian Graves appeared in the doorway, his long coat dulled by travel and framed in afternoon light.

Zinnia stared.

"Okay. That man screams villain origin story."

Killian looked at her like he was cataloguing threats—and enjoying it.

"You must be Zinnia Hart."

"And you must be the very intense hot guy my best friend conveniently failed to mention in all these years."

A smile ghosted over his mouth—more predator than polite.

"Charmed."

"You're not, but points for effort."

Sage muffled a laugh into her sleeve.

Killian's eyes met Seraphina's. Something unsaid passed between them.

She gave a small, guarded nod.

From the far side of the room, Saffron cut in. "She's awakening."

Killian went on alert. "What? I thought she was mundanii."

Seraphina locked down the spike of anger—at herself. Missed signs. Missed everything.

"I never sensed anything. But she has a mark—and it's reacting."

Killian moved in, all that quiet authority wrapped in steel. "Show me."

Zinnia wasn't sure she wanted Mr. Tall, Dark, and Dangerous looking at anything on her. She glanced at Seraphina, who looked unsettled. Decision made, she tugged her collar down.

As soon as it was exposed, the Scriptorium contracted. Candle flames flared then guttered low. The sigils in the walls kindled, faint and fleeting. The mark flushed red and rose from the skin.

Killian's mouth pulled tight. In surprise and recognition.

"Well. That's unexpected."

Saffron barely moved, but the temperature in the chamber dropped anyway. "It's definitely not a birthmark."

Killian's focus sharpened. "No. That's a seal."

Zinnia snapped her shirt up and spun to face them. "A what now?"

"It belongs to the Les Revenantes. A coven long believed extinct. Their power was woven into the Veil."

Killian didn't scare easy. He'd seen too much.

But this? This was a glitch the Council was going to arse-pucker over.

"That's French, right?"

Zinnia's brain was wrecked and trying to reboot. Apparently, language trivia was the best it could manage.

"Yes. It means The Returned."

Saffron didn't say it. No use lighting a match they couldn't put out. But if Brinnan got to Zinnia, it wouldn't be chaos. It would be annihilation.

"They weren't royalty. They were guardians. Gatekeepers. No one spoke of them unless necessary."

"Gatekeepers of what?"

"The Veil."

Killian didn't give her time to catch up.

"It's a boundary between this world and something worse. That mark means your blood was sworn to protect it... or release it."

Zinnia wasn't buying what he was selling. "No. I'm not—this isn't—" The words stacked up in her throat. "I lift weights. I do Pilates. I ride motorbikes. I sob over Disney. I am not a—"

"You are."

Killian didn't soften the blow.

"Or you wouldn't be standing here. That seal only wakes when the line stirs."

"But I'm not related to any of you." She looked at Saffron. "Right?"

"No, you're not Bellarose. But it appears your bloodline has survived in secret. You were hidden and forgotten."

Saffron held back the rest. Zinnia was already carrying enough.

Zinnia folded her arms tight across her chest. She was holding it together—barely.

"So, my life has been a lie? Wow, do my grandparents have some explaining to do! Why is this happening now?"

"No one chooses their awakening, Zinnia. It chooses the time and place."

Killian didn't want to say it. But he pushed it forward anyway.

"If the Veil trembled, Brinnan may have felt it."

Zinnia's head snapped toward him. "Who the hell is Brinnan?"

Saffron let the silence spool out before cutting it off clean.

"That's a large story, nutshell version. He's my half-brother. A narcissistic warlock who has left a trail of ruin—and ended my life in the process."

Zinnia's mouth hung open. Her limbs no longer felt like they belonged to her. Brother hit hard. Ended my life hit harder.

Killian held her eyes. "If you're the last of the Revenantes, that doesn't make you a weapon."

He let that land.

"It makes you a door."

Zinnia's hands turned to ice.

Not a warrior. Not a hero. A door.

More like a goddamn ignition switch.

"This can't be happening."

"Zinnia. This is your truth." Saffron moved closer. "Your magic has started to breathe. Whether you believe in it or not, it believes in you."

Zinnia dropped into the nearest chair.

"I came here thinking you'd joined a cult. Instead, I'm apparently the legacy of a long dead coven with the key to hell branded on my neck."

Seraphina eased down beside her.

"I should've told you more. I thought I was protecting you. But now—"

Zinnia looked at her, everything shaking inside but nothing on her face.

"I'm scared out of my mind. And I'm so freaking overwhelmed."

"I know."

"Yet I'm still here."

"I know. That alone proves your strength, Zin."

Zinnia was not ready for any of this—but she was clearly out of options.

"What happens now?"

Killian delivered the truth.

"We find out exactly what's waking in you... before someone else does."

The candlelight shuddered. The house exhaled.

And the Veil quivered.

***

The shadows inside the study had shifted. Brinnan loomed over the scrying bowl, its carved runes pulsing with blood light. The reflection staring back wasn't his own.

It was hers.

Zinnia Hart. She was in Saffron's house as if she belonged there. The crescent on her neck flared beneath the water, catching fire under his magic—a live brand answering its master's call.

He exhaled, slow and soundless, fingers steepled above the pool.

So. Finally, he had a name and a face.

The Les Revenante line hadn't died. It had lain dormant—until now.

His movements gathered—precise and lethal, the narrowed world of a predator just before the pounce.

And Malrik hadn't told him.

He'd trusted Malrik with surveillance.

Instead, the bastard had gone rogue—followed the girl, tracked her, and said nothing.

You saw her with Seraphina. You saw the mark. And you dared to keep it from me.

Brinnan stepped back from the bowl, frost spidering across the stones as his magic focussed in response to fury.

The runes in the walls pricked to awareness—bloodhounds with their noses up, already tracking.

The study was no longer quiet.

The door creaked open.

Malrik strolled in—dripping shadow and swagger, casual as sin. He leaned into the doorway, unaware the air had shifted. "You called?"

Brinnan kept his eyes locked on the city, like he was counting the bodies it hadn't buried yet.

"I did. I've had a breakthrough."

"You have?"

There it was—feigned ignorance.

Brinnan turned. "Yes. It seems you've had one too."

Malrik went still.

"You saw her. Saw her with Seraphina. Saw the mark begin to stir."

He didn't deny it. "I wanted to be sure."

"And in the meantime, you were hoping I wouldn't see the fire on the horizon."

Malrik shifted, tension building. "If I'd told you every time something flared, we'd be neck-deep in false alarms."

Brinnan spoke over him. "This was not a flare. This was the Veil shuddering."

The old magic voiced itself beneath the floor—dangerous, ominous, unmistakably there.

"You said she was a mere curiosity." "And yet we both know she's a door."

Malrik stepped in. "We agreed—"

"You mistook agreement for equality."

The temperature dropped. The lights dimmed.

Malrik's hand shifted subtly toward the dagger at his belt.

This was going sideways fast.

"You kept secrets too. Les Revenantes weren't just keepers—they were openers. And you want to use the girl to get through the Veil."

Brinnan's mouth curled, cold authority settling in his frame. Insolence would not be tolerated.

He acted. One sharp snap of his fingers.

The runes in the floor ignited.

The room bent.

Malrik's knees slammed into the slate.

Magic crushed in his throat—hellborn claws locking around his chest, squeezing his heart in a deathtrap.

He dragged in breath through clenched teeth.

"You don't need to—"

Brinnan came closer. "I do."

The pressure didn't ease. If anything, it tightened.

"Because you've proven something invaluable." Malrik's mouth filled with dust. "You only believe in leverage."

Brinnan stopped in front of him.

"And leverage—"

He let the lesson land.

"Cannot be trusted."

He placed one hand over Malrik's brow, reciting a phrase stitched from ruin.

Malrik seized once—and disintegrated. Not in blood. In smoke and cinders—an imprint of absence. Just obliterated.

Brinnan stood untouched.

With a casual flick of his fingers, he summoned a perfect illusion of Malrik—breathing, speaking, whole—into the doorway.

It would mimic him. Echo him. Deceive long enough for the real betrayal to begin.

Brinnan returned to the scrying bowl.

Zinnia's face hovered above the water—distant now but not gone.

The mark had chosen.

The Veilborn stirred.

And if she was the lock…

Brinnan would become the key.

***

Zinnia woke to stillness.

198

Not silence—the room breathed with soft sounds: the distant caw of a raven, the hush of wind through old trees, the creak of timber beams settling into morning light. But it was a holy kind of calm, long-held and suspended, like the world beyond the windowpanes stood at the edge of remembering something sacred.

She blinked up at a ceiling framed in dark wood and gold-leafed trim, the bed cloudlike beneath her and far too elegant for reality. Down-stuffed pillows collapsed under her shoulders as she sat up slowly. The quilted linens rustled softly, weighted with age and care.

Heavy brocade curtains hung open, letting the sunlit haze spill over polished wood floors. A fireplace glowed faintly in the corner, still sighing with the embers of a dying flame.

Above the mantle, the painting of a crescent moon over twisted cypress trees darkened at the edges, as though something beneath the canvas stirred. Same shape as the one branded into her neck. Nice touch. Was the house going to hang her medical records next?

It was all too much. She swung her legs off the side of the mattress and ran a hand through her hair. It still smelled faintly of wood-smoke from yesterday's fireplace, and maybe something else—clove? Patchouli?

Her gaze swept across the carved vanity, the mirrored armoire, the emerald chaise lounge. The details were absurdly rich, as if someone had conjured it straight from a design coven's group chat.

Her whole apartment could fit inside this room. Twice. With space left over for the ghosts of all her regrets.

Yesterday she was yelling at her phone for ignoring her on texts, and now she was... what?

A maybe-witch from a maybe-extinct coven. A girl with a literal magical brand on her neck, hunted by a warlock, sleeping in a house full of dead things and demons.

She exhaled so deeply it made her feet tingle.

Her fingers drifted to her nape, tracing the mark that had changed her life overnight.

It stirred with knowing—not hers. She didn't have a bloody clue. It had been keeping its own counsel, holding a truth she'd been blind to.

"Okay, Zinnia. You've survived worse."

"…Maybe," she added.

A knock came at the door.

Without waiting for an answer—because boundaries were clearly optional in magical strongholds—Samthrax appeared.

"I brought coffee." He strutted in like Lucifer on a spa day.

"Scalding, judgy, possibly cursed—a bit like me."

He wore a crimson velvet robe dramatic enough to resurrect Puccini, and fuzzy slippers shaped like snarling hellhounds. Steam curled from the chipped mug in his clawed hand.

"Do you… not believe in doors?"

"I believe in them." Samthrax adjusted his attire, perfectly prim. "I just believe I'm the exception to them."

She took the drink, almost reverently. "Thank you. I think."

"You're welcome, Witchlet."

"Don't call me that."

"But you are one."

He draped himself over the foot of the bed like a pampered puppy basking in a sunbeam.

"Sort of. I mean, fledgling. Late bloomer. Door to a terrible end-of-all-things power no one's prepared to handle. You know, the usual."

Zinnia let out a groan and sipped the coffee.

Damn it—it was perfect. Bitter, rich, slightly burnt. Attitude brewed in a cup.

"Why are you here exactly?"

Samthrax stretched, tail flicking lazily behind him. "Well. Killian left before sunrise to go snarl at some council elders. Seraphina's elbow-deep in a cauldron making something that smells like regret and basil, and the twins are reenacting magical duels using forbidden texts as weapons. So, naturally, I thought—let's check on the emotionally fragile no longer a mortal and see if she's falling apart."

"You're terrible at emotional support."

"I told you—I'm not an emotional support demon."

"You literally said you were."

He shrugged. "It was a brief, self-indulgent phase."

Zinnia set the mug down, leaning forward, elbows on knees. The sunlight caught her tattoos—inked runes, phoenix feathers, crescent moons she'd once thought were just aesthetic.

Now… she wasn't so sure.

Samthrax tilted his head. The antics dropped for a second. "You okay?"

She didn't answer right away.

Am I?

She wasn't screaming. She wasn't hiding under the covers. That had to count for something.

"I'm… overwhelmed."

Understatement of the year.

"This whole situation. I'm trying to catch up, but it's—" She exhaled. "A lot."

He nodded. "The world you knew came apart. That takes time to grieve."

Zinnia didn't answer right away. She stared, because clearly the apocalypse had arrived.

"Did you just say something insightful?"

He flicked his fingers in mock salute. "Don't get used to it. I'm contractually obligated to ruin the moment in about—"

He checked an invisible watch.

"Twenty-five seconds."

They sat in companionable silence. Outside, wind rattled the high windows.

"This bloody thing is getting on my very stretched last nerve." She pressed a palm to her neck. Samthrax lifted his head. "Hmm?"

"It's… humming. Again."

"Might be reacting to your proximity to power."

She stood, heartbeat ratcheting up. The walls of the room whispered behind her, the enchantments old and rich with breathless tension. Something was pulling at her.

"I need to talk to Seraphina."

"Yeah. You probably do."

Zinnia levelled him with a look that said why are you still here?

"Well, scoot along, demon boy. I need to get dressed."

Samthrax didn't even pretend to be innocent. "Wanna hand?"

Zinnia showed teeth. Not friendly ones. "Wanna lose one?"

He backed off, palms up—but not sorry.

"I'll be outside. Totally not listening. Definitely not hoping for wardrobe malfunctions."

Zinnia waited until she was alone. She pulled on yesterday's clothes—because she hadn't packed for a crisis—and stepped into the hallway where Samthrax lounged against the wall, arms crossed, tail lazily curling behind him.

She joined him without a word, brushing a hand through her hair in a vague attempt at presentable.

He looked her over like he was considering dinner.

"Familiar ensemble."

"Bite me."

"Tempting."

Zinnia rolled her eyes but didn't fight the smile this time. The demon radiated smug menace, but there was something else beneath the mischief—an odd, unexpected charm.

And damn it, he was growing on her.

The corridor unfolded like a cathedral in miniature—arched ceilings veined with faded gilding and cryptic glyphs, sconces cradling flames the colour of tarnished ivory, every inch humming with ancestral magic. Sound itself seemed suspended.

Zinnia barely heard her own footsteps.

Her neck burned insistently.

It throbbed with her heartbeat now, as if each step forward was unlocking something deeper.

Samthrax matched her stride, tail flicking once behind him. No expression. No tells. "You might want to brace yourself."

Zinnia didn't slow. "For what?"

"Sometimes. When the blood remembers, it doesn't come in gentle waves."

Samthrax gave a low sound—half scoff, half warning. "It comes more like a tsunami."

Zinnia said nothing. Her throat was a fist.

They descended the stairs. The scent of citrus and crushed sage becoming stronger with every step. Through the archway to the main parlour, firelight flickered. Shadows danced along the stone.

Seraphina stood in front of the hearth, sleeves rolled up, grinding something dark and viscous in a mortar. Her braid hung damp over one shoulder. Tension clung to her.

She looked up as they entered.

Seraphina took in Zinnia's pale face—the exhaustion etched beneath her eyes, the faint glimmer of magic unravelling around her. She didn't miss a thing. "You felt it again."

Zinnia gave a quick nod.

Seraphina set the mortar down without breaking eye contact. "It's accelerating. That's… concerning."

"Good morning to you too," Samthrax chimed in as he flopped into a wingback chair, boots kicked up on a footstool. "I've fed her coffee, so she's now fortified."

Seraphina ignored him. She crossed the room to Zinnia. "Let me see."

Zinnia pulled her shirt aside.

Seraphina reached out, and it flared under her touch—silver bleeding through the lines, as if something beneath the skin wanted out.

Seraphina wasn't sure she trusted what she was seeing. "I've never seen anything like this."

"Well, that makes two of us. It feels like it's going to tear out of my spine."

Seraphina's hand eased back. "I don't know what stage of awakening you're in. This is inherited bloodline magic. I don't know much about your coven at all."

"At the risk of repeating myself, that makes two of us. I'm a literal stranger in my own body."

Saffron appeared in the doorway without a sound, her presence the slow shift of dusk itself. She wore her death lightly—there and not, blurring at the edges, the boundary between worlds thinning where she stood. Zinnia didn't need to close her eyes. The grief knew the way back in. "Saffy. I still don't know what to say to you."

"No words are required, my dear. Listen instead."

Zinnia's mouth parted, but nothing made it out. The floor chose that moment to vibrate—just once. A low current pushing up beneath their feet.

Seraphina felt it crawl up her spine. "That's the house."

Samthrax quit lounging. He flicked a finger at Zinnia. "And it's responding to her."

Zinnia's arms locked around her middle. "What does that mean?"

Saffron moved further into the room.

"It means the bloodline is no longer dormant. It's resonating—with this place. With the Veil."

"Can you tell me more about it?"

"Not much more than we already have. Truth is, very little is known."

Saffron didn't speak again right away.

Zinnia had zero answers. And at this stage any scrap counted as a win.

"It's a membrane between our world and something else. Something old enough that most records are myth, and the rest are warnings."

Zinnia was torn—Saffron didn't need magic to see it.

"When the Les Revenantes were entrusted to guard it, they were just given instructions. Don't open it. Don't disturb it. They were keys. When they vanished, we thought their line was broken."

"It wasn't." Killian walked in, stripping off his coat with one hard pull.

His attention snapped straight to Zinnia.

Saffron didn't take her eyes off him. "You're sure."

He gave a single nod.

Then he crossed to Zinnia—close enough that the room seemed to shrink. "We need to prepare. The Veil isn't still anymore. I felt it crack an hour ago."

Zinnia's blood threatened to curdle. "What kind of crack?"

"The kind that makes the things locked away start hunting for an exit."

"If Brinnan finds out—" Saffron's words hovered.

Killian knew the horse had bolted on that one—if he'd sensed the shift, Brinnan had too.

Zinnia needed a stiff drink or ten after these reveals. "You think I'm gonna open it?"

Saffron sensed Zinnia's spiral. Understandable. Not ideal.

"Intentionally? No. But your blood might. It remembers what your mind doesn't. The magic isn't tame. You have to learn to wield it—or it will wield you."

Zinnia knew her back was up against the wall. How the fuck is this her life now?

"I didn't ask for this."

Killian knew no good would come from sugar coating facts to provide false comfort.

"No one ever does."

The fire crackled. Tension pooled in the room—dense with old secrets and new danger.

Zinnia didn't say anything at first. Just dropped into the nearest chair, elbows braced on her knees.

"Then I guess someone better teach me how to survive this."

Killian lowered in front of her, all that coiled strength held in check. "We will."

Zinnia's eyes locked with his. Something unflinching stared back—resolve, yes, but also a challenge. And trust.

Far below, buried in vaults carved from graven stone, a presence stirred.

It had felt her.

The Veil knew her.

And it was eager.

Sixteen

"Once in every doomed bloodline, a poor bastard wakes up with a glowing mark, a destiny they didn't order, and a front-row seat to the end of reality. Congratulations, darling. You're the human equivalent of a cracked seal on demon Tupperware."

— Samthrax, swirling bourbon and making end-times chic again

The storm had passed, but the sky had not forgotten.

Rain traced pale veins down the glass, streaking the penthouse windows with thunder's final shiver. Brinnan stood motionless at the pane, the city sprawling beneath him in a haze of cold light and poised silence. From this height, New Orleans was a sleepless wound—glistening, distant, ready to bleed.

His study exhaled darkness.

Slate tiles glimmered under scattered candlelight, dulled with old ash. Bloodroot, damp stone, and burnt sigil-ink lingered in the air—the perfume of unfinished rituals and worse things whispered in dead tongues.

Books lay in calculated chaos across the floor, their pages half-open like relics paused in prayer. The glyphs writhed in slow cadence along the parchment, syncing with some hidden rhythm. One volume wept dark smoke from its spine. Another trembled without wind.

At the far end, the scrying mirror quivered—not illusion, but residue.

A sliver of truth that refused to recede.

Two shapes lingered in its reflection.

Seraphina Bellarose.

And Zinnia Hart.

Brinnan's own image hovered between them.

He did not move.

Instead, he let the absence wrap around him, while the sound of the Veil slithered up his spine in its old, soul-deep song. One no human throat could carry without splintering.

Zinnia's seal had stirred—not broken but remembering how to open.

And Seraphina—the Shadowkeep had already called her name in blood.

For weeks, he'd operated in fragments and supposition.

Now the picture had come into focus.

He stepped toward the mirror, brushing his fingers across its surface. The scryglass shuddered beneath his touch. The threads inside vibrated, not with power—but with fear.

"It's always the matriarchs."

The words weren't bitter. They were something close to respect.

He turned, robes whispering behind him like smoke trailing marble, and approached the dais where the Volucris Noctem lay—one of the lost tomes of the elder dark. Its cover was stitched from the hide of a banished beast, its pages bound in hex-thread, etched with rites that answered only to blood.

Not the original Grimoire—that remained locked within the Shadowkeep, breathing behind wards older than empires—but a kin to it. A shard of the same ancient hunger.

The tome twitched under candlelight.

Brinnan knelt before it—not in worship, but recognition. It was a weapon. And now he had ammunition.

He rose and turned toward the fireplace.

Above the mantle, the fresco flared—a figure with wings of char, eyes like dying stars, arms outstretched over a world divided. One half aflame. One flowering with decay.

A tyrant, the myths called him. A heretic. A godless king.

Brinnan met the stare, unfazed.

He wasn't carving a new path. He was completing what had already begun.

Let them think this was about revenge. Family. The Keep.

Let Julian believe this was about control.

Their visions were small.

He had seen farther.

Seraphina was the key to the Shadowkeep—the lock to a prison shaped like a sanctum.

But Zinnia?

Zinnia was the invitation.

Les Revenantes had never been wardens. They had been thresholds. Their power had sealed away darkness—But it could also welcome it through.

And behind the Veil... the Veilborn stirred.

Not demons. Not spirits.

Predecessors.

The original architects of ruin.

The hum had begun—in the Codex, in the deep-folds of the world. The Keep was no longer enough. He wanted what lay beyond it.

And when the gate gave way, Brinnan would stand at the breach—not as heir or exile—but as convergence.

A brief knock broke through his reverie.

Brinnan didn't look away from the fire. His gaze slid to the base of the mirror, where Malrik's blood had dried in a ring of rusted crimson.

The traitor had seen Zinnia. Known she was with Seraphina.

And said nothing.

He'd wanted a chance to trade one secret for another. A coin for his own agenda.

Now he was salt and ash. A lesson to all who confused usefulness with indispensability.

Brinnan adjusted the cuffs of his sleeves.

"Enter."

Julian stepped in, boots damp, coat shedding faint traces of rain. His expression was unreadable, but something hung behind his eyes—tension, maybe. Doubt. Or the first taste of suspicion.

"The tracking wards failed. Someone's shielding them. Possibly Killian Graves."

"Let him."

"Do we shift strategy?"

Brinnan turned. "We don't hunt Seraphina alone anymore."

His voice went low—the kind of low that said nothing was up for negotiation.

"We take them both."

"Both?"

Brinnan smiled. Or whatever passed for it.

"Seraphina is one half of the equation."

He started pacing. Each step landed like an unseen countdown.

"And the girl with the mark?" Julian placed the question with studied care.

"Zinnia Hart."

"That's her name?"

"It's confirmed. She carries the crescent seal."

Julian didn't react. Just stated it. "The Les Revenante."

It wasn't news. Not really. He'd guessed the second he saw Brinnan's reaction to her. The silence. The shift. Like everything had finally lined up in his head.

"She's not dormant," Brinnan, cool as ever. "The seal is active."

Julian didn't sigh. Not out loud. "You knew before now."

"I had reason to suspect."

Of course he did.

Julian said nothing. There was no point pushing—it wouldn't get him the truth. Brinnan never handed over the whole picture. Just enough to keep everyone moving in the direction he wanted.

"And Seraphina?"

"Still linked to the Keep. That hasn't changed."

"And Zinnia?"

He asked to see how his father would answer. Not because he lacked a theory.

Brinnan shifted his gaze to the blackened fresco above the hearth. The figure carved into stone stared back, its wings stretched wide like a warning no one had listened to.

"She's the threshold. The one thing between here and what waits on the other side."

He faced Julian again. "Two women. Two keys. And together…"

Brinnan didn't leave space for variables—just inevitability. "…they will usher in a new age."

Julian stared at him. No reaction. Not outwardly.

Inside something shifted.

He'd read the same histories. Knew what the Les Revenantes were. What the Veil was. What came with it.

But this wasn't about legacy anymore.

It was strategy.

Brinnan was ten moves ahead, already orchestrating outcomes Julian hadn't even considered. He'd seen that look before—right before things got sacrificed.

He let the question die in his throat. He knew the answer without asking: his father didn't see people. Only pieces.

Zinnia. Seraphina. Malrik.

Him.

All just part of the design.

Julian's fingers twitched at his side. He curled them into a fist before the spark could catch.

Brinnan was planning to use them all.

The only question was who he'd cut loose first.

And Julian wasn't about to let it be him.

***

The Enclave — Late Evening, Maison Bellarose

The fire had reduced to embers.

Zinnia lay on the bed in the same sprawling room she'd stayed in the night before. The sheets were soft as rose petals, but sleep wouldn't come—the aftermath of the day settled over her, heavy and unmoving.

Shadows from the hearth crawled slowly up the far wall, painting her skin in orange and coal.

She couldn't stop staring at her hands.

Once, they had flinched at slammed doors. At raised voices. At him. Now they were still—but not because she felt safe. Because whatever was waking within her didn't flinch for anyone.

Fan-fucking-tastic. I'm not a witch, she thought. I don't have magic. I have meltdowns. I have bad taste in men and a mark that feels like it's trying to rewrite my DNA from the inside out.

But the burn at her nape said otherwise.

She reached back and touched it. It braided through her, quiet as smoke in stone—woven deep, part of her now. Her phone sat silent on the bedside table. The lock screen stared, frozen mid-blink. Fourteen years of birthdays, brunches, all-night playlists. Crying into Seraphina's arms the evening she'd fled her ex. And through it all—this had lived beneath her skin.

A secret she didn't even know she was keeping.

She swung her legs off the bed and pushed herself upright. The

212

wood floor was warm under her bare feet. The house creaked, old bones shifting around her. Beyond the arched window, the Crescent Enclave thinned the night, every glyph etched in starlight across the distant spires whispering truths she wasn't ready for.

A door, Killian had said.

You're not a mistake. You're a door.

Zinnia wrapped her arms around herself and paced the perimeter of the room. She wasn't claustrophobic. But tonight, the walls pushed in like they were waiting for her to snap.

Who was she? Right now, she felt like a damn landmine one step away from exploding. She didn't know what was beyond the Veil. Had no idea what the hell that even meant. But Brinnan was after it. And that was enough to make her want it locked up forever.

She eased back into bed, the sheets cool against her skin. Her eyes fluttered closed—not because she wanted sleep, but because it was coming for her whether she was ready or not.

And the moment darkness took hold—the dream began.

She stood in black water.

Still. Endless. Quiet as breath before a scream.

The sky above stretched in all directions, streaked with crimson clouds, stars spinning too fast to be real. The surface beneath her feet rippled—but not a drop touched her. She drifted there, untethered, the edges of the world folding and unfolding around her.

Out of the dark, a woman appeared.

She wasn't walking. She was arriving. Dressed in layered fabrics that shifted in airless motion, skin carved from moonlight, eyes that burned without heat—silver and azure, too vast to belong to something mortal.

Zinnia tried to move. Couldn't.

The woman's voice rang through her—not into her ears, but her blood.

"Gateborn."

The word struck Zinnia's chest with physical force. Her knees buckled, but she didn't fall.

The figure reached out and touched her sternum—silver light poured into her where their skin met.

"You were hidden well, but time unmakes even the oldest bindings. The seal remembers its purpose."

Zinnia shook her head. Not no—only disbelief.

"I don't understand."

The woman tilted her head. Not cruel. Not kind. Just… endless.

"You will. When the Veil shudders, the Gate must choose. Either to open… or to hold."

"What do you mean?"

The words left her mouth, but she didn't feel them. Like they skipped her throat on the way out.

"The boundary between worlds. Between what was imprisoned… and what should never be born."

Behind the woman's eyes, Zinnia saw wings of bone. A city burning in reverse—structures rebuilding themselves from flame. A forest that sang with screaming wind.

A vision.

Or a warning.

"The key is waking. The shadows remember your name, even if you do not. You are the last Les Revenante—child of return, blood of passage. If the Veil tears, you will be the first devoured. Or the only one who can shut it."

Oh Shit.

"What do I do?"

The woman leaned in. Her breath was cold as midnight.

"Survive long enough to choose."

She was gone before the words finished settling.

The water shattered, brittle as glass.

Light swallowed everything.

Zinnia shot upright in bed, drenched in sweat, heart galloping as if trying to escape her chest.

The fireplace had died down. The room steeped in night.

Her birthmark was no longer dormant. It was a brand that had sprung to life.

A whisper—not hers—unspooled inside her mind:

"One opens the Keep. One opens the Veil. And one must decide which door remains shut."

Zinnia sat alone, fists clenched in the bedsheets.

She wasn't a footnote anymore.

She was the weapon. The question was—who'd get to pull the trigger first.

Seventeen

The Scriptorium had brightened with the scent of freshly ground coffee and something bordering on mischief.

A new, gleaming espresso machine—far too modern for the old-world gravitas of the room—hummed proudly atop a polished stone table between two rune-carved bookshelves. It blinked, hissed, and emitted tiny clouds of steam as if daring the age-crusted tomes to argue with its presence.

Samthrax stood beside it in an apron that read COFFEE FIRST, THEN CHAOS, wielding a barista wand topped with a miniature version of his own leering face, like a maestro conducting the end of days.

"Latte?" he chirped—grinning, all fang and no shame. "Flat white? Pumpkin sacrifice macchiato? I'm open to all forms of caffeinated worship."

"Where did you get that?" Sage stared at him. It had probably cost some per unsuspecting schmuck their soul.

"Amazon Prime. Two-day shipping and a minor blood offering."

Her mouth curved. Not quite a smile, but close. "I, for one, am grateful. Hook me up with a latte—double shot."

"You're welcome. No one should face this crapfest without chemical assistance."

Killian stood by the centre table, arms folded. That expression? Half commander, half addict in withdrawal. "I'll take a double long demon."

"You want sass or espresso?" Killian didn't answer. Just arched a brow—the kind of look that meant paperwork. Or pain. Samthrax muttered something in infernal and snatched a mug. "Coming right up, dark lord of decaf."

Saffron hovered a few feet away, her presence dimmed at the edges as she eyed a stack of glyph-bound volumes like they might talk back. "Oh, how I miss the simple pleasures. Coffee. Pastries. Corporeal digestion." She made a show of sighing. "Dead life is terribly under-caffeinated."

In the corner, Sebastian had claimed a leather armchair, feet slung over an ottoman, cradling a cup Samthrax had labelled Death Roast in sharpie. His hair stuck up at all angles, and his expression was all corpse-in-a-wind-tunnel chic—rumpled, grim, and barely awake.

Sage perched cross-legged on the arm of his chair, a pen tucked behind one ear, a highlighter in her braid, and an aura of scarcely leashed anxiety vibrating around her. She was writing something aggressively.

Zinnia padded across the floor to where Samthrax orchestrated the machine with the intensity of someone preparing to summon a small apocalypse. Her face was pale, her shirt wrinkled from sleep, and her eyes ringed with exhaustion.

Her gaze flicked to the others—Sage sitting on Sebastian's chair, Seraphina steady as a fixed star, even Samthrax orbiting his own absurd little solar system. They all looked as if they belonged, pieces of the same impossible puzzle. She felt like a smudge on the outskirts. For a moment, Zinnia wished she had somewhere she fit that cleanly.

"I'll take whatever Seraphina's having."

Samthrax, normally a volcano of snark, blinked at her with the wide-eyed awe of a demon who'd glimpsed his favourite sin in human form.

"Coming right up, Slayer of My Blackened Heart."

Seraphina approached quietly. She reached out and brushed Zinnia's arm. "You okay?"

"No. Not even a little. I had a dream—actually, more like a visitation. And I think I'm officially done pretending I understand any of this."

Her voice wavered, her words trailing off.

Sage looked up quickly, all her attention snapping to Zinnia.

Sebastian leaned forward, mug forgotten.

Killian set down his coffee without tasting it.

"Tell us everything."

Zinnia wasn't sure where to start?

None of it made sense—but somehow, it was all real.

"I was in this endless water, and the sky was all kinds of wrong. There was a woman. Tall. Veiled. She didn't talk as such—it was internal, like telepathy. Called me 'Gateborn.' Said the Veil remembers me, and when it tears, I have to choose whether to open or close it."

"She spoke to you directly?" Saffron was busy lining things up in her head.

"More like she poured the words inside me and let them set."

Seraphina's expression tightened. "She said the Veil remembers you?"

"Yeah. And something about being the last of Les Revenantes. Blood of passage. She said if it opens, I'll either be the first devoured, or the only one who can shut it."

Nobody said anything.

Samthrax placed his coffee down with a strange delicacy, his usual theatrics gone. "Well. I regret waking up today."

Killian turned to Saffron. "Do you have the invocation we need?"

Saffron caught his meaning immediately and nodded once, moving toward the long shelf of grimoires behind the desk. Her fingers glided across spines older than some languages. "There's a summoning we have never used," she told the room. "Reserved for heir-marked bloodlines when all other lines fall. I didn't think it would ever be required. Boy was I wrong."

Sebastian's voice broke the stillness.

"Wait—summoning who?"

Saffron didn't look up.

"Not who. What."

Her hand hovered over a sealed book nestled in a circle of preserved ash and warded ivory. The cover was parchment-pale, etched in ink that bled between orange and black, shifting in patterns that didn't obey logic.

She faced Killian. "I can't do this one." She glanced down at her flickering hands. "There are rituals only the living can perform."

Killian nodded, silent understanding passing between them. He reached for the book and handed it to Seraphina with deliberate care.

The weight settled in her grip—not heavy, but grave. The moment she touched the leather, it responded—warming, thrumming faintly beneath her palms. Her fingers tightened on the spine.

"This is a blood rite. It's tied to lineage."

Zinnia didn't know what that meant exactly—but it sounded like it was gonna hurt.

Sage gripped the fabric of her leggings. Even Samthrax—normally the first to crack a joke or lounge with devilish charm—stood perfectly still, red eyes fixed on the circle.

The summoning mark had been etched into the floor long ago—a permanent fixture in the Scriptorium's foundation, dormant until activated. Sebastian leaned forward on his knees. Seraphina led Zinnia into the ring. Symbols already burned on the surface, rimmed with powdered moonroot and braided hexstring, the edges laced with crushed vireleaf—the kind that only grew where magic had ruptured and reformed. The scent was sharp and sweet. The glyphs bulged and settled like veins. Shards of mirror around the perimeter caught broken glimpses of them all.

Seraphina felt like Zinnia looked—nervous as hell. "You can step out if you want to."

Zinnia shook her head. "I need to know. I've got to understand what I am."

Her nape ached—each throb a steady, insistent drumbeat.

Seraphina nodded, then lowered herself to the floor with practiced grace, kneeling the way one would at an altar.

Her voice shifted.

Not louder. Deeper.

She began the invocation in the old tongue—words that had no parallel in the Mundanii world. They cleaved through sound, sculpting silence into form. Each syllable twisted the light.

The candles flared. Dust lifted from the floor. Every breath in the room caught, held, and didn't release.

Zinnia's balance faltered.

The mirror in the northeast corner wrinkled inward—not on its surface, but behind it. It split the image of the chamber open, revealing what waited on the other side.

A shape emerged.

Not through the mirror, but into it. A woman—not a woman— floated above the stone. Her body was draped in layered fabrics that moved without wind, her form more absence than substance. Something vast and unnatural bled into the room. Her eyes burned beneath shadowed hoods—silver with no light, stars that had died a thousand years before they were seen.

Everyone took a step back.

Even Killian.

Even Saffron.

Zinnia couldn't move. Her body didn't belong to her anymore. Her skin buzzed. Her thoughts scattered.

The spectre tilted her head, and when she spoke, her voice didn't enter through ears.

It entered through blood.

"I see you."

"Blood of my blood."

"Gateborn."

Zinnia's legs gave out again. Seraphina caught her—arms tight around her waist, holding her with everything she had left.

Zinnia hadn't been wrong. This woman—this being—was beyond intimidating.

"I don't know what I am. But I want to understand."

Zinnia couldn't seem to get a full breath. Standing? Also not going great.

Her blood had already agreed to something her mind hadn't signed off on.

The Les Revenante's veils moved—subtle as thread tugged by unseen hands.

"The time has come to remember what your soul forgot."

Sage was trembling. She didn't even try to hide it.

"What's beyond the Veil?"

The figure pivoted to face her.

"Not death. Not demons. Not gods. But beginnings that failed. Unborn things caught between silence and scream. They hunger—not for destruction, but for arrival."

Sebastian's mouth shaped a question he hadn't dared ask—until now. He pushed the words past the tightness in his throat. "Then what's inside the Shadowkeep?"

The spectre turned her shrouded face toward him. "The second key."

The moment stretched—unsettling in a way that left you changed before you even knew why.

"Zinnia is the gate."

"Seraphina is the key."

"Both open."

"Both bind."

No one spoke. The words hung in the air, like fate had just stepped into the room and shut the door behind it.

Zinnia stared at her hands, as if they might bear the hieroglyphics of this new truth. Whatever had opened inside her was tearing against every inch of who she thought she was.

Seraphina didn't think much of this particular responsibility. She'd rather tame snakes.

Killian was certain this was not going to end well. "And if the gate opens?"

The space around the figure deepened, heavy with unspoken consequence.

"Then the Keep also fails."

"And the world will not fall—it will revert."

Saffron was holding it together—for now. But this had Armageddon written all over it. "And what do the Veilborn want?"

Its wrappings lifted by degrees—revealing nothing. Only more dark beneath.

"To unmake mortality. To return to the time before choice. Before consequence. A perfect silence."

Zinnia's hands shook. Her insides swept sideways, nerves jittering on the wrong frequency. "What do I do?"

The voice cut across every wall.

"As I told you last night. You survive long enough to choose."

She vanished between one breath and the next.

The mirror slammed shut—not with sound, but with the finality of something that wouldn't open again. The circle flared once—then went still.

And somewhere deep inside Zinnia, a low hum stirred to life. Not fear. Not power. But a countdown.

Her legs gave out. Seraphina lunged forward, catching her before she crumpled fully—arms locking tight as her frame started to shake, lowering them both to the floor. She couldn't tell where her body ended and the pull began.

Tears tracked down Sage's face.

Sebastian stared at the wall.

Saffron was a pale flare of sorrow.

Killian stood like a statue just before the crack.

Samthrax had nothing clever to say. For a long time, no one moved. No one could. What lingered in the aftermath wasn't emptiness—It was the shape of something unknown, already unfolding beneath the surface. Zinnia sat in the middle of the summoning circle, Seraphina's arms around her, a humming behind her eyes that refused to subside.

The Les Revenantes voice had been a rupture. Her truth, a saltline in a wound.

And Zinnia stood flayed by both.

Seraphina swallowed hard, feeling the tremble in Zinnia's shoulders.

She pulled back just enough to look at her. The room was still heavy with aftershock, but the decision inside her demanded release.

"Zin."

Zinnia looked up, eyes hollow. The bruised crescents beneath them told the story: too much in too little time.

"I think you should consider moving in."

The words didn't quite compute. "Huh?"

Seraphina was bone tired, but one thing was clear: she had to protect Zinnia—and she would.

"Into the estate. With us. You're not safe out there anymore. And after everything we've seen, everything you've heard—there's no going back. Not to the life you knew."

Zinnia sat up straighter, rubbing her arms. She wasn't just touched by magic. She was entangled in it. Claimed.

"I mean, it's lovely. In a gothic death-trap kind of way. But I'm still wrapping my head around the 'possessed mansion with built-in security curses' aesthetic."

Samthrax pushed to his feet in a single, exaggerated motion, eyes gleaming.

"I'd be delighted to help you wrap your head around the aesthetics. Or anything else, really. I come with a very… hands-on approach."

He wiggled his eyebrows. "I give extremely immersive tours."

Zinnia wasn't sure whether to hit him or laugh—but the ridiculousness helped.

"Do any of those tours end without a restraining order?"

"Only the boring ones."

Killian raised a brow. His voice was quiet—like a cliff edge right before the fall.

"Keep talking, and I'll silence you with a binding so old it predates your sense of humour."

Samthrax grinned. He knew annoying Killian was dangerous. That only made it more fun. "Cruel. Stylish. And wildly unappreciative of my sparkle."

Sage, perched on the arm of a nearby chair, looked over at Zinnia. "Z, you're already part of this."

Sebastian couldn't think of anything worse than Zinnia stuck alone in the Mundanii world. She wouldn't last. Not with what was going on. And that didn't sit right.

She was like his second mum—the one who swore like a trucker and always went to bat for him when his mother went full overprotective.

"Yeah. You're family. You belong with us."

Saffron floated closer.

"And there's something to be said for proximity when magic this old begins to move. You're safer amongst those who know how to stand their ground."

Zinnia felt the words like a gut punch. Probably because they were right. On her own, she'd be screwed. And not in a fun way.

Her hand curled around her shoulder in a quiet attempt to steady herself. Her nerves were buggered—nothing a few shots of tequila couldn't fix.

"Okay, look… the last few days have been a lot. I'm talking Netflix-limited-series-with-a-warning-label levels of plot twists. But—" she glanced around the room. "—the truth is, I've never felt safer than I do with all of you. And I'm pretty bloody grateful not to be facing this alone."

Relief hit Seraphina. No way did she want to bury her friend—or face her voodoo-hoodoo grandmother.

"Great, it's settled. Perk of being a witch—I can have all your things moved here with a snap of my fingers. Which is far safer than you going back for them."

Zinnia lifted her hands in mock prayer. "Thank God. I'm so over wearing the same getup, they're starting to stand up when I take them off."

Samthrax leaned forward, all pretend reverence. "And I vow to only disturb your rest for matters of absolute urgency. World-ending doom. Blood moon prophecies. Possibly an espresso emergency."

Zinnia crossed her arms. That brow went up like, really?

"Deal. But if anyone tries to recruit me into a secret prophecy cult, I'm sending you the therapist's bill."

Samthrax pressed a hand to his heart, wounded.

"I would never! We're far too disorganised to be a cult. Think of us more as a… metaphysically convenient friend group."

Killian's scowl said stop talking—now. "If anyone tries to recruit you, I'll make them wish they'd chosen a quiet death instead."

Zinnia stood slowly, brushing phantom dust from her jeans as she took in the surrounding faces—old friends cast in new light, strangers bound by something deeper than blood.

"So, do I get a key? Or is this one of those flick-your-fingers situations—you know, like in Charmed?"

Samthrax couldn't contain his grin. "Sweetheart, if I could flick my fingers and solve problems, I'd be on a beach with a margarita, zero responsibilities, and Lucifer for company."

"Don't let us stop you from trying." Saffron was positive that would be the highlight of her afterlife.

Zinnia was almost smiling. "So… no key?"

Seraphina stepped forward, hugging her. "No key. The wards will recognise you now. The house knows who's safe. Welcome home Zin."

Zinnia liked the sound of that.

***

That night, after the laughter had faded and the last of the candles burned low, the house began to settle.

Killian had departed earlier, duty-bound to Council business. Seraphina and he had stolen a sliver of the evening after dinner— just enough time to press close, to lose themselves in each other like the world wasn't tilting on its axis. It hadn't been long, but it was real, and he left with her essence clinging to his skin.

Now the Scriptorium had fallen into tranquillity.

Samthrax snored softly in a floating armchair, midair and mid-dream, a book titled Forbidden Hexes and Questionable Life Choices open across his chest. The twins had gone to bed. Even the glyphs along the windows had dimmed, their gold fading into dusk-tone, tucked into the rhythm of the house's dreaming.

Seraphina sat in her favourite chair near the hearth, a mug of peppermint tea cradled in her palms. The steam had vanished long ago. She hadn't taken a single sip.

She stared into the fire, uncertain if something was about to break—or already had.

The flames held their shape gently, untouched by urgency. A curl of wax slipped down the side of a forgotten candle, its glow steady and unbothered. And—quiet as moonlight—Saffron appeared.

She didn't enter so much as arrive, drifting through the archway in a sweep of pale light, subdued—more ghost than corporeal. Seraphina didn't startle. She didn't even look up. "I thought you'd gone." Her system had glitched. A full emotional crash. Like being dropped in the middle of a war she'd never asked to join.

"I go. But I remain."

Saffron hated the distance. She'd give anything to rewrite their history.

"I'm not bound by force, Seraphina. I chose to stay—for you. To see you through what's coming."

Seraphina let out a tired breath, her affection showing on her face. "Only you would make staying after death sound noble."

"But I'm glad you did."

All the years between them hung in the air—undisturbed, but heavy.

Seraphina's fingers tightened around the tea. The words tasted like something scraped from a wound.

"I keep thinking about what we became… after I left for the Mundanii world."

Saffron moved forward, her form catching in the firelight. She stopped just shy of the hearth's golden circle.

"Mistakes were made, on both sides, my love."

That same goddamn ache. Still there. "I left. And you didn't stop me. You didn't ask me to stay."

The silence that followed wasn't empty.

Saffron couldn't undo the past. However, they could face it.

"You didn't want me to."

Seraphina looked at her.

"You were so angry." The control Saffron wore so well slipped, just for a second. "And I didn't know how to reach you anymore. Every time I tried, I found another door closed. Another wall raised."

Seraphina turned away, her eyes prickled but she held it back.

"I closed them because I couldn't live with what I'd seen. What I'd lost. I thought if I left it all behind—magic, legacy, you—I could protect my kids from it."

"I wasn't trying to hurt you, mum. I was just trying to survive."

Saffron moved closer, her outline casting soft shadows across the worn rug. "And I wasn't trying to control you. I was trying to hold on. You're my daughter, Seraphina. The last thing I ever wanted was to lose you."

Seraphina hadn't seen it. She'd been too wrapped up in her own wreckage to notice.

"You didn't say that. Silence did all the talking."

"I know. And I let too many years pass in that silence."

"I thought you judged me for leaving the way I did. For rejecting all of it."

"I didn't judge you." Saffron ached to hold her daughter. But that kind of comfort wasn't hers to give anymore. "I feared for you and the kids. I didn't understand you. But I never stopped loving you."

The dam inside let go. Tears came before she could stop them.

Seraphina leaned forward, head bowed over her hands. "Truth is, Mum—I wanted to come back more times than I can count."

Letting that out was like tearing something open.

"But it felt like I couldn't have it all. A normal life. The kids safe and unaware. And you."

Saffron knelt beside her daughter, fingers passing through the arm of the chair like mist through silk—but still, her presence was real and comforting.

"I know."

Saffron's heart was breaking, so much time lost.

"And I should've made it easier for you to choose me. I let pride speak when love should have. I wanted you to stay so badly I forgot how to let you go with grace."

"I'm tired of being angry. Tired of pretending I don't miss you."

Saffron blurred gently at the edges, her emotions trailing around her as shifting colour.

"I love you, Mum."

Seraphina couldn't remember the last time she had said those words to her.

"I always have. Even when I didn't know how to show it."

If Saffron still had a heart that beat, it would've stopped right then.

"Oh, my beautiful angel. I've loved every piece of you—even the ones I didn't know how to hold."

They sat there for a long time.

Not to fix what had been broken. Not to rewrite the past.

But to acknowledge it. To grieve what silence stole. And to let something new take root in the hurt.

The fire licked at the mantle's base. The shadows melted inward. The old house, weathered and aware, wrapped itself around them.

Mother and daughter. Legacy and choice. Forgiveness slowly learning how to speak.

From his floating chair cocoon, Samthrax sniffled—loud and unapologetic.

"I'm not crying," he declared, voice wobbling with theatrical dignity. "My tear ducts are performing a highly advanced sympathy ritual. Happens when love and pain collide."

He dabbed at his eyes with a black handkerchief embroidered with tiny skulls.

"This is why demons don't do family dynamics. Too many feelings. Not enough fireballs."

Seraphina glanced up, half-laughing through the wet shine of her tears. "You're insufferable."

Samthrax sniffled again, draping himself across the arm of the chair with wounded grace.

"And yet, utterly unforgettable."

Eighteen

"Some gates open with keys. Others open with blood. But the worst kind—the oldest kind—open with choice. And the cruel truth of legacy magic is this: it doesn't wait for readiness. It arrives. It demands. And it decides what survives."
— *Council Archives, Restricted Tome VI: On Conduits and Cataclysms*

The Council chamber of the Crescent Enclave didn't hum with power. It seethed.

Vaulted ceilings arched overhead like the ribs of some long-dead beast, carved with sigils meant to suppress ambition. Incense, iron, and ego hung heavy in the room. Twelve chairs ringed the table—though only ten were filled. One remained vacant in memory of the Blood War. The other had waited two hundred years for its heir—and still sat unclaimed.

Killian Graves took the head seat, palms pressed to the surface, eyes hard.

"Her name is Zinnia Hart. She's of the lost coven Les Revenantes. The crescent seal is confirmed. The prophecy's fragments align. If she falls into the wrong hands, the Veil will tear."

A murmur slithered through the circle.

Councillor Edevane—the eldest of the lot, pale as wax and twice as brittle—spoke. He always had to be first. Couldn't help himself.

231

"You say confirmed, but we've seen no official attunement. No ritual. No registry. For all we know, the seal could be a forgery—some glamour meant to spook the Council into chaos."

Killian's jaw locked—mostly to keep from saying what he was actually thinking.

Self-important bastard. Still thinks this is about politics.

Patience: gone.

"You're welcome to visit Maison Bellarose and test it yourself. But bring a priest and a pyre—because if you misstep near that mark, you'll see exactly what she's connected to."

Eyes flicked toward the seal burning in the air behind him—Killian's version of show and tell. One councillor started to raise a hand. Then thought better of it.

Yvane leaned in. All calculation. "And the Bellarose girl?"

"Seraphina has reclaimed her heritage. The Keep's wards responded to her blood. She is officially the key to the Shadowkeep."

Conversation stalled—dense with unspoken power plays—until it shattered.

"That's two active legacies. In one household?"

And here we go.

"Yes. And that's exactly why I'm telling you now."

Edevane zeroed in.

"Or perhaps you're telling us because you can no longer contain it."

One thing he could count on: the Council always folded into the same old fear.

"I'm not here for your blessing. I'm here to warn you. Brinnan knows about both of them. And he's moving."

Several councillors glanced at each other.

Yvane spoke before anyone else could. "You want to shield them? From us?"

"No. From him."

Maltren cleared his throat. The stone half of his face didn't move. "And if we vote for protective custody?"

Here it comes. Killian locked on.

"Then I'll invoke ancient right. Trial by Warden blood. You will not lay a hand on them unless you intend to draw mine first."

The moment congealed with unsaid things.

Not because of the threat—but because of what it meant. A Warden invoking blood-rights hadn't happened in over a century. And the last time it did? An enclave burned.

No vote passed. No approval was given. Only a silence heavy with implication.

Killian rose without dismissal and left the chamber, torchlight running the line of his coat.

And behind him, in the corner of the Council Hall, something shifted.

A watcher peeled from the wall like ink from parchment—and slipped into the dark.

***

The clock in the Scriptorium struck three. No chime. No bell. Seraphina lay curled up on a couch, half-draped in a throw, the embers behind her glowing soft as bruises. She'd drifted somewhere between sleep and thought, her mind blurred by fatigue.

Something stirred beneath her skin. Not in the room—in her.

She stood. Not fully awake. Not entirely asleep. Her body moved on instinct.

She crossed the space without noise, stepping over a book Sage had left behind, past Samthrax, who snored midair in a crooked float, one hand wrapped around a half-eaten macaroon.

Her fingers brushed along the rear bookshelf—until they found the two volumes etched faintly in runes visible only when moonlight struck them.

233

The shelf groaned and swung open, revealing the hidden threshold. It was colder than it should've been. Damp as breath against glass. Steps spiralled downward into blackness that offered no reflection— the path to the Shadowkeep.

Seraphina descended.

One step. The next. Her bare feet were numb to the chill beneath. She didn't blink.

Something called.

But not in words.

Her mind slept. But her blood listened. That was the problem with legacy—sometimes, it moved first.

The passage swallowed her whole. The door stayed open behind her.

The further she walked, the more the light forgot her. The walls pressed close, whispering in a tongue no longer spoken aloud. Symbols flickered as she passed—resonating within her soul like old scars.

Her right hand prickled inward, too deep to scratch. She raised it. A thread of silver luminance stretched between her palm and the corridor ahead, not a tether, but a summons spun from something older than will.

Down.

Deeper.

The magic here didn't have temperature. It had weight.

At the bottom of the stairwell, the door to the Shadowkeep listened with old iron, eager for the key.

The locks clicked shut, then open again—metal with a mind behind it.

Come closer, they beckoned—dragging with the gravity of old oaths.

Seraphina stepped forward, hand rising toward the centre ring. Her eyes were wide, unblinking.

And utterly empty.

"Seraphina!"

A voice broke against her, muffled by the veil of trance.

Samthrax tumbled down the last stretch of the stairwell, his robe askew, curls wild, collar sigils flaring crimson.

"Oh, hell no—wake up, witch! This is not your midnight stroll time!"

He hurled a vial at her feet. It shattered on the stone, releasing a rush of acrid metallic smoke.

Seraphina stumbled, coughing. Her lashes fluttered. The spell broke. Her knees buckled.

Samthrax caught her before she hit the floor, his slight frame surprisingly solid.

"Back up the stairs, with you. Before whatever's in here decides to answer."

Since when was sleepwalking her thing?

"I didn't even know I was down here. I heard something calling—I think—"

Yeah. He knew exactly what was calling. And congrats to him—he now officially needed a new pair of boxers. He'd lived with those things for decades. He wasn't looking to wake them up.

"I don't care if it offered eternal youth and front-row seats to the apocalypse. You don't come down here alone."

She stared at the door.

The blood-rings clung to the surface, still whispering in the tongue of opened veins.

"I didn't mean to come here."

He was already halfway up the stairs. Fight or flight? Yeah—leaning hard on the latter.

"But the Keep meant for you to. And that's what scares me."

She gripped the railing. It hadn't felt like curiosity. It had felt like surrender. It wanted her—it had called to something buried, and she'd almost answered. And that terrified her.

Before they reached the top, Seraphina paused. Her senses snagged on a detail—a scrap of parchment peeked between two stones near the passage wall. Singed at the edges.

She knelt and pulled it free.

The ink shimmered in a hand both beautiful and severe:

"One shall bear the seal. One shall bleed the lock.

And if the Gate listens too long, it will speak back.

Keep the Keeper silent.

Or the Veil shall not break—it will scream."

Samthrax gave a whistle, all dread and sarcasm. "Cos that's not ominous at all."

***

The clouds hung heavy over New Orleans, like a secret trying not to confess.

And high above it all—atop a tower no mundane map recalled—Brinnan worked.

No candles tonight.

Only flame.

Seven of them, black-wicked and unnatural—fed on oils from extinct roots and fouler things. They ringed him on the floor, dancing against sigils carved directly into slate. Their light faltered—a last exhale, dragged from something unwilling.

Magic saturated the space, dense and unmoving. It pressed into the lungs, heavy with world-old power and unspoken consequence—a ritual poised between invocation and burial.

Brinnan knelt at the circle's centre, bare-chested, eyes closed, a blade resting across his palms. Smoke curled from the crimson offering in the ceremonial bowl before him, trailing skyward in the shape of glyphs that hadn't been taught in centuries.

The mirror shivered—then split into two images.

Seraphina Bellarose. Zinnia Hart.

His voice was a whisper ground down from stone and hunger.

"By crest and seal… by blood and breath… show me the pulse beneath the lines."

The bowl trembled. His veins stirred—not in quivers, but in shapes. It remembered something older.

For the briefest second, the faces in the mirror fused.

And shattered.

Brinnan opened his eyes. Twin sparks of silver fire burned behind his irises.

"They converge. And through them, both thresholds begin to thin."

"When the Veil begins to give," he added, "it won't split like stone—it will seep. In dreams first. Then thought. The blood-marked will feel it. And they won't know what's waking inside them until it's already speaking through them."

He rose fluidly—approaching the altar beside the mirror. The Volucris Noctem sat open, its ink the colour of old wounds. His fingers hovered over the page.

Behind him came a shift. The silvered glass convulsed.

And a shadow peeled itself from the far wall.

Malrik. Or what was left of him.

He wore the same gaunt shape. The same tattoos snaking like venom down his neck. But the eyes were gone. In their place—voids rimmed in emberlight. A corpse lit from within by something that should not burn.

The being bowed. "The council is fractured. Graves remains firm. But there is unease about the two legacies in one household."

Brinnan wasn't surprised. Those fossils were notoriously short-sighted.

"Unease is the prelude to obedience. Fear is the skeleton of every empire worth ruling."

He studied Zinnia's reflection.

"Two legacies in one house isn't instability. It's inevitability. They see fracture."

He gave the words space to settle.

"I see convergence."

Brinnan turned toward the map again. His fingers traced the outer fold of the vellum, honouring the years it had endured. The Keep calls her the same way I call you. Not with chains. But gravity. That was the true shape of power—not possession but pull. Not control, but surrender.

"And when unity becomes collapse… I will be the one standing in the ruin. Unbroken."

The creature held him in its ember-eyes.

"As you wish."

Brinnan regarded the Malrik carbon dispassionately.

"Your body copies the living. But your soul is mine. Do not forget what you are."

"I forget nothing," the creature rasped. "I carry only what serves."

"Then serve."

He turned to the altar, where blood-inked hide mapped the Enclave in layers of rune and ley.

"Killian Graves is their spine. Sever it. Not to kill. To paralyse. Let them think he's still in play, while his influence decays beneath them."

The being bowed once more. "It will be done."

It folded back into shadow, sliding into the mirror like poison down a throat.

The room stilled—but not with peace.

The quiet throbbed.

Five beats later, Julian entered.

The scent of spellfire lingered—acidic, soaked deep into the walls, refusing to fade. The surface swirled faintly, twin flames flickering in its depths—Zinnia's image fading.

"You're tracking them both now?"

Brinnan didn't look up as he folded a curse into a runed satchel. "Their paths are bound. It makes sense to do so."

Julian scanned the room. Something didn't sit right.

"Did I hear Malrik's voice?"

"I haven't had an update from him," he added. "Which is… unusual."

Brinnan turned to meet Julian's enquiring gaze with a smile that never touched his eyes. "You did."

And that told him exactly what his father had done. "You repurposed him."

Brinnan nodded once. "He betrayed us both. I dealt with it. What walks in his skin now serves a greater purpose."

Julian stood very still. His mind moved quickly.

He had always planned to discard Malrik—knew the man's loyalty was a loose thread, waiting to be pulled. But the fact that Brinnan had discovered the betrayal first—had acted, adapted, remade?

That was something else.

If Brinnan could hollow Malrik out and fill him with obedience…

What's stopping him from doing the same to me?

A fault split down his centre—small, but real. Just enough to feel.

He turned to the mirror—Zinnia's silhouette receded into blackness—and masked his disgust behind neutrality.

He didn't care about the girl. And Seraphina? She'd become a sealed chapter years ago. But the way they disrupted balance by existing— that was dangerous to everything Julian had spent his life building.

If the world was going to shift, he wouldn't be standing on the fracture line. He'd be the one drawing the map.

Brinnan returned to the drawn plan stretched across the altar.

"Obedient Malrik will ensure Killian is removed. Better to cut out the infection before it finds the heart, wouldn't you agree?"

What was he going to do, say no and risk the same fate? Not bloody likely.

"Of course, father."

He turned and left.

Down the corridor, past the trembling glyphs and the storm pressing against the penthouse glass—he walked.

But inside, something crystallised.

Brinnan may believe he's the only one holding a knife.

But Julian was done being carved.

***

The Scriptorium never truly slept. Even at dawn, when fog curled against the windows like secrets on cold glass, and the candles burned low along the sills, the room thrummed with energy—not frenetic, but ancient.

Magic stretching its limbs beneath the floorboards.

Zinnia stood barefoot in the centre of the circle. Her shirtsleeves were shoved up. The floor was freezing under her toes.

The crescent lit like a fuse—not searing, but primed.

Sage stepped over the line of powdered mirror glass and rose quartz, practically bouncing with unholy enthusiasm.

"All right. Time to see if the spooky spaghetti squiggle on your neck is more than decorative."

Zinnia gave her a look flat enough to press flowers. "That's comforting. I feel extremely safe."

Sage brushed chalk dust off her jeans, hoping she looked more confident than she felt. "Safety is a spectrum. And you voluntarily walked into a magical world and made friends with a demon. You lost your safe card days ago."

Behind her, Saffron floated serenely, wrapped in an opalescent shimmer that softened the darker edges of the glyphs spiralling outward from the circle.

Zinnia's entire body was one big knot. *Don't get dead, Zin.*

"Okay. Let's do this before I overthink myself into cardiac arrest."

240

Seraphina passed her a carved obsidian pendant, strung on a leather cord. "You'll wear this while we activate your power. It should help ground you. In theory."

"In theory?"

Saffron crossed every ghostly part of her anatomy she could. She pasted on a calm smile. "Magic is rarely binary, dear. It's fluid. Like fire. Or heartbreak."

Zinnia knew plenty about the latter. If she'd known she had magic, her no-good ex would've been express-mailed to hell.

Seraphina stepped back. "When I nod, focus on the mark. Don't fight it. Just… observe."

Zinnia tilted her head in agreement. *In for a penny, in for a pound.*

Seraphina spoke first.

It wasn't a word, not really—more a sound shaped from lineage. Sage joined in, her voice weaving through Seraphina's, a living thread stitching through the wounded dusk. The glyphs flared—gold, violet, followed by that strange, liminal silver that made the shadows recoil, scraping backward along the walls.

Zinnia's spine arched. Her eyes slammed shut. The brand ignited.

Holy shit.

Power tore through her, lit her chest with a second heartbeat—hot and ragged. She gasped, choking on a cry that wasn't hers.

She wasn't wearing the magic. It was wearing her. And it liked the fit.

"Z?" Seraphina was a lifeline across a chasm. "Zinnia, stay with me—"

But she was falling inward.

Through vision not her own—through possibility, not the paths already walked. She saw gates—some open, some sealed. Eyes in the dark. Cities half-buried in ruin.

A voice—not hers—wove through her mind:

"Let us speak, Gateborn."

Zinnia buckled, barely staying upright.

The pressure yanked tight. Her bones shoved against it, rattling inside her, wild and frantic, ready to snap. She screamed—and the circle shattered, tearing reality at the seams.

The glyphs sheared apart in a scatter-burst of smoke and emberdust. She hit the floor, coughing.

Sage got to her first, brushing hair from her face. "You're okay. You're okay. You're back."

Zinnia felt like she'd been dragged through a gorse hedge backwards. "What the hell was that?"

The answer didn't matter. What mattered was the knowing—that something in her blood had reached across the Veil. And something had reached back.

Saffron hovered close, concern stark on her face.

"Your magic isn't sleeping anymore. That was a tether trying to form. Whatever's beyond the Veil recognised your call."

Zinnia wiped her mouth on her sleeve. "Didn't feel like recognition. Felt like a goddamn psychic invasion."

Seraphina could relate. Given last night's fiasco—the one she and Samthrax had decided not to mention.

"It was both. The mark is a gate with your name carved into the frame. Lucky you—you're the lock and the warden."

Zinnia looked at Seraphina, genuinely concerned.

Yeah. Great idea. Give the girl with training wheels the key to Armageddon.

"What if I can't?"

Sebastian had appeared silently in the doorway, a mug of hot chocolate in one hand and a bottle of water in the other. "You will. You always show up when it matters, Z."

Zinnia tried to laugh, but it snagged halfway up her throat.

"You're not alone in this." He crossed the room to give her the water. "None of us are."

She took it and drank deeply. The cold steadied her.

"Great. So, I'm a gate with imposter syndrome and a demon stalker."

"Technically, he stalks all of us." Sage didn't seem particularly bothered by that detail.

Samthrax piped up from a high shelf, where he'd been watching upside down and eating rose-flavoured macaroons. "And technically, you're not just a gate. You're also a conduit."

Everyone turned.

He blinked slowly. The usual quirk gone from his voice. "I served someone once," he added. "Long time ago. Before the Keep. Before the binding. He tried to open the Veil. Bled the conduit dry trying to make it respond. But it doesn't respond. It devours."

Understanding started to creep in, slow and unwelcome.

Zinnia didn't like the sound of that.

She definitely did not want to end up a husk.

That would be hell on the complexion.

"Meaning?"

Saffron knew what she was about to say had all the elegance of heels on black ice.

"It means that if the Veilborn speak through you, they won't be borrowing your voice. They'll be claiming it. And you."

Zinnia stood, every muscle sore. Her heartbeat was still syncopated against the crescent's residual pulse.

Right. That's settled then.

"Okay. Round two tomorrow?"

Seraphina hadn't expected that.

"You're serious?"

"Yup." Zinnia grabbed her jumper off the chair.

"If I'm gonna be the voice for some soul-eating nightmare pantheon,

I'm damn well learning how to throw a fireball."

Saffron actually laughed. It was soft and strange and sad and beautiful all at once.

Samthrax raised a macaroon. "To fireballs and fatalism."

"Shut up." Zinnia didn't mean it.

Her stomach growled loud enough to startle the wards. "I'm starving—what's for breakfast?"

Seraphina didn't have all the answers yet. But she could definitely do carbs.

"Me too. Come on—we'll do pancakes."

Sage stayed seated. She'd been itching to try out what she'd learned. "I'll follow you guys shortly. I just want to finish up my practice."

Seraphina nodded, already half-turned toward the door, but her thoughts lingered—on the mark, the power, and the weight they were all trying so hard to carry.

Once Sage was alone, she lit a low bowl with a flick of her fingers. No words. No ritual. Just focus. She was getting good results with her magic.

The water quaked and then grew clear as a scryer's eye. From its depths, a figure surfaced. Tall. Familiar. Sebastian.

But he was screaming, it wasn't a death scream. It was something worse—his body unzipped in bands of shadow, his eyes feral, seared with a rawness that had nothing to do with power.

And everything to do with loss.

The image collapsed into ink.

Sage stared at the swirl of black spreading through the bowl. Whatever was coming wouldn't arrive with fanfare. It would arrive through him. And it would shatter them all from the inside out.

She left the Scriptorium, schooled her features, and joined everyone in the kitchen for breakfast.

Nineteen

The council chamber crouched beneath the pre-dawn sky, heavy with unspoken judgements. Incense burned low in braziers, curling against the copper tang of sweat and temper. Ten councillors sat hunched like crows in their shadowstone thrones, gazes hard with suspicion.

Killian stood at the head of the table, coat unbuttoned, gloves off, jaw tight with warning.

"You called me back at this ungodly hour for a ruling. So, make one. But understand what it means."

Edevane leaned forward, eyes yellowed and hungry. "We discussed this after you left. We all agree that containment is our right. They are volatile—one marked by the Veil, the other tied to the Keep. You expect us to wait and hope they don't break?"

Killian fought the urge to hex the fool into oblivion.

A snap of his fingers and the problem would be solved.

"I'm not asking."

Yvane gave him the kind of look that usually came before a duel.

"You think we fear you Graves?"

Killian stepped forward.

Challenge accepted.

"No. But you should."

Something familiar shifted beneath his skin, not violence.

Yet.

"Try to cage them—with chains, with threats, with your antique politics—and I'll turn this chamber into a memory made of ash. I don't need permission. And I don't need backup. You already know why."

The room fell still.

No ruling came. And no one dared stop him when he turned on his heel and walked away.

Outside, the sky had just begun to peel open. Dawn unravelled across the horizon in threads of saffron, cutting the Crescent Enclave into knives of shadow and light. The cobbled paths glistened with dew. The glyph lanterns had dimmed, winking uneasily.

Killian didn't burn—he locked down. A pressure-system of rage held behind his ribs, ossified into something cold and precise. The leash wasn't restraint. It was strategy. And the second he let go, it wouldn't be fury. It would be annihilation.

He hated politics. Always had.

He hadn't wanted New Orleans. Not the ghosts. Not the power games.

But when his mentor—Aramis Veklen, the last Warden of the Black Vale—called him home from the ruins of Prague, Killian answered.

He'd owed him too much. And Veklen had never asked for favours. Just this one.

"You are the vein in the mountain." Killian could still hear him— gravelled, worn thin from too many battles. "But veins don't choose when to be mined. It's the world that comes for them—splits them open and takes what it needs."

He had buried him three months later under a glacier.

Grief took the post for him.

He ground his teeth.

Now, years in, he stood at the helm of an Enclave that mistook power for permission.

Babysitting egos the size of small kingdoms.

Every council meeting was more like an autopsy than a strategy session—probing a dead system, pretending it still breathed. Each one chipped away at the lockbox. The one holding the part of him that didn't compromise, didn't negotiate, didn't care about rules or robes or the poetry of power. That part wanted to play hockey with the Council's heads and see how far a hypocrite's skull could bounce off a floor.

His boots struck the corridor with ruthless precision.

The outer ward glyph above the archway flickered, then held—a stutter Killian didn't like. The sentry who should have been posted was gone.

The warmth leeched out, leaving behind a stillness threaded with warning. Just a shift that settled beneath his sternum and whispered: *move.* The lanterns swayed slightly, shadows pooling longer than they should've, lines distorting into impossible geometry.

A dissonance.

He didn't slow.

Old magic stirred in his spine—not the kind polished for wards and councils, but the kind that answered only to blood and instinct.

And it was listening now.

A line pulled tight beneath the skin of the world—and then snapped.

Shapes peeled from the walls—too tall, too thin. They slithered upright, dragging boneless arms behind them, heavy with the residue of regrets that refused to die. Killian's breath misted. "Brinnan. You bloody coward."

The first shadow lunged.

It didn't walk. It bent toward him, mouth sewn shut, the limbs unspooling into serrated black blades that wept ink as they flexed.

Killian didn't draw a weapon.

He didn't have to.

He let the mask slip, and the thing he kept buried looked out.

They came fast. He moved like reflex—weaponised.

Something invisible buckled around him.

He raised one arm—his fingers curled—and the shadows surrounding him screamed. Not out loud. Not to ears. But to the marrow.

He pulled from the place he tried to never use.

Dark strands lashed out from beneath his coat—not fabric, but raw myth—unwritten and unkind. Vortexes of voidlight spiralled from his chest, streaming toward the enemy, slick and fluid as oil. They struck the nearest shadow—it folded in on itself, devoured in silence.

A second creature attacked.

He didn't dodge.

He absorbed, turning the strike into a counter—his shadow racing up the creature's arm and imploding it with a burst of inverted light.

The street behind him shattered. The glass screamed three buildings down.

Another came.

Killian turned toward it—and his eyes weren't eyes anymore.

They were pits of burning coal.

He opened his mouth, and the word wasn't spoken—it just happened.

A weapon dressed in language. A prayer for annihilation.

It unwrote sound, peeled back silence like skin, left the air raw and flayed.

The shadow exploded.

But one remained.

At the edge of the courtyard.

Watching.

It didn't attack.

It wore Malrik's shape—but not his soul. His smile was too smooth. His stance too perfect.

Killian's lip curled.

Guess the warlock had pissed Brinnan off royally.

"You."

The creature cocked its head.

"The last bled slower."

Killian took a step—then staggered. Pain detonated across his chest, sharp and merciless. His shirt clung wet against him. Seamed with thin surgical cuts that wept red.

He dropped to one knee, refusing to give in.

The glyphs embedded in the stone beneath his feet still trembled.

The thing didn't move.

"Tell Brinnan. Next time, I'll open all the doors."

The creature smiled and dissolved—a smear of shadow staining the dawn light.

Killian forced himself upright. His body screamed. His magic wanted blood. He made it swallow the urge whole.

Temptation hissed under his skin. One more word, and he wouldn't come back from it.

There was no time to heal.

No time to rest.

The war had started.

And the ones he loved? Unguarded.

***

The kitchen at Maison Bellarose smelled of cinnamon, scorched maple syrup, and safety. Sunlight spilled through leaded glass, throwing colour like confetti across the table. Calm saturated the plaster in a way that felt rehearsed.

Seraphina stood at the stove, her curls pulled back in a loose braid, sleeves rolled to her elbows as she flipped a pancake with practiced ease. A cup of strong coffee steamed beside her, untouched.

"I'm telling you." She threw over her shoulder. "This batch is going to be edible. Maybe even good." Samthrax clung to the chandelier like it might save him from a terrible fate. "Witch, please. If I wanted to gamble with my afterlife, I'd summon a god. Not your cooking."

"Keep running your mouth, and I'll hex a mute button into your skull."

Zinnia sat cross-legged on the counter, cradling a mug of something dangerously caffeinated, her shirt sleeves stretched over her knuckles.

"You really have a death wish, don't you?"

Samthrax struck a pose mid-air.

"Multitudes, darling. Most of them lethal. Along with oodles of charm and a dash of drama."

Sebastian didn't look up from his plate, a half-devoured stack of pancakes in front of him. He swatted away Sage's fork with a syrupy one of his own. "Mostly drama. And this is your third helping."

"Demons digest differently." Samthrax patted his stomach. "Besides, grief burns calories."

Zinnia sipped her coffee with the devotion it deserved.

"What are you grieving?"

Samthrax rested a hand on his chest, all mock sincerity. "The untimely death of my respect for this family's breakfast etiquette."

Sage laughed under her breath, though her eyes flicked toward Sebastian with an unease she hadn't voiced yet. The vision still sat at the back of her mind. But today—this hour—was bright. And she was tired of bad news.

Saffron drifted through the archway, her aura muted in the morning light. She didn't speak—just hovered by the table, regarding the others with an expression that mixed pride and sorrow in equal measure. Her form flickered once before steadying.

It didn't go unnoticed. Zinnia's smile faltered. "You okay?"

"I'm here. And for now, that's enough."

Seraphina added to the pancake tower. "One more round and I swear I'm sitting down."

Sage gave her mother a wry look. "You said that two rounds ago."

The batter hissed in the pan. "Yes, but I remembered you all eat like rabid squirrels."

More laughter—lightness born in the fleeting moments the havoc chose to spare.

A deep, visceral boom reverberated through the house—no door had been touched, no hand raised. The entire structure flinched. Mugs jittered. The windows shimmered, fine cracks crawling outward in deliberate lines. Somewhere upstairs, a mirror toppled and burst like brittle ice. The chandelier swung wildly on its chain—Samthrax yelped and hit the floor.

Sage stood in a flash. "What was that—"

Seraphina was already moving, her pulse shifting into battle-tempo. "Wardline."

The wards exploded in light—flaring a sick, violent red that bled into violet. The house's defences screamed, a raw, torn sound that clawed through the halls.

Samthrax stepped back from the glow, lips pursed. "Oh, no. That's a we're-about-to-be-turned-into matching décor set kind of colour combo."

Zinnia was the first out of the kitchen.

They sprinted through the hallway, down the steps as the front door slammed open on its own—a living house flinging itself into attack mode.

Zinnia braked fast. "Shit. Is that my mark?"

No one had time to answer.

A sound unfurled through the dark. Not a roar. Not a scream. A voice, carried on the wind.

"Open what is sealed. Or bleed in its place."

The message was clear. Brinnan knew about Zinnia—and now, she was also in his crosshairs.

Killian's Escalade growled into view, headlights slicing through the haze curling over the scorched lawn. Light splintered against the crescent glyph still smoking in the grass.

He parked just past the wardline, engine grinding to a halt.

The door opened.

Killian stumbled out. Every movement telegraphed pain. His coat was torn, one sleeve shredded to the elbow. His shirt stuck to him, the fabric puckered over wounds. His face was chalk white. Each step forward was an act of defiance against gravity.

He took two steps—and his knees gave way.

He collapsed with a grunt, barely catching himself on a single hand.

Seraphina didn't think—she just moved. She dropped beside him, arms already around his shoulders. Her magic flared instinctively, warmth spreading across her palms.

"Killian—what happened?!"

She didn't care about anything else right now. The glyphs could burn. The Veil could scream. But in that moment, there was only the brutal singularity of him. Hurt and bleeding.

If she got her hands on the bastard—or bastards—that had done this, she'd bury them in the backyard and sleep just fine.

"Ambushed. On the way back."

Every word fought him. But he forced them loose.

She pressed her palm firmer to his chest—magic already stirring, hot and sure. "By who?" "Veil-touched."

His shoulders dropped. Thank God they were safe, they could deal with the rest later.

"They tracked me after the meeting."

He saw the crack in her composure and filled it with the closest thing to comfort he had left. "I'm OK."

But Seraphina could see it—he was lying. The shielding around him had been ripped. As though some unseen presence had read every line of it, undoing it strand by strand with the care of a butcher in prayer.

"The Council." Killian preferred pompous gits. "Demanded you and Zinnia be turned over. Protective custody, they called it."

"Well. That's a hard no." Zinnia would rather tweeze her soul through her nostrils than kiss the ring of some dusty institution.

"I said the same. But they won't wait long. Brinnan sent something to greet me. One of them was wearing Malrik's face."

The name hit, like a corpse dropped in still water.

Seraphina wasn't surprised.

Ambition had made him reckless, and that was as good as a death sentence.

"Malrik's dead?"

He didn't answer. He didn't need to. Whatever had come for him in the dark corridors of the Crescent Enclave had once been Malrik… and now it was something else entirely.

Saffron moved toward the boundary where grass met scorched earth, her gaze fixed on the smoking glyph.

"And this is Brinnan's way of letting us know he's coming."

A deep knowing unfurled inside Zinnia.

"They're trying to divide us."

She looked at them—found family, compass point, reason to stay upright.

"We need to make damn sure that doesn't happen."

The wind curled through the grass. The scorched glyph still smoked.

***

The others had gone back inside, pulled reluctantly by Saffron's insistence and Sage's unsteady hands. Zinnia had lingered, sharp-eyed and unwilling, but Seraphina had waved her off.

She needed to be alone with Killian—it was time to stop dodging the conversation she'd been avoiding since the second he walked through the door.

She caught his arm before he could collapse again and helped him down onto the stone bench beside the ivy-strangled porch.

He winced as he sat. Most of the wounds had already sealed under the pressure of magic and sheer willpower. The heat radiating off him was off—not feverish, more like too much taken.

"Let me help."

He didn't say no.

She knelt as if the moment might collapse if she didn't hold it steady. Her fingers moved with a healer's care and a lover's ache, tracing bruises—trying to make sense of the flesh that almost wasn't.

He bit down hard but refused to pull away.

Her hands faltered. A tremor slid through her magic—grief woven under the rhythm of her pulse. The weight of nearly losing him pressed into every breath she took.

"Seraphina. I'm okay."

"No. You're bloody well not. And don't you dare lie to me about that."

A laugh tried to rise—dead on arrival. She'd always called him on his bullshit.

She looked up, eyes too bright to hide anything. Anger. Fear. And under it all—relief.

"Do you have any idea what it felt like, seeing you get out of that car, bleeding?"

"I—"

"No. Don't answer yet." She wasn't ready for him to speak. If he did, she'd lose her nerve.

"I told myself after everything, that if I just kept my distance… if I was focused on the twins, the magic, this damned prophecy—then maybe I could survive the idea of you not being part of my life."

Killian's expression shifted. He wisely stayed quiet.

"I built a life like a fortress. Told myself I was safe without you. Told myself love was a luxury I couldn't afford. But every decision—was me trying to outrun what I felt."

She pressed a palm to his chest—not to heal, just to feel his heart beating.

"I saw you, and for a moment, Killian, I thought I'd lost you. And it gutted me."

Silence settled between them. It muted everything but the truth.

His hand came up slowly. He cupped her face, thumb brushing the edge of a tear she didn't know had fallen.

"I'm still here, and I won't leave. Not unless you ask me to."

"I won't be asking you to do that."

Killian leaned forward, forehead touching hers. His presence—solid, even now—was a gravity she hadn't realised she still orbited.

She was so tired of pretending. That ended here.

"I never stopped loving you. Even when I tried to forget. You were in every choice. Every corner of my heart I buried to survive."

Killian closed his eyes. She still loved him.

He'd tear the fucking world down for a second chance—if that's where this was heading.

"I felt it. Even when I didn't want to." He gave her the truth, unarmoured for once.

She nodded slowly. Talking herself into saying the rest.

"I want the life we left behind like cowards. I want the future we pretended we couldn't have because it hurt less than hoping."

She pulled back enough to meet his gaze.

"I want you here. With me. With the twins. I kept telling myself I was protecting them by keeping you at a distance. But I realise I wasn't. Please say you'll move in with us."

His answer came without hesitation.

"Yes."

Relief hit like absolution. He hadn't dared to hope—and now here it was.

He reached for her hand, fingers tangling with hers as if they had all the time in the world.

"I'm done fighting for everything but you. I choose us first. I choose love. And I really want to get to know our children."

Seraphina closed her eyes and let the tears flow freely.

Not from grief.

From the unbearable relief of finally being allowed to fall—and knowing someone would catch her.

And this time, she wouldn't run from the future. She'd shape it.

Twenty

"Found family means cursed secrets, emotional shrapnel, and pancakes that might start a portal war. Love and legacy, baby. Normal's not on the menu."

— Samthrax, emotionally constipated but trying his best

Killian stood by the window in the Scriptorium, stance born of habit not peace. He was watching the twins—studying them. Their ease. Their brightness. Their youth threaded with shadows no child should carry.

Seraphina moved closer to him, her hand brushing against his. He caught it. Held it. Didn't speak.

They had agreed—after blood, after confessions, after nearly losing each other again—that this was no longer a secret worth keeping. Not for the kids. Not for themselves.

Sage sat curled on the couch, tracing idle symbols into the throw pillow, unaware the fabric had begun to warm and shine.

Sebastian leaned against the mantle, braced like he might require the support. The stare he aimed at their parents? Detached. On the surface, sure.

But underneath? Not so much.

"Kids."

Seraphina silently hoped they would take the news well. Sage, she'd be fine—probably even thrilled. But Seb? That one could go nuclear.

"We need to talk."

Sage looked up instantly alert.

Sebastian didn't move. His gaze—cool as glass. And just as breakable, if you knew where to look.

Killian edged in closer to Seraphina, that subtle lean. All intimacy, no apology.

"This may shock you… but your mother and I—"

"Are back together?" Sage jumped in, her expression sliding straight into delighted mischief.

She'd called it. And yeah—this? Best news all week.

That caught Seraphina off guard. "How did you—"

"You've had moon-eyes for each other since he got here." Sage waved a hand like she was bored of being right. "You're not subtle. He looks at you like he's trying to remember a spell he never actually forgot, and you keep eyeing him like he's dessert and you skipped breakfast *and* lunch."

That hit his funny bone. Not that he laughed. Killian just let the moment land, then shut it down and turned to Sebastian.

"And you?"

Sebastian didn't answer immediately. He held his father's eyes while mulling over his crazy life.

A week ago, he'd thought calculus would be the hardest part of his month.

Now? His mother was a legacy witch. He was the other half of a prophecy. His grandmother could walk through walls. There was a demon in the kitchen who ate sugar and drank coffee in equal measure. And his father—the man he'd once considered a footnote—stood five feet away, freshly wounded, talking about becoming a family.

It was more than a lot.

It was insane, but what the hell.

Sebastian shrugged, feigning nonchalance. "As long as this doesn't mean you two start kissy facing in the kitchen where I eat…"

Sage tossed a paper ball at her brother. "Oh my God, you're the worst."

Sebastian lobbed it right back. "You love it."

"I tolerate it." Sage turned to their mother and Killian, reining the attitude in just enough. "But seriously… this is good, right? You two being together again?"

Killian opened his mouth, but Sebastian beat him to it.

"I'm not going to pretend this isn't weirding me out. It is."

His fingers tapped against his elbow. He took a moment, trying to gather the words that fit.

Killian didn't interrupt. He waited.

Sebastian's gaze drifted to his mother… and returned to Killian.

He wasn't great at verbalising what was in his head. It usually came out all kinds of wrong. But this? This he was getting clear on.

"You've stood between us and danger every time without hesitating. You've literally bled for us, and that counts."

Seraphina moved to his side, her hand finding his arm—light and steady. Sebastian didn't look at her. His eyes stayed on Killian.

"I know what lives in me. I can feel it. The dark. The pull of it. And I've seen the way you use it—not just as a weapon, but with control. I need you to teach me how to do that too."

Killian knew the feeling all too well. Fearing yourself, not knowing if mastery is even possible. "I will, son. I know that darkness. I've carried it longer than you've been alive. But it doesn't have to own you."

Sebastian swallowed, nodded once, then looked away as if he couldn't hold the moment and his composure at the same time.

Joy bloomed so fast across Sage's face it nearly unbalanced her. She bounced once on her toes, blinking and beaming brighter than the chandelier.

"So, we're really doing this? Like… family dinners and shared holidays and arguing over who enchanted the last slice of cake to scream when you cut it?"

"I believe that was your demon." Killian didn't even try to hide the dry amusement.

Sage's pulse thudded hard. She was smiling too big, and her hands didn't seem to know what to do with themselves.

"Um… is it weird if I… Can I call you Dad?"

The question hit Killian like a spell aimed dead at the heart.

He cleared his throat—a thousand unsaid things in the space between syllables. "You can call me anything you want. But… that? That would mean more than you know."

Sage grinned so wide it hurt. Tears slipped free before she could stop them. She wiped them away fast, but the smile stayed.

"I always wanted someone like you." She kept her eyes on his. "Strong. Quiet. Dangerous—in the cool way. I mean, Mum's badarse, obviously, but she's a lot more 'hex your soul' and a lot less 'knife to the throat.'"

Seraphina wasn't sure how to take that. "Sage, please."

"What? It's a compliment."

"Her love language is creative violence." Sebastian dropped that like it was objective truth.

Sage elbowed him. "You pretend stoicism isn't emotional repression. Let me have this."

Killian looked at them both—his kids. His blood. For a man who'd spent his life in discipline and control, the emotion that flooded his chest came like a tide breaking a dam. Fierce and uncontainable.

He moved forward, resting a hand on Sebastian's shoulder, brushing his fingers gently through Sage's curls.

"I'll protect you. All of you. No matter what."

Seraphina folded her arms around herself, just for a moment. "We know this doesn't erase the years apart. Or the confusion. Or how fast it's all moving. But this… this is real."

Sebastian stared at the fireplace again. And slowly, something inside him let go.

It wasn't normal. It wasn't simple. But it felt right.

"It's all good with me. But if you start doing cheesy couple nicknames, I'm launching myself into low orbit."

Killian's mouth kicked up at one corner. He had to admit—the boy had a sense of humour.

He was going to need it for what was coming.

"Duly noted."

Sage beamed. "Oh my God, we have to tell everyone." She was already halfway out the door.

Seraphina hadn't realised how heavy it had all been—until it wasn't anymore. The relief came in a rush. Almost dizzying. Years of secrets gone, just like that.

They settled into the leather chesterfield tucked in the alcove, his hand covering hers. His thumb brushed her wrist, as if searching for proof she was still there.

Sebastian pushed off the mantle and dropped into the nearest chair, one foot thunking onto the coffee table—casual as a dare.

Seraphina looked over at her son. "Do you think they'll take it well?"

"If by take it well you mean Samthrax will have five sarcastic comments and Z will threaten mild violence, then yep."

Killian didn't argue. The kid wasn't wrong.

Sage called out from the foyer. "Alright, Grams—enough with the ghostly gallivanting! We've got news and a pot of coffee, so time's ticking!"

Saffron appeared in the doorway, every inch the serene spectre— until she opened her mouth. "Ghosts don't gallivant, darling. And we certainly don't need coffee. Though by all that's holy, I do miss it."

Samthrax entered, steaming coffee in one hand, half-finished cinnamon twist in the other. His curls were a tactical disaster, but somehow still smug about it. The mug read: I'm hexually frustrated. "Ugh. Who sprayed emotional stability in here? If this turns into a group hug, I'm combusting."

Sebastian took in his appearance and gestured lazily. "You lose a fight with a cursed broom?"

Samthrax sniffed. "It's called feral chic, wonderboy. I summoned caffeine and confidence. Both stuck."

Zinnia followed behind, unbothered, sipping from a black cup etched with a silver crescent. "Why do I feel an intervention coming?"

"No intervention." Sage had stopped bouncing and taken a seat. "We're doing the Big Reveal."

Zinnia looked between Killian and Seraphina. Her expression said it all: well, duh. "So… are we congratulating you two on finally admitting what everyone else already knew?"

Samthrax leaned in. "Ten bucks says they start making out, and we all have to blindfold ourselves and bleach our eyeballs."

Zinnia's face didn't move. "Make it twenty, and you've got a deal."

Sebastian fished a crumpled bill from his pocket. "Make it fifty, and I'll bring the bleach."

Seraphina shook her head, smiling despite herself. "Okay, clearly you already know. But I'm saying it anyway: Killian and I are officially a couple. He's moving into the estate. And we'll do our best to keep the eye-bleach moments to a minimum."

Saffron lit up. "Thank the gods. I was about this close to lighting a fire under both your arses."

"Because you never meddle." Seraphina didn't even bother to inject sarcasm—her mother wasn't slow on the uptake.

"Only when it's necessary." She turned to the twins, already shifting gears. "And you two?"

Sage was way ahead of her grandmother. *Two parents were far better than one when it came to getting away with shit, surely.*

"We're good with having Dad in our lives. If Mum ever says no, we now have backup. Options matter."

Killian barked a laugh before he could stop it. Seraphina didn't need words—just the look.

The maternal warning system that said: *Don't even think about it.*

"Checks and balances." Sebastian was only half joking. "It's only fair."

Zinnia tried to contain her mirth—but failed. "Honestly? I think it's great. You two have been hovering at nuclear flirtation levels. It's been kinda painful."

Samthrax sipped. "You know I get to call you 'Dad' now, right?"

Killian looked like he had swallowed his tongue. "No."

"Let me have this one thing."

The laughter that followed wasn't loud. But it was real.

Seraphina glanced around the room—this strange, stitched-together constellation of blood, legacy, and beautiful misfits.

They didn't know what was coming. But for this moment? They were whole.

And that, she thought, was more magic than anything else.

Twenty One

The flames in Brinnan's study burned black.

They danced low in the corner hearth—hungry, unnatural. They consumed nothing, yet still they fed like tongues of ink lapping at the stone.

He stood motionless before them, hands folded at his back, expression carved from polished malice. Behind him, the penthouse windows showed no sky—only a churning wall of mist. The city's heartbeat had been swallowed by storm and summoning.

He had called a presence through.

Not a demon. Not a spirit. Something older than myth. Older than decay. Something the world forgot on purpose.

The silence vibrated—brittle and strained, like a violin string pulled too tight. As if the laws of sound had fractured and now spoke in their own tongue.

Out of the fire, it came.

It did not arrive. It manifested—a rupture in the logic of space. Reality sagged inward, forced to make room for something that

264

refused to fit.

It wasn't cloaked in darkness.

It was composed of what existence had to forget. A shape sewn from collapsed timelines, entropy flowing like cloth. Light recoiled from it. Not in fear—light had no agency—but in refusal, as if even photons rejected proximity to what it was.

Its form was unstable, in flux. It churned with gravitational indecision. The ghost of a face surfaced—unravelling quasars coalescing into the vague suggestion of a skull—then scattered like dust before meaning could settle.

No eyes. Only convergences: red data-points, silver spirals, black apertures blinking in fractal sequence. They didn't see. They computed.

It radiated silence—not the absence of sound, but the cancellation of frequency.

Evil was too narrow a name. What stood there transcended intention entirely.

It was the Umbra Vitae.

A forsaken master of passage. Keeper of forbidden thresholds. The whisper behind sealed doors.

Brinnan inclined his head. "Thank you for answering my call. You know what I ask."

The being did not move, but its voice followed—a dry rasp, like a dead leaf dragged across slate.

"You seek the spell of unmaking. Not to destroy, but to become a shadow among shadows. To pass beneath wards not meant to bend."

Brinnan was steady as a rock. "I require passage through the old tunnels below Maison Bellarose. The protections are layered and complex. I must reach the Shadowkeep unseen."

"You are known to the wards. And what is known… is watched."

Conviction radiated off Brinnan. "Then un-know me."

The Umbra extended a hand.

Not flesh. Not claw. A curl of living dark—slick with void, twisting in defiance of form. The air around it thinned.

"One spell. Written not on page, but into space. Etched in fire. Remembered by pain. Once burned, it cannot be undone. Once used, it cannot be unbound."

Brinnan remained quiet, understanding there was more to come.

"You will not be man when you pass, you will be memory of form. And you will hunger."

Brinnan's lips curled. "I already do."

The Umbra's head inclined. It pointed to the far wall.

The hearth erupted—black and red fire exploding outward. A sound followed—not loud, but piercing, like a needle threading through bone.

The figure's hood rose—disturbed by nothing.

"It must be earned. Watched by no god. Spoken by no name."

The shadows on the wall convulsed.

In their wake, writing unfurled.

Twisted script etched itself into the surface—long black ribbons of living heat. Each line hissed as it formed. The plaster beneath began to blister and blacken.

The lost language of the First Mouth.

A tongue never given voice—because to speak it was to invite what waited to hear.

One word sank darker than the rest, as if ink had remembered how to bleed.

Thal'vesh.

Brinnan stood in reverent stillness. His lips moved, though no sound escaped.

He wasn't reading. Wasn't memorising. He was going to become.

The spell was never meant to be cast. It was meant to embed itself.

Dread moved ahead of the Umbra Vitae, whispering truths Brinnan longed to hear.

"You will pass unnoticed. You will unmake your shape into the absence of presence."

Satisfaction filled Brinnan. "This is what I choose."

"Once spoken. You cannot return unchanged. The Keep will close behind you. Gods will not look. What dreams beneath will not remember. This is the price of becoming unseen."

Brinnan's words came soft—too soft to be harmless. "I am done being seen. I intend to be obeyed."

The being bowed its head.

And folded backward into flame.

The hearth collapsed into silence. The wall smoked, exhaling the spell in a final benediction.

Brinnan turned toward the scrying bowl on the side table.

One breath. One drop of blood. It struck the surface, rippling into silver.

The liquid curled.

A face formed—Julian, seated in his study. Shirt half-undone, fingers pressed to his temple, as if sleep had become foreign. The instant the vision anchored, he stiffened.

"Father?"

"Come. Now."

Julian didn't argue. He never did when Brinnan used that tone.

He stepped through the summoning arch minutes later, boots echoing across the black tile. The moment he entered, he stopped.

Something was wrong.

The air in the room was thinner. Brittle at the edges. Bitter on the tongue.

His eyes drifted to the wall—where the exiled script still smouldered.

Julian's mouth tightened. "What the hell is that?"

Brinnan didn't look at him. "A solution. And a necessity."

Julian folded his arms, discomfort threading through him. He didn't like the way the magic crawled beneath his skin.

"What are we solving?"

Brinnan moved—not pacing, but circling. Mapping a perimeter. Drawing the outline of a new reality.

"They're strong. Killian. Seraphina. The demon. The twins. Alone, manageable. Together? Not so much."

Julian kept his mouth shut. His father didn't tolerate interruption.

Brinnan went on. "What the test proved is what I suspected: their strength isn't in raw power. It's in cohesion. Timing. They move like instinct—like they were always meant to fight side by side."

He turned back to the wall, where the final glyph still pulsed faintly— Thal'vesh.

"That kind of unity doesn't break with force. So... we don't push."

He looked at Julian. And smiled. "We slip."

"So, this incantation—what, allows us to sneak in under their nose?"

"Yes. It lets us cease to exist in the way the protections define presence. The house won't even know we're there."

Brinnan gestured to the burning script. "It's not subtle. But it's effective. Seraphina will come when I call. I'll weave this into her dreams. Draw her down while they sleep. No warning. No resistance. No war."

"You think she'll just walk into the Keep in a trance and open it for us?"

Brinnan gave him a look that asked, how had evolution failed so completely. "I don't think, I know. Seraphina's power is tied to legacy. But her mind is tied to her heart. I only need to pull the right thread."

Julian said nothing.

His silence wasn't consent—but it wasn't protest either. And Brinnan read him perfectly.

He gave a thin nod. Satisfied.

"And the Gateborn?" Purely rhetorical. Julian already knew the answer.

Brinnan was almost gleeful in his response. Very out of character for his father.

"Zinnia will be the Veil's mouthpiece. It's not her I want. It's what will respond to her."

Julian's stomach churned. The sound of Brinnan's conviction twisted inside him.

This wasn't the plan. Not the original one.

Brinnan had moved the pieces again. Realigned the board without warning, without consultation. And he'd done it with the calm certainty of a man no longer interested in power—but in transcendence.

Julian had spent years preparing—positioning himself as heir, shadow-master, eventual usurper. His path had been slow. Precise. Patient.

But this?

This was different.

This was Brinnan leaving the mortal scale behind.

Julian realised, with a quiet chill, that he might not be ready.

His mind flashed to Malrik.

Ambitious. Predictable. Useful—until he wasn't.

Brinnan had hollowed him like a gourd and filled the husk with obedience. No second chances. No sentiment. Only efficiency.

Julian knew the calculus. He'd seen it applied.

And he knew—if it turned on him—there would be no pause.

No mercy.

His throat was dry.

If I wait too long...

He didn't finish the thought. He didn't need to.

Once Brinnan entered the Shadowkeep, he would have what he

needed. Control. Access. Power enough to remake the world's foundation.

And me?

Julian smoothed his features into something neutral, measured and loyal.

But inside?

The clock had started ticking.

Julian Bellarose had no intention of becoming another ghost discarded on the altar of someone else's divinity.

Brinnan turned to the Thal'vesh, lifted his hand, and pressed his palm to the central glyph.

The room went black.

Words scorched their way across the floor, twisting into a spiral of ember-lit script.

But it wasn't flame.

It was the absence of light, curling upward into a ring. A circle of hunger. A wound in the fabric of creation.

Brinnan spoke the invocation. Once.

The language tore through the air—brutal and elegant. Julian couldn't understand it. Not fully. But it struck him anyway.

Not in the ears. In the bones.

The words embedded under the skin like hooks of fire.

His body convulsed. Then dissolved.

So did Brinnan.

Two shadows left the tower. Neither cast a reflection.

And far below, beneath the stones of Maison Bellarose… the Keep remembered old footsteps.

***

Maison Bellarose, 1:00 AM

Seraphina didn't stir in the usual way. Her eyes didn't flutter open, there was no gasp, no sudden lurch into wakefulness. She simply stood.

One moment she lay warm beside Killian; the next, she was on her feet—barefoot, dressed only in her nightshirt, the hem brushing her thighs as she walked slowly toward the door.

Nothing moved in the bedroom. Killian, anchored by the protective wards, remained asleep. Whatever magic pulled her from bed was needle-fine and subtle. The careful slip of silk through a seam—not a severing, but an undoing.

Her eyes were open. But they saw nothing.

She drifted with eerie grace, fingertips gliding along the wall in the dark. Her palm lit from within—silver threaded with green, stitched through with a third colour that didn't belong to this world.

Neither spellborn nor human.

It flexed. Then again.

She reached the Scriptorium.

The wards remained still—no flare of defence, no resistance. Only a nod of acceptance.

She passed the velvet chairs. The books quivered faintly in her wake. The drapery—long untouched—swayed in the heatless breeze she carried.

At the far bookcase, her hand rose. Glyphs carved in oath-bound secrecy snaked across the spines of age-darkened tomes. The moment her fingers touched them, the runes flared once—the case creaked.

The wall surrendered with the slow grace of something remembering how to yield. And the entrance to the Shadowkeep yawned open.

Deep within the house's foundation, a ward fluttered. Confused. Not enough to raise an alarm—just enough to wonder what it had missed.

Beyond the door, the stairwell spiralled into its roots. The scent shifted—not old books and candle smoke, but stone gone damp with years that never dried. Rust that had never known iron. Air that had forgotten the sun.

Her bare feet touched the first step. Then the next.

She descended—compelled—into black.

The darkness didn't repel her.

It curled toward her. Welcoming. Familiar.

A leftover promise made in a dream not her own.

And far above, behind a bedroom door that hadn't moved in hours, the protections didn't twitch.

Because no part of them recognised the threat.

***

Maison Bellarose — Upstairs, 1:05 AM

Samthrax woke suddenly.

An eye opened. Then the other gave up and joined it. He lay sprawled on the couch he'd claimed in Sebastian's room, one leg dangling off the side, hair a full-blown rebellion against gravity and good decisions.

He felt it in his fangs first. That old tension—shadow rubbing against shadow. A displacement.

A presence breached the boundary beneath the estate.

He pushed himself up and blinked once. "...Houston, we've got a problem."

With a grunt, he yanked a T-shirt over his head—inside out, naturally—and crept from the room without waking Sebastian.

In the hallway, he tapped two fingers to the floor. "Hey, ghostie. Rise and un-shine."

A distortion flexed in the night. The temperature dipped. Saffron emerged, her form wavering—like someone had traced her in frost with a trembling hand.

"Samthrax, why in all that's holy are you calling me at this hour?"

He tilted his head, more serious than usual. "Tell me you don't feel that."

She paused, narrowing her eyes. "Something's brushing the bones of this place."

"Exactly. And not in a 'hey-let's-have-tea' kind of way."

They moved swiftly through the halls. Samthrax's bare feet made no sound on the floorboards. Saffron floated beside him.

They slipped out the kitchen's side door and crossed the garden in silence. At the far edge, the iron gate marking the old tunnel entrance rose in stark silhouette against the night.

Samthrax bent down, running fingers over the threshold. His touch came away smeared in essence—not liquid. Not blood.

It stank of way worse.

Whatever had come through didn't belong.

He swore softly, in a language the world no longer claimed.

Saffron glanced at him. "We reinforced the lower wards. No one should be able to pass."

He looked up, eyes unusually sober. "Yeah. But something has."

They exchanged a look—the kind shared only by those who had seen too much.

And lost too many.

***

The tunnel breathed around them.

It wasn't air—it was the crawl of what had survived the unspeakable. The stone held a rhythm not meant for walking—funeral-paced and time-worn. The walls sweated with age, salt bleeding through seams. The ceiling sagged with old growth, damp and heavy above their heads.

Brinnan moved ahead without sound. More outline than man. His shadow-cloak absorbed the weak light like oil drinking flame. The concealment held. The wards registered nothing.

Julian followed.

Each step scraped deeper into a myth he'd once dismissed as

exaggeration. Not the tunnels—he'd known those existed. But the spell. The way it wormed beneath the skin, carved itself into thought and soul. It wasn't magic. It was consumption.

He glanced up. Roots broke through overhead, twisted in the shapes of old limbs. Water bled from the hairline splits. The ground vibrated.

His eyes locked onto his father's form.

"You always knew about these tunnels."

Brinnan didn't look back. "I was raised on this estate. I learned its bones before I learned my own."

They reached a narrowing curve that opened into a vast, forgotten chamber.

A pale wound cleaved the far wall. Cold spilled from it—deep and ageless.

The breach point. The hidden entrance to the Shadowkeep's spinal corridor.

Julian slowed. His gaze skimmed the floor—wet with glyphs cut into the stone, symbols of dominion and restraint. Old magic. Darker than Brinnan had shared.

His nerves lit up—sudden and involuntary.

This wasn't the plan.

Brinnan hadn't told him about this route until an hour ago. Julian had his own strategy. His own timeline—years in the making.

Now? Everything was accelerating. And he was no longer in control.

"You're sure she's coming?"

Brinnan's demeanour radiated unwavering confidence. "She's already halfway down the stairs. I gave her a memory—one laced with longing."

Julian's unease grew. Not because he cared about Seraphina. But because he hadn't foreseen this kind of manipulation.

A tool used without noise. Without resistance. Total control... without force.

That was terrifying.

Julian's mind spun with recalculations.

He had counted on letting Brinnan take the fall—draw the blood, pay the price, and leave the scraps behind. Instead, he watched the man shape prophecy in his palm.

And now Julian wasn't sure he'd done the math right. The numbers weren't just shifting—they were multiplying without him.

He glanced at the fading spellmark under Brinnan's sleeve—Thal'vesh, glowing faintly beneath the skin.

He would have to move fast. Once inside the Keep, there would be no margin for hesitation.

Brinnan turned toward him, as if attuned to the shadows threading through his thoughts.

"You still doubt?"

Julian knew better than to show weakness. "I doubt everything. But I don't make moves without options."

Brinnan's smile bent the rules of what a human expression should be. "Good. You'll need that edge."

He looked back to the fault in the stone.

"She'll open it in trance. There will be no struggle, no alarms. And once I have the Grimoire and the portal, she's unnecessary. The Gateborn will follow soon enough."

Julian didn't respond. He thought again of how Brinnan had unmade Malrik—hollowed him out and turned him into a sheath for something foul.

How quickly loyalty became liability.

He'd be next.

Unless he moved first.

Brinnan placed his palm against the stone.

It responded like flesh beneath his hand—flexing, resisting, then relenting.

The fault groaned open. A seam peeled wide enough for two shadows to pass.

Beyond it, the Shadowkeep exhaled.

Julian shivered.

Not from chill.

From the stark realisation that his father had outmanoeuvred him.

They stepped into the dark.

And waited.

****

Down the stairwell, Seraphina took the last step.

The final note of the descent cascaded outward—like a bell tolling through the ruin where faith once lived.

Her eyes were open but unseeing, irises glazed with the pearlescent sheen of trance. The sigils around her wrists—usually dormant— flickered faintly, reacting to long-forgotten magic.

Behind her gaze: a place she knew. Wild roses, overgrown. Sunlight. Killian's voice in the distance—softer than they had ever been in reality. Urging her back. Drawing her home.

But something in the light was wrong. Too golden. Too perfect. A fiction her mind believed in the guise of truth. A lie wrapped soft as a lullaby.

She walked forward. Barefoot. A whisper of cotton brushed against her skin.

Somewhere under the silk-thin dream, a piece of her screamed.

But it was too small. Too quiet. The story was louder.

The doorway yawned open—she passed through it.

The Shadowkeep welcomed her.

A vast, circular space beneath the earth—its walls ribbed with old bone and glistening stone. Pleas for release echoed through it. The imprisoned Grimoire called to her—not with words, but with a tug at her nerves, the kind that knew where the soft parts hid.

She stepped to the edge of the podium's reach—and stopped, still as glass before the shatter.

Behind her, Brinnan came through the doorway.

A formless silhouette unspooling into his usual shape. Thal'vesh clung to his shoulders, twitching at the edges, refusing to settle. His eyes, when they found Seraphina, gleamed with the satisfaction of plans fulfilled.

Julian followed. The room allowed him to pass without acknowledgment.

He was awestruck and apprehensive all at once. He'd never set foot in the Keep—only heard what it was supposed to hold. Things even nightmares refused to remember. Treasure trove didn't begin to cover it. With luck, he'd get to crack a few locks.

They moved to the centre. Seraphina didn't react.

Julian watched her. She'd hate knowing how easy it had been to bend her.

"She opened it."

Brinnan nodded. "As expected."

He reached toward her—not touching, just hovering his palm near her temple. "She's adrift in the dream I chose."

Julian's eyes landed on the grimoire. He felt it immediately.

Not with sight—but with something buried beneath thought.

A pressure grinding against his shadow. A weight clawing at his soul.

It wasn't asking politely. It wanted out.

"This is where you remove her?"

Brinnan's focus remained on Seraphina. "She has fulfilled her function."

Julian frowned.

Not because of doubt—because of the tone.

So absolute it left no room for partnership.

Behind them, the chamber walls shivered.

A sound—too high, too faint for mortals.

But not for demons.

***

Samthrax crouched beside the iron gate at the garden's edge, his clawed hand hovering over the entrance to the old network beneath the estate. The residue clung to his fingers, congealing like blood under the moonlight.

Knowing rose—bone-deep. Not shadow magic—this was older. The kind of power that named things and made them kneel.

It was rooted under the barrier. A curse with petals, blooming only for the marked.

A cold spasm slid across his shoulders. His nostrils flared. Every instinct sharpened. He tilted his head, ears homing in on a sound most creatures would never hear.

A click. Gear meeting gear. Stone accepting command.

The door to the Shadowkeep.

It was open.

Samthrax's pupils slit wide. Demonic energy sparked in his throat. "Shit."

"What is it?" Saffron knew when Samthrax got serious, that meant things had just gone to hell.

Samthrax rose to his feet, claws flexing, expression carved from an emotion so rare on him it was almost unrecognisable—fear.

"Seraphina's down there—someone's made her open the Keep."

Disbelief rippled through Saffron's form. "No. That's—she wouldn't—"

"She did. Or more likely, she was puppeteer'd. That door only opens to her blood. Someone twisted their way into her mind—and there's only one arsehole alive who could slip past the wards and do it."

He held up his hand. The black residue glistened. Realisation hit like a freight train.

"This is Thal'vesh. It doesn't break, it bypasses."

He was going to tear that bastard apart.

"It's old. It's vile. And it works."

He turned to Saffron, fangs bared. "Get Killian. Wake the whole damn estate. If they're in the Keep, we're already late."

Saffron didn't argue. She vanished mid-breath.

Samthrax ran.

All speed. All fury.

The kitchen door exploded open. He tore through it, claws hammering the floor. Light flared along the glyph-etched walls. The house stirred. Pages fluttered. Shields rose.

Every protective rune screamed awake.

He hit the Scriptorium like a bomb.

The hidden passage behind the bookshelf gaped wide—waiting.

The moment Samthrax crossed the threshold, the shift took him.

Gone was the flirt. The chaos gremlin. The smirking devil-in-drapes.

What descended was demon. True demon.

His skin blackened, runes crawling to life across his chest and neck. His horns curled behind him like blades ready to impale. Wings erupted from his back—not feathered, but serrated, rimmed with heatless black flame and crusted with flaked bone-char and scorched sinew.

His spine lengthened. His jaw unhinged with a low, grinding click. His mouth opened—a cavern of fangs made for banishment, not speech. His eyes burned: concentric rings of fury and ruin.

When he roared, the underworld stirred.

"Brinnan!"

Stone shook.

The spiral corridor narrowed, but Samthrax didn't slow. Air

recoiled. Magic fled.

He landed.

The Shadowkeep waited. Samthrax stood at its opening—not the irreverent menace who lounged in chandeliers or flirted shamelessly.

This was something else. This was dangerous.

He had come to guard what mattered.

Brinnan might wield shadow. Julian might deal in betrayal. But Samthrax had walked through ages that burned entire realms to ash—and he hadn't broken.

Brinnan and Julian wanted war? Then bring it.

He was what war broke against.

And nothing—nothing—was getting past him.

At the centre of the chamber stood Seraphina.

One arm extended toward the podium at the Keep's core. She was in a trance so deep it might have been death, if not for the silver thread of breath at her lips.

And at her back—Brinnan. Wreathed in the folds of the Thal'vesh. His form barely there. A shadow worn like skin.

And beside him, a spectre of silence and calculation—Julian.

Samthrax growled low. The sound reverberated through the Keep. His entire body shook with thinly veiled violence—rage held just behind the bone.

"You bastard." Power punched through the syllables. "You broke into her mind."

Brinnan turned. His mouth curled. "Spare me the theatrics, demon. She's perfectly fine."

His confidence in his ultimate success was apparent.

"We're here for the Grimoire and the Portal. If you agree to turn a blind eye while we go about our business, perhaps we can come to an arrangement?"

Samthrax stepped further into the chamber. Memories surfaced—

of his own time caged within these walls, not so long ago. He didn't want to be here. But he wasn't letting these two-rewrite reality while he stood still.

His wings arched—vast enough to smother the corridor's light.

He loomed, horned and burning, his voice all about infernal.

"Not likely. I know bullshit when I'm looking at it, Brinnan."

Brinnan's smile didn't reach his eyes. It rarely did.

"Interesting and unexpected—a demon who protects. Nevertheless, it's too late. You can't stop me."

Samthrax opened his mouth in a parody of a grin. Not kindly. Not human.

Flames licked up his arms, catching in the seams of his skin.

"Watch me."

And he lunged.

***

"Killian!"

The voice tore through the dark.

He was on his feet in an instant, magic spilling from his hands before his brain caught up. Saffron stood at the foot of the bed, her aura spasming—too bright. Too erratic. Panic in lightform.

"Seraphina's opened the Keep."

He didn't speak. Didn't ask questions.

He slammed his palm against the sigil panel by the door.

The wards responded with a screech—high, flayed, furious.

Doors banged open along the corridor—wood cracking like gunfire.

Sage stumbled out, her nightshirt still softly sparking from the enchantments she'd fallen asleep reading. Behind her, Sebastian emerged—T-shirt twisted, one hand half-formed, magic already leaping to his palm. Zinnia followed, hair in wild spikes, wearing a monstrous green Shrek tee that looked suspiciously borrowed.

Samthrax was nowhere in sight.

Zinnia covered her ears with a pained expression on her face. "What the hell is that screaming?"

Killian sliced through the uproar.

"Seraphina's in the Keep."

Everything stopped. Time didn't break—but some mechanism within it stalled.

"No. Mum wouldn't do that." Doubt flickered through Sebastian. Would she?

"She's in a trance," Saffron met his eyes. "Samthrax found the entrance tampered with. Something passed through into the tunnels. He told me to wake you while he went after her."

Killian was already moving.

Down the stairs. Into the foyer. The others fell in behind him, feet pounding, energy wild and untethered. Magic surged through their veins—an unspoken alarm in every heartbeat.

He flew into the Scriptorium.

The chandelier above spun slowly—its glow had turned ruddy. War-blood red.

The hidden passage at the rear stood ajar.

Killian pivoted to face them. The light seemed to pull back from his silhouette.

Darkness bled from beneath his feet, spiralling upward in slow, deliberate arcs. It wrapped around his shoulders, sank into his shirt, laced down his arms in virulent veins of shadowbound magic. A plume of vapour escaped him—not from cold, but from the force building inside.

When he spoke, it was a command. Not loud, but immovable.

"No one enters until I do. Stay close. Do not touch anything unless I say so."

The house braced itself.

He turned to the twins, meeting their gaze—his children, yes, but also his last line of defence if this went wrong.

"You may need to channel the prophecy magic. Together."

Sebastian's eyes widened. His core blinked once, and the rest of him missed it. A slow ribbon of darkness slipped across his vision, settling beneath his pupils like thunder learning to speak.

"I don't know if I can. We haven't used that kind of power yet."

Killian got it—his son's magic was barely under control on a good day. But this wasn't a good day. They were out of time.

"You don't have to know how. You only have to trust each other."

Sage's fingers closed around the obsidian pendant at her throat. Her face was calm like she was already braced for impact.

"I've got him."

Sebastian looked at her. Not questioning. Just seeing.

And the fear, though it didn't leave him, took a back seat.

Zinnia cracked her knuckles. "I don't know what I can do, but I'll do it anyway."

There was no bravado in her voice. No bluff. Only raw honesty—and a courage born from the wreckage of too many days survived when survival shouldn't have been possible.

Killian looked at her for a second longer than the others.

"You're more than you realise. When the moment comes—your instincts will be louder than fear."

The Les Revenantes words threaded behind her thoughts: You are chosen. You are remembered.

She gave a single, exact nod. Her eyes blazed.

Killian turned forward.

Shadow gathered around him—an armour of long knowing and intent.

He raised a hand.

The glyphs lining the stairwell stirred with luminescence—silver and red. Not in warning. In recognition.

The Keep had opened for Seraphina.

Now, it made way for him.

"Let's finish this."

He stepped into the dark.

Behind him, the twins followed—light and shadow, prophecy and potential, side by side.

Zinnia came last.

A current surged through her.

Her fingers tingled, raw with power that had no name yet.

She didn't look back.

Because ahead—monsters had begun to move.

And no gods stood guard at the gate.

Twenty Two

Cold climbed the stairs in curling sheets, clinging to the walls.

Energy bristled, raw and feral, quivering through the beams, worming into the stone with a fever's sting.

Not the clean hum of the wards or the warm pulse of protection. No—this tasted of evil. It stretched the skin too tight and made your heartbeat stagger.

The deeper they descended, the more the world narrowed.

First came footfalls. Then breath.

Until all that remained was the low, seismic throb of rising seals, stirring for war.

They reached the bottom—and the instant their feet touched the stone floor of the Shadowkeep, it answered. The air slammed into their lungs. Choking. Dense.

The walls groaned—no metaphor, no illusion.

Veins of forsworn sigils fractured and spat light, raking along carved rock. Fire chewed through nerve. Crimson bled, threaded with oil-slick blue.

Above, the ceiling flexed—like wet rope strung to breaking.

The Keep was awake. And it was not pleased.

The first shockwave hit. Demon magic.

Wild and furious.

A bolt of raw power screamed across the chamber—black and red—smashing into the far curve of the wall in a blast that rattled the spine of the room.

Stone smoked. Glyphs hissed. Dust fell in a fine, silver rain.

"Move faster, you bloody peacocks!"

No panic. No plea. Straight up command.

Samthrax welcomed the old him back. Personal growth could wait.

Right now? He wanted to destroy something.

Killian didn't acknowledge. He just moved. Body primed.

Shadow flared up his arms—hot, deliberate, lethal.

His shirt whipped around him, every step pure, controlled rage.

"Eyes open. Stay sharp."

Sage flinched at the flare of wardlight, but her stride never broke. The pendant at her throat had gone ice-cold—narrowing her focus like a noose. Her fingers twitched, already tracing the first sigils she'd taught herself in secret.

She promised herself she would freak out later.

Right now, she had to move.

"We've got this."

Tension knotted in Sebastian's chest. Darkness pooled at his fingertips, twitching beneath the skin.

He wasn't ready. Not fully.

But Sage was beside him. And their magic moved toward each other, drawn. Rising.

Something else rose with it.

That familiar whisper. *Let go. Let it all go.*

It brushed the edge of his mind—hungry. He blinked hard, forcing it down.

Not now. "Please hold the line. Don't get freakin' possessed down here."

Zinnia's mark blazed white-hot, searing through fabric. The tang of scorched spellwork slammed into her nose—bitter, metallic, chemical.

She gritted her teeth, took the fear and hammered it into resolve.

"Alright, monster-boys. Let's see what the new girl can do."

Killian swept the chamber with a soldier's eye—quick, trained, brutal.

He found Seraphina.

Two hits at once. First, a burst of rage—*raw, blinding,* Brinnan's violation burning through him.

Second, the Oh, *shit.* Because now he saw what she was doing.

She stood dead centre, one hand on the sarcophagus housing the Grimoire.

Eyes wide. Unseeing.

Her other hand trembled—caught mid-air, trapped between casting and recoil.

Like even her instincts couldn't decide if this was salvation or suicide.

Fine cracks spidered beneath her palm. The artifact inside floated—humming, impatient to be free.

Brinnan stood beside her, whispering something into her ear.

Zinnia's blood turned to ice. "She's definitely in a trance—"

Killian didn't wait. He lunged. Dark power burst from his hands in writhing bands, smoke-wrapped and furious. The ground cracked under his boots. "Get away from her!"

Brinnan pivoted. Slow. Lazy. Smiling. He showed no reaction. Made no move to dodge.

Killian's magic slammed into his chest—and passed straight through. He skidded to a halt. *Shit. That didn't bode well.* "He's not even real!"

"Thal'vesh! He's cloaked—not present the way the Keep defines presence! You can't hit smoke with a blade!" Samthrax realised he probably should've led with that.

"Then how do I make him solid?"

"Via blood-shadow! He's riding banished magic. You need something older. Yours—and Seb's. That spell only bows to extreme darkness."

"And Seraphina?"

"She's caught in a memory-loop. He's got her running it like a cursed lullaby with no off switch."

Killian turned to the twins.

"Sage. Sebastian. Break it. You're blood—that might be enough to cut it loose."

Sage stopped breathing.

Talk about being thrown in at the deep end.

"What kind of loop?!"

No one answered.

Seraphina's hand pressed harder against the glass. The Grimoire shuddered.

She was unlocking it.

Sage's instincts kicked in. She grabbed Sebastian's wrist and pulled them both into the warped radius of air.

Pressure thickened.

Sound distorted.

Light bent.

The magic here refused entry—guarding its own.

"I can see it."

Sebastian's throat went dry.

He couldn't see squat. "What is it?"

"She's chasing Dad's voice. She doesn't remember choosing us."

Sebastian steadied himself.

"Then we remind her."

Sage nodded. "Follow my lead."

They dropped to their knees—one on each side of Seraphina—hands hovering above cold stone. Reality writhed. Dream-magic snapped.

Sage reached for her pendant.

"On three."

Sebastian gave a quick nod.

Here goes nothing. "One… two… three—"

They struck the floor, palms to sigil.

Twin star-veins erupted—Sage's bright, celestial; Sebastian's slow, molten, like gravity breaking open.

The bind cracked. The spell screamed.

Tendrils of shadow lashed their arms, their throats—trying to choke the connection.

But they held.

"Mum!" Sage had to break through this madness.

"This isn't real. Brinnan put you here. We are now. We're here!"

Sebastian was having a shot of anything alcoholic if they got through this. *Age be damned.*

"Dad's here with us! We're a family, Mum. Completely dysfunctional. But it works. Choose this moment." The illusion flickered. A fracture crept through it, light peeling at the edges, unravelling outward in broken filaments.

Seraphina's head twitched.

Her fingers curled.

A sudden, seething screech tore through the chamber.

The stone wailed.

The glyphs vibrated in protest, dragging the heat from the room.

Brinnan spun—his eyes burning wild, his features warped, barely human. "No!"

He hurled a searing shard of black entropy streaked with violet flame.

It surged at the twins, snarling with intent to unravel.

But Killian was already moving.

His arm snapped up—magic roaring in his blood, boiling to the surface.

A tendril of shadow burst from his palm—not cast but born.

Fast as thought.

Furious as vengeance.

It whipped through the air, caught Brinnan across the chest, and bound—a living chain of smoke and ancestral wrath, tightening by the second.

"You touch my children again, and it will be the last thing you do."

The promise landed before the words did. Killian wasn't threatening. He was delivering a fact.

Brinnan snarled, magic breaking off him in sharp bursts. Waves of raw power scorched the Keep's edges.

But the tether held—blood-forged and rage-locked.

This wasn't supposed to hold. Not against him.

Behind him—Sage shouted again. "Mum—listen to me. You already made the right choice. You're ours."

Sebastian's eyes glowed. Darkness crawled beneath his skin.

He didn't command it. But it wasn't pushing back.

Whatever lived inside him… was learning his rhythm too.

"Come back to us. Come back where you belong."

The dream-snare shattered. Magic ruptured. Light detonated.

The spell blew apart. Sigils ripped from the floor.

Runes tore free from stone. Arcane remnants scattered like ash.

Seraphina gasped—lungs pulling air she hadn't known she'd missed.

Her eyes snapped open. Wide. Wet. Clear.

Bloody Nora.

Her children.

She'd nearly lost them. Not to war. Not to magic. To a lie. A dream that wasn't even hers.

Her hand fell from the glass. She staggered, caught herself—chest heaving, skin cold. Her soul felt torn, scraped raw, like it had clawed its way back into her body.

The Grimoire shrieked once—high, furious, demonic—and sagged into stillness. Contained and unopened.

Seraphina blinked hard, vision swimming.

She saw Sage and Sebastian—kneeling, panting.

Eyes locked on hers.

And she knew.

Knew where she was.

Who she was.

What they'd just pulled her back from.

Behind them, Brinnan screamed—not with fear, but fury.

He exploded out of Killian's tether in a shockwave of force.

The shadows peeled away in shuddering sheets, shattering the glyphs clinging to his limbs.

Killian moved. Fast. Shadow wrapped every inch of him—a deep magic scarred by history.

He opened to it. The dark knew him, and he knew it. That was enough.

Power surged.

Seraphina turned to him. She looked ready to kill Brinnan herself. "Stop him."

Killian didn't need the order twice.

He raised both hands.

And the darkness obeyed.

***

Across the chamber, Samthrax bellowed—lunging for Julian with the force of a thousand storms.

He had Julian's shadow cornered.

291

Pinned against the stone, the shape convulsed—warped and splintering, a reflection barely holding form. Tendrils of demon magic clenched around it, woven from fire, ruin, and old power that didn't ask permission.

The Thal'vesh still cloaked Julian in half-presence, but Samthrax had fought things worse than shadows older than lies.

His grin turned predatory. Horns arched. Fangs bared. This?

This was personal.

Sigils flared beneath him—alive with heat that had nothing to do with flame.

The runes answered his rhythm: slow. Deliberate. Lethal.

He crouched low, claws raking glowing lines through the stone. "Oh, this is going to hurt you in ways your daddy never warned you about."

Julian's shadow shrieked—a tangle of static and despair.

Samthrax rumbled with dark amusement—a sound refracted through several dimensions, layered in octaves not meant for mortal ears.

It had been centuries since he'd done this.

Not since the fall of the Umbral Sanctum.

Not since the Chains of Varn still steamed with the screams of their last betrayer.

But the flow returned. Instinct. Hunger honed into protection.

He didn't aim for the shadow.

That would've been too kind.

Instead, he reached for the tether—the root.

The thread that bound Julian to the veil.

He remembered what it felt like to be pulled from the dark before you were ready.

This was gonna sting. Good.

His fingers curled through the oldest of the floor glyphs, tracing the pattern not in arcana, but in memory.

The boundary tore.

Thal'vesh screamed.

And Julian came apart.

There was no elegance to the return. No grace. Only the wet, ruptured sound of magic being turned inside out.

Reality buckled—then spat him out.

Julian hit the Keep's floor hard. Shoulder first. Limbs sprawling. Runes scraping skin. He skidded through chalk-scorched glyphs, coughing on dust and pain.

The impact hollowed the ground around them.

He wheezed, lungs trying to remember how to draw air. "What—what the hell—"

Everything felt inside out. And he knew this demon was only getting started.

Samthrax didn't wait. He roared a word spoken before the world took shape.

Pulled from the dead language of the Third Gate.

Reality ripped.

A vertical wound opened behind Julian—stitched in shadow and light, lined with sigils meant to hold gods.

And through it came the Hellwraith.

Born from evil.

All chain and claw.

A body haloed in smoke, bound by iron script. Each length of binding dragged a rune of ensnaring—words forged to imprison what no prison ever could.

Julian twisted, eyes wide. "No. No—wait—"

He scrambled backward, boots skidding across the floor, but the chains were already flying.

They snapped forward and locked around his chest, his legs, his arms, his throat.

He screamed—not from pain, but from disbelief.

This wasn't how his story ended.

The Wraith dragged him closer, ignoring his flailing, his shouting, his curses.

"Father!"

No answer.

"Help me—"

The other side of the chamber offered nothing back.

Samthrax tilted his head.

Light spilled from his claws—molten, unnatural. "No rescue arsehat. Not this time."

He stepped forward, towering over the boy who'd tried to wear a crown in his father's image.

"Straight to hell. Express service and no return trip."

Julian howled as the Wraith yanked him backward.

Into the tear. Into the dark. Into the maw.

A razorburst flared from the rift—final and blinding.

The chains retracted. The rift sealed.

The aftermath scraped against the edges of sense.

Samthrax didn't move.

He let the last curl of smoke vanish from his fingers, his eyes burning with that bottomless, older-than-sin fire.

He exhaled once—steam bleeding from between his teeth.

One threat down. One to go.

He turned slowly toward the chaos still erupting.

The Grimoire pulsed in its cage.

Brinnan unravelled across the chamber.

And Julian's scream rang through the stone.

And somewhere behind that sealed seam of reality, he was still echoing. Still screaming. Or maybe… something else was.

Samthrax cracked his neck and stepped back into the fray.

"Let's finish this."

***

The Keep came alive.

Not with sound—but with pressure that gripped the skeleton itself.

Magic clawed through the room.

Sigils blazed on the walls.

The Grimoire stammered in dissonant beats, flaring with warning, fury, hunger.

Across the floor, Brinnan burned.

Not in flame.

Not in agony. In power.

His form had begun to unravel—his face flickering in and out of human shape.

Something old and terrible surged beneath the surface, breaching the seams of his illusion.

He was no longer a man.

He was something born from history's blind spots and bloodied pages.

Ruin had crowned him.

Darkness poured from his spine in slow, deliberate waves—heavy with ritual, soaked in intent, dripping the memory of sacrifices carved in screaming flesh.

His robes disintegrated into smoke.

Fissures spidered beneath his skin, and from the opened seams, raw shadow bled out—unbound, sentient, ravenous.

Killian stood across from him, body locked in purpose.

The two of them held each other in their gaze—one forged in order, the other in undoing.

Killian didn't know what Brinnan had become. But whatever it was, it reeked of ending. "You've lost."

Brinnan was all teeth.

Exultant. Lit from within by something unholy.

The moment he'd chased—here. Almost complete.

"You think this is defeat? You fool. This is ascension."

He raised both hands—and the keep convulsed.

A faultline tore wide at the chamber's core.

From it, tethers surged—dark ropes of thought-born magic. They writhed, lashed, seeking purchase.

"Incoming!" Sebastian was already moving.

Killian threw up a ward.

It caught the initial tether—the force slammed him into a column. Dust exploded. His head snapped sideways—but he didn't fall.

Another tether unfurled—whipping past Sage, reaching for the Grimoire and missed—the third found its target.

Zinnia.

She turned—too late.

The shadows swallowed her legs first. Next her waist. Her throat followed.

Claws of dark energy clamped around her wrists, wrenching her arms wide.

Her mark flared—white-hot, wild.

But the tethers didn't burn.

They fed.

She gasped. Magic surged—raw, untrained, violent.

But the bindings didn't snap.

They didn't crush her.

They claimed her.

With the certainty of prophecy. The precision of fate.

No. Not like this. I am not going to die today.

"Zinnia!" Sage's scream ripped the air.

Brinnan turned toward her—his face no longer human, his voice an invocation.

"Gateborn."

He said it not with awe, but with ownership.

A benediction.

Zinnia thrashed, every nerve screaming.

The power inside her tried to break free—but the bindings only tightened, drawing strength from what they held.

"You are the beginning. And the end. The lock. The key."

Killian moved—but Brinnan's spell was already at work.

He didn't cast her.

He offered her.

"May the Veil open."

The tethers reached their limit—then snapped like rigging in a storm.

And hurled Zinnia into the portal.

One brutal motion.

Air folded around her.

Her scream tore through the chamber—full and final.

The portal flared—pale silver, veined in ink-dark magic.

It sealed shut.

No trace left.

Just—gone.

Everything stopped.

The Grimoire quieted—its radiance fading, its hunger retreating.

Seraphina dropped to her knees.

Sebastian stood frozen, hands twitching with power and disbelief.

Sage didn't move.

Her fingers still reached for a girl who wasn't there anymore.

Her mind refused to follow. If she acknowledged it, she'd break.

Samthrax howled.

A sound old as grief.

Old as fire.

Old as every god who failed to listen.

The Keep heaved. Glyphs sputtered. The ceiling groaned.

His wings ignited—shadowfire racing through the veins of smoke and wrath.

He turned to Brinnan.

He wasn't fury.

He was pure vengeance.

"You're not walking out of here." His voice split in four—low, divine, death-bound.

Brinnan laughed—once. A hollow bark of something already lost.

In the next breath he vanished.

Through shadow.

Into absence.

The portal sealed.

Magic imploded, curling in on itself like muscle gone slack.

Silence returned—so heavy it pressed on the ears.

The Keep was still.

Only the imprint of Zinnia's scream remained.

And the promise of retribution.

Twenty Three

"We thought the story paused when she fell through the portal.
We were wrong. That was the ignition point. And now?
Now we burn our way through time to bring her back."
— Samthrax, demon-forged, grief-armored, flame-bound and ready

The Council Chamber did not stir. It bore witness—and nothing more.

The great onyx table sat at the heart of the room; a monolith etched in dead tongues and bound by blood-inked sigils. A dry, metallic tang clung to the air, as if the room itself remembered sacrifice. Above its centre, the Looking Dome swirled, casting flickering visions in coldfire and flame across the walls.

Twelve seats encircled the table. Only nine were occupied.

Within the Dome, the final moments of the Shadowkeep battle played out in spectral detail. A three-dimensional mirage—shivering light and memory, stitched into momentary truth. Zinnia's body arcing through the air. Her scream. The portal closing.

Even after the vision faded, the moment hung suspended—an unstruck bell, heavy with what lingered.

Edevane finally exhaled. A sound like wind through a crypt—one part theatre, one part self-soothing. Relief settled over him. He hadn't realised how close it had come to unravelling.

"It's confirmed. The Gateborn is gone."

No remorse. Just the pleasure of eliminating a complication.

Yvane's crimson nails tapped against the table. A coded rhythm—her version of a blade to the throat.

She could smell weakness. She scented it on him.

"Yes, but not slain—only displaced. That was never part of the original plan."

"Displaced is better than here." Salen tossed in from the far end. He hadn't spoken in half an hour. His silence always meant something was already in motion.

"Plans bend." Maltren delivered it as doctrine, not opinion.

The carved side of his face caught the Dome's fading light—his other half unreadable by design. He enjoyed these cracks in consensus. They made room for him.

"As the Veil bends, so do our designs. This one may yet snap."

Edevane leaned forward a fraction. Always the scholar. Always ten steps ahead in theory. Never comfortable when chaos veered off-script.

He spoke to the Dome, not the others. They didn't deserve the full shape of his genius.

"It was never about destruction. It was containment. The Grimoire. The portal. The Keeper and the Gateborn. Too much in one place. Too much risk."

A chill crept through the chamber.

Yvane offered the barest shift of acknowledgment—just enough to imply consent.

She conceded. Not because she was convinced. Because the move served her.

"We agreed when the prophecy resurfaced, that should the legacies converge, intervention was required. With her absence, the chain weakens. Therefore, the threat lessens."

"For the moment." Maltren stayed silent after. Not out of caution—out of discipline.

The best pieces were never visible until checkmate.

"And the Keeper? Seraphina still remains." Varas didn't sit so much as recline in ownership. Dusk-magic clung to her eyes the way her ego clung to her soul. "She opened the Keep under trance influence."

Yvane folded her hands and schooled her features. "That's forgivable. Her line is bound to Maison Bellarose. We can use that."

Maltren didn't move. "Killian will not allow you to use anything."

And he would know. He'd buried better plans than this.

"We're not asking." Yvane didn't need volume. Authority came dressed in certainty.

The Looking Dome flickered again, then began to hum—a low, bone-deep sound, barely audible.

This time it showed the aftermath: Killian knelt beside Seraphina, arms braced against the bloodied ground, his head bowed—not just in grief, but in fury. The twins, clutching one another. Samthrax, pacing at the chamber's edge, fire rippling across his skin, unable to be still.

"And the demon?"

Varas made no effort to soften the question. Precision was its own kind of cruelty.

"Will he become a threat?"

"He's dangerous," Salen drawled from the shadows. "And angry. But he's tethered."

"For now." Edevane wasn't one to hedge bets—and this case needed to be monitored.

Silence followed. It wasn't passive—it was individual assessment.

Edevane shifted again. Just enough to show intent.

"Do we call it?"

Varas arched one perfect brow. "Initiate Phase Two?"

Edevane delivered the facts like he was delivering a sermon. "The

Keep is awake. The Gateborn is gone. The Grimoire nearly freed. This was only the first breach. There will be more—whether from inside or beyond."

Yvane smiled. The kind of gesture that meant the decision had been made hours ago. "Then we make sure she never comes back."

Her fingers moved again—three taps this time. A message sent through the mirrored relay beneath the table.

Her agent would be in place before the next breach.

Maltren spoke before consensus could form. "And if she does?"

No one answered. Because they didn't know.

But all eyes turned once more to the Looking Dome—now empty. Where Zinnia had vanished into the portal.

And they began to plan. Not for her rescue.

But for the reckoning her return might bring.

***

The Scriptorium felt suspended, the wreckage contained but not yet understood.

The table had been cleared of everything but candles. Dozens of them, their flames wavered against the windows, trembling in the draft.

The room carried the trace of spent magic—shadowfire, blood, and silence.

Killian scanned the chamber. Everyone was there. And still, it felt empty.

He had barely spoken since they'd returned. His gaze hadn't left the door. Like if he watched hard enough, the impossible might reverse itself. Like sheer intent could drag her back.

He'd seen war. Lost men. Killed worse.

But this? This was a hole. And he was already falling.

Seraphina's hands stayed folded in her lap, knuckles drained of colour. Her curls stuck to her temples, sweat-damp and unkempt.

The look on Zinnia's face when she realized no one could save her—
She couldn't scrub it from her mind.

Magic simmered under her skin—too fractured to wield, too wild to trust.

Saffron hovered behind her daughter. Dulled by grief. Anchored by rage. And beneath both: guilt.

How had she not seen this coming?

Sage moved in slow, deliberate lines in front of the tall bookshelves. Her fingers dragged over the spines without focus. The pendant at her throat hummed—a leftover heartbeat of magic. Her face was pale, her features swollen from weeping.

Fury and despair took turns holding her together. One to keep moving. One to stop the scream trying to claw its way out.

Sebastian had dropped into the chaise the second they got back. His shadow-magic twitched beneath his skin, agitated. His knuckles were scraped. His eyes were bloodshot.

But not from crying. That would've been release. And letting go meant admitting she was gone.

He wasn't ready to make peace with a universe that allowed that.

Samthrax sat on the edge of the table, one sleeve torn, boots crusted in ash and mud. His jacket lay forgotten somewhere in the corridor. Shadows curled from his shoulders in lazy spirals. His face unreadable.

He held a mug in one hand. The steam had long since faded. It read: *I Came. I Saw. I Set It On Fire.*

Should've added: And it still wasn't enough.

The irony hovered, bold as graffiti on a crumbling wall.

No one spoke. Each of them trying to make sense of something so senseless.

"We have to get her back."

The words tore out of Sage. She hadn't even known she was going to say anything. But now that it was out—there was no maybe in it.

No room for debate.

Zinnia was family. And anyone who stood in the way of that? Was a problem.

Samthrax didn't speak at first. Not because he was calm—because anger like his needed time to aim.

This was more than grief. It was something that set worlds on fire.

Zinnia was gone. Ripped from the fight. From him.

And the worst part? It had happened right in front of him.

But he knew the portal and it wasn't random. He knew the shape of that magic. Knew the taste of it.

It had purpose. Coordinates, if he could just find them...

"I saw where the portal was attuned. But not where it landed."

Seraphina closed her eyes—and the moment came rushing in.

Zinnia hadn't begged. Hadn't panicked. She'd resisted. With everything.

She swallowed around the lump in her throat.

"When he pulled her. She fought so hard, but I couldn't reach her."

"None of us could, Mum."

The words sat bitter in Sebastian's mouth. He desperately wanted to hit something. Violently.

The taste of blood still clung to his molars. One more second. That was all it would've taken.

He'd felt it—how close they were. Right there. Breathing distance from pulling her back.

He had no idea who to hate more—Brinnan, the Council, the universe. Or himself.

Killian hadn't meant to speak. But the truth pushed through anyway.

"She didn't stand a chance against what Brinnan's become. I fear none of us do."

Saffron moved to the window. Her fingers brushed the glass, where faint lines of wardlight still shimmered across the panes.

"She's not dead. I'd feel it. The tether would snap. But it hasn't." She placed a hand over her heart. "She's out there. Somewhere."

Sage pushed Sebastian's legs aside and dropped onto the chaise beside him. She needed her twin to ground her. Her throat burned, her lungs stuck between reality and belief.

"Z's alive. We just… don't know where."

Samthrax's eyes flared.

"Not where. When."

The room went still.

Killian straightened. Whatever lived in him did the same.

"You're sure?"

Samthrax jumped up and started to pace.

"The portal wasn't stable. It wasn't anchored to place—it was cast to disrupt the flow. That's why it sealed the way it did. The spell didn't banish her. It rethreaded her. He threw her into the current, hoping to open the Veil. Instead… she entered a river of sorts."

Sebastian leaned forward, eyes sharp. "So how do we follow her?"

Samthrax gave him a look edged with reluctant respect. "You don't follow a current like that. You map it. Or intercept it."

He let that land.

"Or you find a way to call her back."

Hope didn't knock. It barged through Sage's door.

"Okay. How do we do that?"

Something lit behind Seraphina's eyes. Not insight. Instinct.

"The Grimoire."

Hang on, Zin. We're coming.

Killian's shadow magic surged to the surface—alert.

"The portal."

Saffron snatched the thread and pulled it tight.

"And the power that made them both."

They all looked at each other. One broken family. One stolen girl.

One war sharpening its teeth in the dark.

Samthrax stood, stretching with a groan that didn't match his swagger or his centuries. The light caught his profile just enough to show the deep exhaustion beneath his charm.

"Well. Looks like we're going on a time hunt."

Sebastian's sarcasm came on autopilot. No room for awe, not yet.

"Is that even a thing?"

Samthrax's smile lacked anything good. "It is now."

Faith hurt. But Sage clung to it anyway.

"We'll get her back."

She wasn't sure who she was trying to convince—herself, or the universe.

Seraphina didn't answer. She rose instead. Walked slowly to the threshold still hanging open behind the bookshelf—the entrance to the Keep.

The surrounding air was colder there. The light bent around it. The wound in the house had not healed.

She stared into that darkness for a long moment. At last, she reached forward—and closed the door.

It clicked softly into place.

When she turned, her eyes were made of steel and shadow. She had failed once. She wouldn't do it again. Not even the dark would stop her.

"We find her. No matter what it takes."

Killian met her gaze and gave a single nod.

One by one, the others followed. Still reeling. Still raw. But united.

And somewhere, far from where they stood... A storm opened its eyes.

***

The mountain did not have a name. It had lost it long ago—swallowed by time, by quiet, by snow. There were no roads here.

No stories. Only ice and ruin, and presences too old to remember their beginnings.

Inside the hollowed core of that mountain, the dark moved. Not shadows.

Shadow.

It poured along the walls—slick and endless—pooling across the black stone floor in silence that devoured even the ghost of sound. The chamber had no entrance. No exit. It was not part of the world as most knew it.

And yet—he was there.

Brinnan stood at the centre. Though stood was no longer the word.

His human shape had reformed, reassembled from memory and malice. Eyes. Hands. A mouth that remembered how to shape words. But it was all chosen. Worn. A suit of flesh designed to keep mortals comfortable.

His true self was the thing beneath—the presence behind the presence—the shadow that filled the chamber's seams, watching from silver-threaded gaze that blinked from alabaster and smoke.

He had become what the old books feared. The creature that nightmares begged not to meet.

A Shadow Ascendant. A god of thresholds. A prince of absence.

And yet... He was not whole.

He moved to the rim of the obsidian platform, where a single shard of black glass hovered in midair. Not a mirror. Not a bowl.

A rift in reality—thin, slivered, stitched into being by spellwork and raw want.

He reached out and touched it. A ripple broke across the surface. The distortion flared.

And then—an image. Zinnia. Tumbling through the portal. Spiralling through non-linear space. Gone—but not. Her light still moved. And it had landed.

He simply didn't know where.

"I miscalculated. The mark should have opened the Veil as soon as she entered the portal. Instead, she held the door shut."

A low hum answered. Not a voice. Just the chamber, responding.

The pressure in the room rethreaded around him.

Brinnan turned away from the shard.

Behind him, the shape of a being began to coalesce.

The Umbra Vitae.

It arrived without motion. Without beginning.

Eyes resembling twin dying suns sank into view, veiled beneath its shifting cowl.

"You failed."

Its voice screeched like wind scraping rust from bone.

Brinnan's smile didn't belong to the man he used to be. It belonged to what he had become.

"No. I transcended."

"You misaligned the portal."

"No. I underestimated the Gateborn's power." He turned fully, shadows folding around him becoming a cloak of absence. "But in doing so, the Thal'Vesh broke the tether. It opened the path I needed. I gave the spell what it asked for. And it gave me something I hadn't planned."

He stepped forward. "Divinity."

The Umbra's cowl rippled. "You are not divine. You are unfinished."

"I know." But not for long.

He turned his palm upward. A single thread of silver-shadow shimmered across his hand, dancing like smoke trying to remember fire.

"Which is why I still need the Grimoire. And the portal. And her."

The Umbra did not move. "You would chase her through the current?"

"No need to chase. I can walk it. She's not lost. Just drifting. I only have to find when."

"You risk unravelling your form. You walk roads not meant for flesh."

"I've shed my flesh." Becoming what he was now—that had been the last step, not the first. This was better.

Everything held. The chamber. Him. The dark between them.

"There are more portals. More Veil-breaches. I can feel them clearly. I will thread the strands—pull the river tight. I'll find where she landed."

The Umbra moved. It knew.

"You will use her to stabilise your new form."

"I will use her to anchor my reign."

The glass shifted again. Zinnia's eyes appeared—wild with power. Unyielding.

"She's becoming." Victory hovered—close enough to take. Brinnan could feel it lining up. "But she's not there yet. That's my window."

He turned away. His current appearance still held the boyish arrogance of the man he once was. It no longer suited him.

"I'll need another face soon. The world will be looking for this one."

Without gesture or word, his form began to shift. Bones lengthened. Skin blurred. His eyes glowed. Hair bled from silver to void. A new mouth. New hands. A smile full of fresh teeth.

But the eyes? They burned the same emerald green.

The mountain stirred beneath the stone—not a tremor, but something deeper. An assent. A submission.

Brinnan stepped away from the shard. His voice dropped to a whisper of iron.

"Begin the descent."

The mountain groaned. Tunnels opened—not through rock, but through reality. Rifts peeled outward, stitched by shadow, leading to cities, ruins, timelines still warm with life.

And the god that had once worn human flesh walked forward. Not to conquer. Not to announce. To wait. To gather. To hunt.

And when he found her—*he'd be the end she never saw coming.*

Sneak Peek: Witchmarked

Book Two of The Bellarose Legacy

The story continues…

***

One

"They call it falling through time.
But it wasn't a fall. It was a tearing. A choosing.
And maybe… a beginning that already knew how it would end."
— Zinnia Hart, inconvenient oracle, reluctant weapon, temporal accident

Zinnia Hart didn't fall.

She was ripped—violently, unforgivably—from one reality into another. No grace. No mercy. Only a full-body teardown, as if the universe had reached in, grabbed her spine, and yanked.

A heartbeat ago, gravity had rules. The next, it wanted her gone. Not just from the world. From herself.

This wasn't travel. It was erasure.

The moment stretched, warped, as though her atoms couldn't quite agree on the direction of time.

She dropped through something deeper than space—past history, past memory, past logic.

Every scream she'd never let out, every fear she'd buried so deep even she forgot it existed, got fed into the gears of whatever had her now.

The portal didn't open. It cracked wide—teeth first—and bit down. Hard.

She spun. Tumbled. Felt her thoughts shred like wet paper.

No up. No down. Just relentless momentum and the sensation that her insides were being unpacked and rearranged without anaesthetic.

Blackness surrounded her—thick, damp, alive. It folded against her ribs. Wrapped itself over her lungs. Slid past the place where her soul was supposed to sit.

She felt seen. Violated. As though the dark wasn't content to observe. It wanted to wear her.

Pulling her apart as if searching for a precise piece—and not finding it.

Every nerve fired. Then nothing. Then everything again. Rinse and repeat.

She tried to scream. But the noise? It got caught—spliced, frayed, inverted. Like her voice didn't belong to her anymore.

But a single thread held. The mark. Born with it. Branded by it. That silver, fire-lined tether that had never meant anything—until now.

It was molten steel inside her skin. A fuse that hadn't gone off yet. And it wouldn't break.

Not for this. Not for them.

Because something was in here with her. And it wanted in.

It slid fingers—slick, invasive—up her spine, searching.

For a seam. A crack. A weakness.

And when it couldn't find one, it spoke. Not in words. Not in language. In decree.

You belong to us.

But the mark? It snapped back. Not quiet or subtle. It detonated.

Her blood ignited—silver current surging as if from a spell that hadn't been taught, only inherited. Born in bone. Sealed in vow. Fuelled by rage that never burned out. It wasn't just fury. It was inheritance—holy, hunted, and stamped in the bones of her bloodline.

The thing trying to take her?

It flinched. And she ripped free.

One heartbeat chained to the void—the next, slingshotted out, body first.

What followed wasn't impact. It was like being tackled by a planet with a grudge.

She didn't arrive—she collided.

Twigs snapped. Stone slammed into her ribs. Air bailed on her as though it had better places to be. Her spine caught the brunt. Her skull caught the echo. Her face took the rest.

She lay on her side, body twitching, brain fried. Her heart wasn't just pounding. It was a riot in her chest, trying to punch its way out first.

She blinked. "How the hell am I still alive?"

The question ricocheted inside her head, not as a jest, but as a genuine plea for understanding. Every fibre of her being screamed that survival was a mistake, an anomaly in the universe's design.

She should be dead. Maybe she was. What if this was the after part?

Everything hurt—but not in a way that meant broken. No red-flash agony. No wet, sucking puncture sounds. Just a full-body chorus of fuck this.

She tried to move. A single leg cooperated. The other filed a formal complaint. Her left shoulder felt as though it had fought a meat grinder and lost. Her brain? Still buffering. Stuck somewhere between now and whatever the hell that was.

She cracked an eye open. The sky was bare. No satellites. No planes.

No city glow bleeding from the bones of civilisation.

Just stars. Raw and exposed. Hanging overhead—pure judgment with a front-row seat.

She turned her head. And the trees stared back.

Haggard yew and rowan, bark warped like scar tissue, branches curled into claws.

She sucked in a breath. The air hit her throat dry and sharp, steeped in the heavy musk of a world that didn't know her name.

She coughed. Spat a string of green. Rolled onto her back. Maybe it would help. Maybe gravity would cut her a break.

The forest floor was a leech, draining warmth from her spine, its clammy embrace whispering secrets of ancient sorrows and forgotten tales. A shape slithered past her elbow.

Right now, she couldn't care less.

Everything under her felt alive. Not passive alive. Aware alive.

Her T-shirt was toast—Shrek's face twisted across her chest like even he'd noped out of this reality.

Mud. Blood. Magical whiplash. The full travel package.

Her arms were sliced up. Her thighs ached. Her whole body was a brutal memo she hadn't signed off on.

But it was her magic that really had the attitude.

Still awake inside her. Still pacing. Still testing the edges of her skin, a wolf pressing against a cage it had no intention of staying in.

Not calm. Not curious. Predatory. It had moved in like a hostile roommate—redecorated the walls, changed the locks, and hung a "fuck off" sign in the window of her soul.

She yearned for the simplicity of her former life. Of toothpaste caps and grocery lists and daylight that didn't come with strings attached.

Destiny? Could suck it.

Gateborn? Les Revenantes? Veil-ripping prophecies?

They could all line up and kiss her arse.

She was so not that girl.

Someone show her the nearest Starbucks—she had questions, complaints, and zero interest in being anyone's magical heir apparent.

Right now? She wasn't sure if she was the weapon… or the idiot standing in front of the trigger with a confused look on her face.

She licked her lips. The taste of copper hit as if it were memory with a vendetta, and the resonance of a forgotten god still clawed its way through her bloodline.

A reverberation that didn't belong to this century. Didn't belong to her.

The magic flexed. Took inventory. Sniffed the air like a creature with an appetite and a score to settle.

It wasn't just awake. It was conscious. And whatever it was—it had her number.

And she was at the top of its *goddamn* to-do list.

About the Author

C.M.N Rogers is a New Zealander living under Australia's dazzling skies, where she writes dark, deliciously magical fiction for readers who like their fantasy tangled with trauma, blood oaths, and just a hint of redemption. Her books aren't just stories—they're wild, witty adventures into bloodlines, ancient magic, and the divine chaos of alchemising adversity into power.

When she's not conjuring epic tales, she's a tarot-reading, dog-obsessed sass-master who loves probing the mysteries of the soul. Whether she's trekking foreign lands with a grin, dishing advice on finding your inner light, or debating whether coffee should be considered a food group, she's always knee-deep in life's quirks and questions.

As founder of **House of Nine Press**, she's all about helping others navigate life's labyrinth with a wink and a nudge. Keep your eyes peeled—she'll soon be unleashing her BookTok energy as **@cmnrogers.author**, where shadowy spoilers and witchy wisdom await.